BEAUTIFULLY BUILT

LAKE HAVEN SERIES - BOOK TWO

TRISHA MADLEY

Copyright

Copyright © 2024 by Trisha Madley

All rights reserved.

No portion of this book may be reproduced in any form without written permission from the publisher or author, except as permitted by U.S. copyright law. This ebook is licensed for your personal enjoyment only. This ebook may not be re-sold or given away to other people. If you would like to share this book with another person, please purchase an additional copy for each person. If you're reading this book and did not purchase it, or it was not purchased for your use only, then please return it and purchase your own copy. Thank you for respecting the hard work of this author. To obtain permission to excerpt portions of the text, please contact the author at trishamadley.com

All characters in this book are fiction and figments of the author's imagination.

Publisher: Independently Published by Trisha Blinkiewicz
Editor: Elaine York, MNM, Allusion Publishing
Cover Designer: Flirtation Designs
Proofreader: Amy Dobbs

BEAUTIFULLY BUILT

Contents

Prologue		1
1.	Chapter 1	5
2.	Chapter 2	12
3.	Chapter 3	18
4.	Chapter 4	23
5.	Chapter 5	29
6.	Chapter 6	37
7.	Chapter 7	43
8.	Chapter 8	50
9.	Chapter 9	58
10.	Chapter 10	66
11.	Chapter 11	71
12.	Chapter 12	77
13.	Chapter 13	82
14.	Chapter 14	86
15.	Chapter 15	91
16.	Chapter 16	97
17.	Chapter 17	101

18.	Chapter 18	105
19.	Chapter 19	114
20.	Chapter 20	122
21.	Chapter 21	130
22.	Chapter 22	143
23.	Chapter 23	154
24.	Chapter 24	162
25.	Chapter 25	173
26.	Chapter 26	181
27.	Chapter 27	189
28.	Chapter 28	201
29.	Chapter 29	205
30.	Chapter 30	214
31.	Chapter 31	219
32.	Chapter 32	225
33.	Chapter 33	231
34.	Chapter 34	233
35.	Chapter 35	239
36.	Chapter 36	247
37.	Chapter 37	251
38.	Chapter 38	257
Epilogue		261
Follow Me!		265
About the Author		266

Prologue

I'm grounded for the millionth time this month. I went to a party with my brother and his friends and my grandmother found out. I'm locked in my room until the day I die according to my Gran.

I'm sure she'll release me in a day or two. She likes to make her point.

Glancing at the backyard, through my window, Benjamin Carmichael sits under the pine tree in the dark of night. My brother and a group of his friends and a few girls whom I don't know are hanging out in our garage.

I can't help but wonder why he is out there all alone.

His back is leaning up against a tree and he's staring down at his beer bottle.

Contemplating whether I listen to Gran or listen to my racing heart, my body moves on its own, and opens the window. I climb out of it, step onto the ladder rung that used to hold the antenna before there was cable or streaming. Now it's been repurposed and has become my escape route from my room. Gran is no idiot, she knows I use it, but thankfully, she hasn't had it taken down.

My feet carry me toward him. My heart beating out of my chest. I've had a crush on him since I can remember. I'm eighteen now, and I think tonight is the night to let him know.

"Hey," I say, my voice cracks.

His big blue eyes look up at me. Even in the dark, I can read the surprise on his face.

"Hi. What are you doing here, Sunshine?"

"Can I have a sip of beer?" Ben looks in the direction of my brother, unsure whether to hand it over or not.

"He doesn't care."

"Yes, he does. And I'm not pushing him. I'm drunk. Not stupid. I don't need to fight your brother tonight."

"Whatever. I'll go get one myself." Standing up, ready to leave, he pulls at the bottom of my shorts.

"Sit down. You can have a sip."

He hands me his beer. It's not like I haven't had a beer before. My friends and I drink, I don't ever do it in front of my brother or his friends, though.

We sit in silence. Ben looks lost in thought.

"What's wrong with you tonight?"

"I don't want to talk about it."

I nod. "I get that. Sometimes it's better to just sit quietly."

"You usually don't know how to stay silent." He teases.

I take a sip and roll my eyes. "Whatever."

He remains quiet and so do I.

"I like sitting here with you," he says, taking the bottle from me and taking a sip of his own.

"You do?" I clear my throat.

"Don't sound so surprised. I like that you are yourself around me. And I can be myself around you." He moves a little closer to me. "Sometimes I wonder what it would be like to kiss you."

"Umm... what?" It's not like I've never thought of it, in fact, I've dreamed of his lips on mine ever since I knew that kissing was a thing. It's just that it's Ben. My crush. He's unattainable.

"You really don't know how beautiful you are, do you?"

"I think you had way too much to drink."

"Kiss me," he demands. "I dare you."

I can't breathe. What happened to my lungs? Have they stopped functioning?

Only he doesn't give me a chance to kiss him before his lips are on mine. I've kissed boys before, but this moment literally feels like a dream. His lips are soft. He moans against my mouth. Heat and tingles shoot through my body. Before I can kiss him back.

"Sunshine?"

"Yes." I don't recognize my own voice.

"Go find your brother and hang out with him tonight. Okay?" His forehead crinkles as if he's in pain.

In shock at his words, I only nod.

Standing up, my only thought is to get out of here. Anywhere but here.

Rushing past the garage, I make my way back up the ladder into my bedroom window.

The realization that he kissed me must have been horrible. I must have been a horrible at it for him to stop and tell me to leave him alone.

Tears fall fast.

He broke my heart in just a few minutes. Shattered my dream of being with him.

After who knows how long, I pull myself away from the self-loathing. The group in the garage has quieted down. But that doesn't matter, because before anything else registers, the only thing

I see is Ben kissing Sarah James in the same spot under the tree in my backyard.

We never spoke of that night again, I never wanted to humiliate myself more by bringing it up because I'm pretty sure he was too drunk to remember.

And all I wanted was to forget my broken heart.

1

There's that piece of shit. He thinks he can walk away from me after what he just did! Tammy Jenkins, one of my closest friends, of all the lousy girls to pick for tonight's...ummm, festivities. They didn't even try to hide their hookup. Here they are, parked only a few feet from all the car haulers, only a short walk from the racetrack. Almost like a giant fuck you to whoever is walking by—like me!

My brother, Jake, and his best friend, Ben, just finished racing and I was heading back to find Lance after it was over with. Ben had taken first place and Jake took fourth. Ben is, by far, the most talented racer out there. But I won't say that out loud.

Lance is only here to place bets and make some money on the races. His family lords over the street racing scene here in the small town of Lake Haven. He must not have won, because he's busy fogging up his truck windows, trying to make himself feel better.

I've stayed away from my brother's group of friends—romantically speaking. I thought it would be better if I dated someone outside of my friend circle...always wanted to find 'the one'. But I know I won't find the one in my brother's circle of friends. They all see me as Jake's little sister, which brings me to my good-for-nothing boyfriend Lance and the situation that I find myself faced with—Lance, the son-of-a-bitch. He told me, "Baby, you're my girl." Now the low-life scoundrel is steaming up his Dodge pickup truck's window and rocking the whole damn thing. Why on earth would he pick my friend, no strike that ex-friend?

"Think, Callie Rae, what would Gran do in this situation?" I ask, to who, I have no idea, since I'm now sitting in the cab of my F-150 by myself. I could call my grandma, but then she'd know my boyfriend left me to go screw the pooch and I'd never hear the end of it. I'm a big girl, I can figure this out.

I sit for a few seconds and the brilliant idea pops into my head, like a ray of sunshine peeking out from behind a tree. I lower my hand, till it meets the baseball bat under the bench seat.

Sweet justice.

Opening the door, I let myself out and casually meander on over to the lifted red piece-of-shit truck holding the very bane of my existence.

It's showtime and I'll start with a taillight. I lift the wooden bat that I've used many times as a child. Like the time, Jake, my brother and his best friend, Ben tried to play a joke on me and told me that the bat would only hit baseballs and not softballs. They said it would crack it. Well, I'm about to crack up this truck with my non-softball baseball bat.

I step up to the truck, aim at the bright red light. Crack. Damn, that felt good. I rear back and take a second to decide where the next spot might be when the big oaf jumps out from the cab. His pants aren't even zipped, his belt is dangling down, and he's looking very much like he just got caught cheating. Jeez.

"What the fuck, Callie?"

"Who do you have your pecker in, huh?" I don't give him time to answer. He doesn't deserve it. "Tammy Sue Jenkins? Seriously?" I say, glancing over at my former friend.

"We were just talking, that's all."

"With your pants unbuttoned?" I remind him just in case his memory has slipped, and he isn't noticing the draft of air down below.

"Callie, you're making a big deal of nothing. I told her brother I'd give her a ride home." He points over his shoulder like her blue house, the same one that I've spent many sleepovers at and ate breakfast there with her entire family—is in the middle of the racetrack. Idiot!

"You don't think I know where she lives? She's my neighbor, you moron. By the way, this street is for racing, not screwing. How stupid do you think I am? We had plans for tomorrow night. Consider this..." raising my hand, I point between the two of us, "O.V.E.R. Done!"

"Callie, stop! I love you, baby. It was just a ride. We were just talking about how awesome the race was and how someday I'd love to race Ben." He stutters and adds, "And of course, how much I care for you."

I haven't been seeing Lance that long. Maybe two months. My friends, Van and Emerson, came home after Emerson left Van to save him from her ex-husband's wrath. She thought she was protecting him, but she ended up in the hospital. I started dating Lance shortly after I got back from visiting her in the hospital.

I wanted to find a love like my friends, Van and Emerson, had. I should have known better. It probably doesn't exist for someone like me. At least I found out sooner than later. But am I really surprised? The guys I've dated are jerks. I watched my mother go through multiple boyfriends. None of them mattered. When she was done, she'd just move on. The only problem was she picked them over me and Jake. If they moved, she moved. If the flavor of the week didn't want to be bothered by us, she didn't want to be bothered by us. Jake and I ended up being raised by her mother, our Gran.

As he confesses his undying love for me, Tammy slips out of the truck. Slamming the door to bring attention to herself, like I didn't know the sleaze bag was in there. To top it off, she tugs at the bottom of her skin-tight dress as she takes a step up on the sidewalk. Awesome...she's scared as hell. I can see it all over her face, of course it probably helps that I'm carrying a weapon. She knows I can throw down, and I will, just as soon as her stick figure struts on over here. I raise the bat again. "I'm going to swing this bat on the back end of your truck if you don't start telling the truth, Lance."

Holding his hands up to stop me, he squeals like the weasel he is, "Wait! Fine. Okay, fine. We were just fooling around. It meant nothing."

Tammy chimes in, her high-pitched voice, squawks. "Of course, it meant something. You asshole! We've been seeing each other for weeks. I'm glad she finally caught us." Her head bobs and bounces as she talks, probably excited to let the cat out of the bag. "Now we can be together in public and not have to sneak around all the time." The words flow so easily from her lips. Like she didn't just confess to backstabbing her friend. I could see if I were another girl, but hell, we've been friends for years. All of us, tighter than ticks.

Lance tenses, his fist clenched at his sides and his eyes dart from me to Tammy. He looks like a rabid raccoon, unsure what to do next.

Tammy has her arms crossed and is obviously freezing. It's a cool South Carolina spring night. Of course, if she would have put some more clothes on, she wouldn't have that problem. But I guess that would have meant there'd have been more clothes to take off in his truck.

"Look, could you just drop the bat, and we can go talk this out?" Lance says, with his hands up in the air like he's approaching a wild animal.

"There is nothing to talk about. You are screwing someone else. So... I'm going to take out my aggression on your truck like a good Carrie Underwood supporter and bid you all a fond farewell." I salute him with my middle finger and then raise my arm, with bat still in hand, and whack the other taillight as I make my way toward the back. The crunch of the plastic spikes my adrenaline. "Good, now they match."

"You stupid bitch. I'm calling the cops." In the next second, he has his phone in hand and is dialing.

"Shit!" I screech. He's a pussy. I know it, he knows it. But his Daddy takes care of all of his problems. Which means I've just caused a huge problem for myself. I'm in trouble for sure. I drop the bat and take off toward my truck. Obviously, in the heat of the moment, I didn't think this through, so I high tail it out of there. The adrenaline must be catching up with me because my hand doesn't want to work when I reach for the door. I try the door handle two times before it opens. Thank the good Lord, I left my keys in the ignition, or I might never get out of here.

I put the truck in reverse, look over my shoulder, and press the gas pedal. Only I don't go far. Nope...the sound of metal scraping echoes in my ears. "Damn it!"

I know what I hit. I don't even need to look. Ben Carmichael's precious Mustang. It sits much lower than my truck. I remember seeing it when I parked but now, I'm not leaving under the best circumstances. I put my truck back into park and raise my head to find the boy I've had a crush on since I was eight —the same boy I'd shared an amazing kiss with who doesn't even remember—coming out from behind the Carmichael car hauler. He must have heard the crunch of metal, or maybe he has just impeccable timing.

Ben doesn't immediately react. Instead, he seems to be taking in the scene playing out before him. His head bounces from Lance to Tammy and over to my truck. He picks up the pace as realization dawns. Even in this moment, when my world is crazy, I can't help but notice how gorgeous he is with his black and gray race suit unzipped at the waist with the top half down around his sides, the sleeves dangle at his hips, and his Carmichael racing T-shirt showing in all his glory. His short dark blonde hair is all over the place because when he rips his helmet off, his hair goes in every direction. Where his is a dark blond, mine is light blond, almost white. I have watched him for hours on end over the years, doing simple things like talking to his friends to complicated tasks such as swapping out a motor, and it never gets old. I shake my head to focus. This is not the time to daydream. One, because I'm in trouble, and two, because he is my brother's best friend and will only ever see me as his best friend's little sister. Lance must not realize Ben just walked up because he heads toward me with Ben right behind him.

While Lance radiates panic, tension, and guilt with his hands interlocked on top of his head, pants still open, swiveling his head back and forth between me and Tammy, Ben is calm, cool and struts toward me with a beer bottle in hand.

As he passes Lance, he raises his bottle to him. Lance freezes in place. Reading his lips, I can tell Ben says, "I got her" to him. He knows if he says one cross word to me in front of Ben, he's going to be the one in need of repair.

Ben isn't like most guys I know. I'm twenty-three now, but at eight years old, I knew then and there he was what I'd hear Gran call a handsome devil. Now he fits that description to a tee. He's tan, muscular, and he's stalking toward me like I'm his prey. Oh, but how I would give anything to be. My thighs tremble at the thought.

His deep blue eyes meet mine. I can't move, his gaze has me locked in place. As he approaches the driver's side door, he motions for me to roll the window down.

Nope. I'm not doing it. I'm not putting down my window, so I shake my head letting him know I'm on to him and I'm not doing what he wants.

Ben steps closer, tossing the bottle in the bed of the truck. Glass shrapnel crashing against the metal, still our eyes are locked on each other. Which one of us will crack first? A second later he taps on the window.

"Come on, Callie? Get out of there. You're causing trouble. I was trying to get out of here, but it looks like my Sunshine is causing a bit of a ruckus with all of these people around you."

I shake my head, and before I can think of locking the door, he opens it. "No!" I try to stop him from opening it, but he's too fast and strong for it to work.

"What'd you do?"

I bite my lip before confessing, "I'm sorry, Ben, I backed into your Mustang trying to get the hell away from my cheating ex."

2

His eyes widen as he takes in the site behind my truck. Oh shit! He really didn't notice. I think he might be frozen, possibly in shock. Maybe I should call the paramedics. A few seconds pass and then he comes back to reality. "Damn it, Callie."

"I'm sorry about your girl Betty." I say, in a sweet southern manner, knowing he likes when I'm sweet to him, but his eyes bug out of his head instead of soften.

Quicker than lightning, he's out of my sight, and as I step down from my truck, he's crouched down, examining the dent I just made to Betty, his beloved Mustang.

"What the hell did you do?"

"I'm sorry. I didn't think there was anything behind me. I looked. I promise."

"Well, then you're obviously blind, or maybe smashing other people's vehicles is a new hobby for you since I just witnessed the scene from one of Carrie Underwood's videos."

"Do they even make music videos anymore?" I joke, trying to lighten his temper.

I get a half smile from him at my attempt at humor, but then he's serious again. Just when I think I might not be in as much trouble as I think, red and blue lights make a real-life photo filter on Ben's face.

Ben's eyes grow bigger than before, and I think I'm about to pass out. He grumbles and stands. "You better hope it's Alex or I won't be able to get you out of this. Thank God the fucking race is over."

The lights blind us as the police car comes up beside us and stops beside Ben. It feels like an eternity until the officer gets out of his vehicle, but when he does, sweet relief floods my soul. "You're so damn lucky," Ben says from beside me as his friend from high school walks over. Officer Alex has come to his rescue on more than one occasion. Since street drag racing is illegal, it's good to have friends who look the other way.

"Benny boy, what's going on? I was a few blocks over when I heard the address over the radio." His eyes take in the scenery. "Did you finally piss Callie off enough that she crashed into your car?" Alex laughs like he always does at my antics. His big stomach and deep laugh make him look like a dark-haired version of Santa Claus. He runs his hand down his beard.

"She did crash into my Mustang, but I wasn't the one who called the cops on her. Can I talk to you over there for a minute?" He nods to the back of my truck, with his casual smile. Ben's calm, which makes me nervous, even my eye is twitching.

"Sure, buddy. Callie it was good to see you." His eyes roam over to Lance, who still has the phone plastered to his ear. "He's the one who called?"

"Yes, sir," I admit.

He chuckles and mumbles, "Moron."

They walk to the back of Ben's Mustang.

I concur his sentiment as I glance at Lance's angry face. I swear if it wasn't so dark, he'd be the color of a stop sign. Tammy is rubbing his arm, consoling him while he's talking on his phone. His hands are flailing and he's obviously distraught over his precious taillights. Or maybe because he knows that Ben's friend won't let anything happen to me. I'm part of the family and everyone here knows it, even Tammy, but she's too selfish to admit it.

I'm not sure what to do with myself. I could go intrude on Ben and Officer Alex, but that might hurt my chances of getting out of this mess, or I could go have a serious conversation with my ex-friend and her new boyfriend—because he certainly isn't mine anymore.

I think the best thing I can do is keep my keister right where it's at. I stay, leaning against the truck for what seems like forever. Looking around, I see Lance is still on the dang phone. My guess would be he's called his rich daddy who happens to be a lawyer. Shit! I kinda forgot about that lucky ace in his pocket. I rub my ear, like I always do when I find myself in a bit of a pickle, which lately is usually often.

A few more moments drag on, and Officer Alex is walking toward me. His usual go-with-the-flow smile is replaced with his serious cop face. I've made fun of him wearing that face when Ben and my brother were in the ones in trouble, but now it's not so funny directed at me.

"Callie." He nods his head, while holding on to the brim of his blue uniform hat.

Nodding in return, I don't say anything, it's best to stay quiet. Wait. Let him strike first so I can formulate an appropriate course of action.

But the dummy doesn't talk. He's staring at me, I'm guessing he wants me to confess, but he can kiss my pale ass, I'm not saying a word. We're in a stand-off as Ben steps beside him.

"Callie, let Officer Alex know it was an accident and your temper got the best of you. You'll pay for Lance's truck to get repaired." His eyes narrow with a hidden meaning that says, "You better agree with me, brat,'cause I just saved your ass."

He's right. It's the best thing I can do. But it boils my blood. That jerk fools around with my friend and they both get off without consequence. I inhale and let the punishment begin. "Okay, Ben's right, I'll pay for the damage, but..." I can't help but want to explain my side of the situation. Surely it's every girl's right to smash up her boyfriend's car, especially when the little slut he's having sex with is still in it. "Alex, I had no other choice. Did you hear what they did to me, it's only fair." Ben flashes a stern look, definitely ready to tell me to shut up, but I don't care. I need to say my peace. "He needs to learn a lesson."

I know I sound like a spoiled brat, but I can't help myself.

Just then Lance barges in the conversation. "You're going to jail. I talked with my dad, and he said I should press charges against you!" He turns, pointing directly at me. "You need to arrest her. Isn't that your job? Read her goddamn rights!"

If he wasn't so dang tall, I'd clock him right in the jaw. "Listen here, you big oaf." I move closer, my finger reaching his chest, and with each word I give him a nice jab. "You will do no such thing. I've put up with your bullshit for far too long. You're lucky I didn't do more to your precious truck...or your cheating, ugly mug!"

I'm ready to keep screaming, but Ben speaks first. "Settle down, Sunshine." His stern voice calls from behind me. His nickname for me stops me in my tracks. I sense him only inches away from me. I'm not sure if he doesn't trust me, or Lance, but either way, he always has my back. As always, his words calm me, melting away the hazy fog of irrational emotions that are threatening to spill out.

Lance takes this moment to add his two cents. "I always knew I was too good for you. Everyone knows it. Your mother is proof that poverty, and failure run in your veins."

Ben is in between us in a second. He wants me to calm down, but he isn't listening to his own instructions. His face lines up directly with Lance's, his finger in Lance's face. "You! You better watch what you say. This isn't the way we handle things. We don't call the cops at a street race. We don't call the cops on girls, and we certainly don't call the cops on my girl." His voice is low, stern and menacing and I love it. *Wait...did he just say my girl?*

Ben's fists are balled at his sides, even in the dark, I can see the veins popping from his arms. He's ready to strike, but he knows as well as I do that he can't, not in front of the law—friend or not.

Officer Alex speaks up, causing Ben to back away and him to take his place. "Now. Now. Boys, please calm down. I need to ask you a few questions, and then we can talk about filing a police report." Officer Alex takes a little notebook out of his back pocket and a pencil. Just like in the movies, he takes the tip of his tiny pencil and places it on his tongue, then moves it to his notepad. "Now, the first step is me writing down why you are parked illegally. And if you would like, I can check the inside of your vehicle and make sure there was no damage done to the inside. Perhaps I should examine under the seats and in the console. I know your truck has great *storage* options."

"What the hell are you rambling about? She smashed my truck. Why are you trying to turn this shit around on me?"

"Because I like Callie," Officer Alex says matter of fact. "And if I recall, you've been in some trouble lately with an illegal substance or two. Isn't that right?"

Lance's face pales. He stammers his words. "I...I...we...don't have to file a formal complaint. I'll figure it out."

"Sounds like a great idea," Alex says. His smile almost screaming, "I thought you'd have a change of heart."

He adds, "As for the rest of you, no street racing on this road next week. I didn't see any racing tonight, but I can't turn a blind eye next time." His wink lets us know he knows exactly what goes on this road, and he also knows that we'll be here every Friday night for the rest of the season. Besides, I've seen him here a time or two as a spectator…and even placing bets.

Bets are the most important part of racing to some. Everyone can make good money if you do it right. You can lose your ass too. Case in point, Ben's father. It doesn't matter who you are—the driver or the spectator or even a crew member. You pick the driver you think will win, they drag race. If your guy or gal wins, you get cash; if not, you better pay up.

"Sure thing," Ben says to him. "Callie will pay for the damages and won't cause any more problems." He looks at me with his stern face.

I back away and nod. "Fine." Holding up my hands in surrender. "I'll pay for the damages, and I'm sorry that you're such a lying, cheating scumbag that I had to take a bat to your truck like the song says, "Maybe next time you'll think before you cheat."

And I sing the rest of the lyrics all the way back to my truck.

3

It's after one in the morning when I finally reach my grandmama's house.

I did have my own tiny apartment for a bit, but I moved back in a months ago after living on my own for six months. I loved being on my own, but Gran's health hasn't been good. She had a minor stroke and is under preventative measures in place, but I don't like the thought of something happening while she is all alone. Plus, this helps me save to open my own salon one day. I work at the local salon for Sally Jones and she's been good to me, but it would be much better to own my own business. Jake lives with Gran, too, but he isn't as reliable as he should be. He also stays at the apartment above the bar some nights when he's had too much to drink, or hooks up with a girl.

I've been with Gran since my mama went to live with boyfriend number seventy-million and two—except for the six months I was gone, so practically all my life. My mama floats in and out, but never stays long. She's the life of the party and fun to be around, but it gets old when you need her to actually act like a mom. Like making you dinner or remembering to buy you school supplies. She had my brother Jake at sixteen and me at eighteen. I don't think she ever grew up. It's okay with me though, as long as I get a few days a year with her, I'm good. Sadly, my father passed away in a race car accident when I was a baby. I don't think my mother ever dealt with her grief or got over his death.

My grandmama is the one who has always taken care of me. Her tough ways are what I've learned and wouldn't trade it for anything in the world. Although, tonight, I might trade her for a lesser sentence.

As soon as I get out of the car, Gran is standing on the porch. Gray hair up in rollers, a flower petticoat and pink fluffy slippers. She looks like she could play the lead on *Mama's Family*.

I can tell by the way her hands on her hips, squinting through her glasses, she's already gotten a call about me. The question is from whom?

"You have a fun night, puddle?" Oh shit, she's using her nickname for me. I'm in deep trouble. You think at my age I wouldn't be scared of my grandmother. But her calling me that is like most people's parents calling them by their middle names. Though it's a seemingly sweet nickname, it only means shit has officially hit the fan. The name came from when I was little and I used to love to jump in mud puddles, and the name stuck, especially when I got into trouble as a kid.

I slowly trudge up the steps, taking one step slower than the next. Wishing the brick steps would slowly disintegrate, so I couldn't experience the disappointment in her face.

"You already know what happened?"

She nods, while her glasses fall down her nose. "You know that officer is so nice. I told him to stop by for some coffee sometime."

"Yeah, he didn't put me in jail tonight, so I'd say he's pretty nice." I pause, waiting for something else, she stares, so I give her a little push. "But...what else did he say?"

"Oh, just that my sweet granddaughter took a baseball bat to her boyfriend's truck. I asked who he was rolling in the hay with, and he told me...Tammy." We say her name in unison.

She gives me a small smile and I go in for a hug, her arms feeling so welcoming. "It's not that I'm heartbroken over it. I dated him for only a couple of months. But it's betrayal, you know?"

Gran nods sympathetically.

"My two friends have been keeping a secret behind my back and made a fool of me," I say, while my head rests against her chest. She squeezes me tighter, and I feel a little lighter.

"Let's go inside. Get to bed. We'll deal with that mess tomorrow. This isn't my first rodeo with a cheatin' fool, ya know."

"Yeah, Gran, but it still sucks."

When I reach my twin bed, I take off my outfit from the day and slip on my pale yellow tank top and light pink pajama shorts. Letting my blonde hair fall over my shoulders, I lie back on my pillow. "Callie Rae, what a mess you've made." I sigh out loud, unsure of what to do or how to feel about my current situation. My mouth gets me in more trouble, but tonight—I lost it. Did I really just smash up Lance's truck with a baseball bat? I don't even know why I care so much. I haven't known him that long. We slept together and it wasn't even that great. To be honest, it was boring. Fast...and he must have missed the entire chapter on foreplay.

"Ugh...how could I be so stupid," I say out loud again to no one at all. Covering my face with my elbow, I try to hide from the night, but my racing heart isn't complying. Sometimes I think I'm on the verge of a stroke, the way my body gets so worked up. I just want to experience the feeling of someone caring about me. Maybe even loving me. If I had to pick someone, it would be someone like Ben. He's smart, he's not afraid of anyone, he's kind, he is serious, but in a good way. He makes me laugh and is protective. The only problem...he would never think of me in that way.

Years ago, when we were in our teens, he kissed me. Turns out he must have been drunk because I found him minutes later kissing Sarah James, her supermodel body wrapped around him like a python. He moved on rather quickly, shattering my young, naïve heart.

Now that I'm older and understand his ways, this is not a surprise at all. He's always jumped from girl to girl. After all, he isn't in town for a long period of time. He's got drag racing to do. Races to win. Money to earn. He jumps from city to city. But lately Las Vegas has been his most frequented city.

I'm just his best friend's baby sister. He has his choice of every beautiful girl in the state and beyond. There is no way he sees me as anything other than a friend. That kiss was nothing to him. He doesn't need to know my feelings for him. Or that he broke my heart when he chose to spend the rest of that night kissing Sarah. But I was a silly young girl who was infatuated.

Honestly, Lance was just a fling. A placeholder for the one and only person who has ever been able to keep my attention. Like I told Gran, I could not care less that he likes someone else. It isn't because I wanted to spend the rest of my life with him or have his babies. It was just the betrayal.

Ben is the only one who has ever kept my heart and attention. Even tonight, he stood up for me when Lance called me poor and a failure. He would do anything for me. Except he won't stay. That I know for sure.

He has been everything I've wanted in a boyfriend or partner. But he has always been unattainable. I'm not sure what to do about my feelings for him. Some days I feel invisible to him, and then there are moments like tonight when I don't think I'll ever be able to escape these feelings I have for him.

Just as my mind starts to slow down and I begin drifting off to sleep, I convince myself about what a dumb idea it would be for me to think that dating Ben was even a remote possibility, a tap echoes outside my window. Glancing over, Ben is staring back at me. I jump, yelping a bit.

Did I conjure him up, like a spell or something? Or have I fallen asleep without knowing it and am dreaming of the man I have less-than-innocent feelings for?

4

I get out of bed. It's not as if he scared me, it was just weird I was thinking about him at the exact moment that he appeared. He crawled up the old antenna ladder outside that reaches up to my window. He's been doing that since we were kids and I'm glad to see that things haven't changed.

Tonight, has been a clusterfuck. I never meant to do any damage to anyone other than that two-timing Lance. So, out of all the people in the world, his is the only car I wish I wouldn't have damaged. Because I know that that directly hurts Ben. I also know the lengths he's gone to pay for it—he even does some side jobs just to pay the monthly payment, race fees, normal maintenance, and countless other things that I don't even know about. He works himself to the bone, and I just backed my ass right into the back of it like it was invisible.

He should be mad at me, want to yell or never talk to me again, but here he is, in all his glory, climbing through my window like he has done for years. The first time he did it, I was eight and he was ten. We were all playing in the woods behind his house. We had an old tire swing hanging and he dared me to jump off of it. Well, me being me, even at eight, I took that bet. Proving that I was so much tougher was not a maybe, it was a must. That was until my foot, somehow, got tangled up in the tire. I fell flat on my face. Once I spit the dirt out of my mouth, and came to my senses, shearing pain in my ankle was all that could be felt.

Trying not to cry, I sucked in every tear, whine, and whimper until the pain became too much. Ben was the first one over, asking if I was alright. His kind words were my undoing. The tears ran like a waterfall. "I hurt my ankle. It hurts so much," I told him with trembling lips.

He looked down at my ankle. His face paled. "We need to get you home."

He carried my little butt all the way home, which turned out to be almost a mile away from his house. It wasn't an easy trek with a whiny girl on his back, while maneuvering the hills, rocky paths, and branches swinging in his face. But he only was concerned with getting me back home, safe and sound. Thankfully, it only turned out to be a sprain, but Gran insisted that we go to the hospital.

On the ride to the hospital, Gran was giving me some long-winded speech about knowing better than to do something so ridiculous, and he held my hand the whole way there. Later that night, he climbed up to my window, tapped on the glass, and waited until I hobbled my way over to let him in my room. We talked for hours about the little things. I think that's when I first noticed him—really noticed him. He wasn't some annoying boy from across the street, or just simply my brother's best friend. No. Ben was caring, kind, and there was a quiet strength about him that I had never felt until that moment. And to this day, he's the only one who makes me feel that way.

He raps at my window again. Squinting his eyes, then bringing his hands to the window to cover the reflection in the glass, giving him a better look. My heart kicks up a few beats, but I try to slow it down. There's nothing new about him being here. I can squash these nasty hormones and my feelings for him that I know won't go anywhere with a little southern attitude.

Raising the pane, I whisper-shout at him, "Benjamin, what if I was naked? You can't just crawl up my antenna ladder and try to climb through my window whenever you feel like it," I tell him as I lift the window a little farther so he can squeeze through the opening.

"Damn, you'd think this would get easier," he says, his breath strained as he lifts his leg over the windowsill and onto the window seat cushion. Bringing the rest of his body into my room, suddenly, the room shrinks.

"That's because you're getting a belly on you," I say, ever so sweetly, but it still comes out a little raspy at my last thought. Yeah, right. I can practically do my laundry on his washboard abs.

He rolls his eyes back at me, knowing I'm full of shit. I guess that it's the relief of seeing him has somehow made everything feel easier. "Sorry, it's so late. I wanted to check in on you. Gran's light went out, so I know she's already in bed. I just wanted to let you know you don't have to pay for anything. I took care of it. I'll fix his lights and the tiny dent you made. Not really a big deal. Betty isn't that bad either." Ben holds up his hands, now much darker than earlier and the knuckles bloodied. "You're lucky I'm good with my hands."

A pang of guilt jolts my heart. I rush toward him and grab his fingers. "Ben? What'd you do?"

He yanks his hands from my grasp. "I just had a quick conversation with Lance after Alex left. I let him know that we don't call the cops on a girl, especially not on you, and if he comes around you again, I won't have a problem handling the situation a little more intentional myself. Sorry, I didn't get there sooner. Although I should have known it would have escalated quickly." He gives me a pointed look.

"You can't threaten him like that? He'll call his daddy on you. Just like he did me."

"I think after our 'talk' that he knows better." This time he reaches for my hand. His face softens and he says quietly, "It was a pussy thing to do. Him cheating on you and then blaming you for the outcome of his own actions."

I don't even care about Lance at this moment. Ben has squashed any feeling I had for Lance with the sincerity in his voice. I swallow, hoping he can't hear the giant lump that just disappeared down my throat.

He should be at home, in bed like normal people, but he isn't normal, and that's what I love about him. Finding my voice, albeit, low and not as sassy as I want it to come out, I say, "Well, thank you. But you're lucky I'm tired and don't feel like continuing this conversation, so you can go home and get some sleep."

"Are you ready for bed?"

"I think it's safer for everyone if I turn in for the night. I've done enough damage for a while."

He shrugs, not his usual response. "You don't agree?"

"Umm...well...Callie, I wondered if you feel like going down to the lake?" His voice is quieter than usual, his confidence not as evident as it usually is. Is he acting almost...shy?

"This late?"

"Yeah, Gran's not going to even know you're gone. Just leave a note that you're going night fishing. It's not the first time we've done it."

He's right, but this will be the first time alone, with him and no brother or other friends around. Ben's big blue eyes flash with anticipation waiting for my response.

And that's just it, because I can't say no to him, never could and definitely won't be starting tonight.

***

The walk to the lake isn't that far from my house. Ben stays pretty quiet on the walk there. Pointing out little obstacles in our way—a random tree branch laying on the ground, a rock that hasn't moved since I've been coming to the lake, and I could find it in my sleep. But he still points it out so I don't trip. We're about to head down the steep hill when he finally starts to talk.

"So, yeah…my dad's gambling has gotten worse. I'm worried about him," Ben confesses.

His dad has gambled forever. Ben has always had to find ways to make extra cash. I'm pretty sure that's why he started racing in the first place.

"I thought he quit gambling." But as I say the words, I know the truth. He hasn't changed or gotten better. Mr. Carmichael has been in and out of jail for as long as I can remember. He and my mom are very similar creatures; only her vices are men and alcohol.

He stops. His head drops and his shoulders sag, if I didn't watch his mannerisms so much, I wouldn't know how uncharacteristic this reaction is for him.

"I thought he was getting better, but a man showed up at our house today. He apparently made a bet, and this guy came to collect." He pauses and lets out a frustrated growl.

"Did he hurt you?"

"No. He just came to let me and my father know the debt has to be paid by the end of the week, and he better pay up." I'm so exhausted of taking care of his problems." He sighs. My heart aches for him. He's being so vulnerable right now. I'm not sure what I should say, so I go with honesty.

"You shouldn't have to. He's a grown man."

"He's my father. If I don't take care of him, I'm afraid of what will happen to him. This guy wasn't violent today, but that doesn't mean he won't hurt him, eventually."

Again, I have no idea what to say. I'm not an expert on parental advice. His words hit their mark, knocking the wind out of me.

The silence between us continues until we reach our destination. A quiet moment between us seems best. I'm not sure the extent of trouble his father is in, but it's clear that Ben is worried.

I know he loves it here. The lake has been the most memorable part of my childhood. Thankfully, Gran's house is so close. We swam anytime we wanted, made bonfires, and had sleepovers. As long as we didn't get too crazy, no one complained. We still have fun at the lake, but now that we're older, no one cares that adults are having fun at the lake.

It's not a large lake by any means, maybe more of a pond, but to us—the lost and forgotten kids of Lake Haven—it is our little piece of heaven.

5

Ben must have been here tonight before he came to my bedroom. There are two beach chairs, logs ready to be lit, and the familiar blue tent that I've seen many nights here, but I usually head home long before Ben turns in for the night. I'd rather recover at home in my own bed, Ben, on the other hand, along with my brother and their friends, use the tent as an oasis so they can recover from their drunken exploits without having to worry about getting home.

There also isn't any fishing gear like he suggested. Only a tent, chairs, and a case of beer. But that is fine with me. It doesn't matter what we're doing as long as I can have some alone time with him. Which seems like a bad idea, but I'm not sure I can leave.

We're sitting in the chairs, the tide washing in and out from underneath the chair. The water is chilly but not enough to deter us. My toes dig into the sand, and I lean my head back against the chair. Relaxing for a moment, not wanting to think about what he told me about a man coming after his father, which means Ben is also in danger. I guess I never realized how serious his gambling addiction was as I stare into the fire, watching flames dance around the logs.

"Callie?" He breaks my trance.

"Yeah?"

"Thanks for coming down here with me. I wasn't ready to head home yet. I don't feel like facing my dad tonight. I'm twenty-six and somehow still dealing with his shit."

"You could ask him to leave?"

"Where would he go? It's actually better if I can keep an eye on him, less fallout to wade through if he's within eyesight." He huffs.

"That's okay, I mean I still live with my grandmother. I get it though. I feel the same responsibility toward her. Your mom died and your father had a hard time adjusting. My mom left and I think it's my job to look after Gran even though Jake is around, he can't take care of her like I can."

"You do get it, don't you. You understand me. You've always been there for me, Sunshine. And I've never been brave enough to tell you that I've had a crush on you for as long as I can remember."

Then he takes my hand and lifts it to his soft lips. And I stop breathing. Lips that I have imagined kissing millions of times over the years. Lips that I've kissed once before. He holds it there for a long moment, as if he doesn't want to let me go.

When he finally releases my hand, he shifts in his chair so that his body is facing me. He's so close, I hadn't realized how close our chairs were until now. He reaches up, his thumb caressing my cheek and he moves it slowly, back and forth. Heat swells under his fingers. Tingles race from his touch. I'm having a hard time breathing but can hear myself practically panting. My body never reacted this way to Lance's touch. I'm no angel. I'm a feisty southern girl who has some experience with boys, but Ben—he's not just some boy, he is my Ben. He's got my nickname all wrong, though. He is *my* sunshine, he brightens everything around him, always bringing light when my sky darkens.

I swallow as he traces his thumb down to my lips. "I wish I hadn't wasted all this time without you." He pauses and I'm about to pass out. "I wish I wasn't afraid of what your brother would think. I wish I would have told you sooner."

"Tell me what sooner?" My voice is breathy.

He smirks. "That I'm so fucking glad Lance has been fooling around with Tammy. That it's more than a crush. I'm crazy about you, Callie. I have been for years. Every time I tried to tell you…there was always something or someone in the way." His eyes glisten. "Miss Callie Rae? May I kiss you?"

Breathing?

Nope.

This is not happening.

Frozen.

Yup.

Every ounce of my body—frozen.

My voice won't work. But my heart is melting at his beautiful words.

His hand threads through my hair and grazes down the side of my face, his thumb brushes lightly over my lips. Total explosion inside of me. Eyes close, and the very thing I've dreamt of happening for years is seconds away from blowing my mind. I peek open my eyes to make sure this isn't a dream just as his lips find mine.

A gentle kiss, featherlight and barely touching, but with so much presence behind it; my world stops. His lips are soft and full. And before I can even begin processing it, he pulls away.

His thumb moves along my jaw line, never leaving my skin while we kiss. Somehow that small little gesture melts something inside of me that I can't describe.

"I don't want to leave you. Not now. Especially not now," he says quietly. His eyes are locked on mine.

I finally find my voice. "You don't have to. I've liked you for as long as I can remember. I never thought you'd see me as anything other than Jake's baby sister."

His hand comes up to brush a strand of hair off my face, then with both hands he cups my face. His calloused thumbs sweep along my cheekbones. Calming and igniting an unfamiliar feeling inside me.

"I've always seen you, Sunshine. How could I not? You walk into a room, and everyone stops. The beautiful blonde, feisty and sweet, strong and kind, who makes the world come to a standstill. I can't tell you how many times, I've wanted to tell you how beautiful you are inside and out. But I never could without your brother knowing."

"I'm glad it's dark out. I must be as red as that fire."

"Don't be embarrassed. I'm crazy about you, Callie Rae. I'm just so sorry I waited this long to tell you. Now... things are complicated. The timing never works out between us, does it?"

Something takes over as his words finally hit me. "What? I don't understand..." I don't get my answer because his lips cover mine to stop me from questioning him more.

The panic settles a bit, but not the passion. The fire burning inside me. The knowledge that I may never have this moment with him again.

I somehow manage to maneuver myself onto his lap, straddling him. My hands, thank God, can finally run through his silk strands. He pulls me to his chest and in this position, I can feel his erection. He wants me and good Lord, I want him, too. No, I need him.

I grind against him, letting him know with my actions all the things that I want from him.

He manages to stand with me wrapped around his waist, never letting go.

"I want to…" He pants in between kissing. "Be with you. Can I…" I place my finger over his lips to stop him.

"I want you, Benjamin Carmichael. Even if it's just for one night. I want you." I know he will change his mind about us in the morning, that the regret for the things that we will assuredly do tonight will weigh heavy. He'll remember who I am. Jake's little sister. The neighborhood girl who likes to cause trouble. The girl who will always live in this small town and not amount to anything big or worthwhile. As my usual dysfunctional thoughts rule my mind, we make our way into the tent.

Ben tugs at the straps of my tank top, laying kisses around my collar bone. His tongue darts down my cleavage. "Take this off." He almost whimpers as he commands me to strip.

I do as he asks. "You are unbelievably beautiful, Sunshine." His eyes never leave my body, as more and more skin is revealed, and a sexy smile spreads across his face.

Pulling me back down to his lips, his hands roam over every inch of me as he kisses me senseless. Making me want so much more from him.

He tugs off my shirt and shorts. The thin fabric practically melts off by itself from the heat of our bodies. Next, I help him remove his t-shirt and jeans. He kicked off his shoes at some point. I don't know when, and I damn sure shouldn't be trying to figure it out now.

My attention gets pulled back as he nips at my breasts. Biting and tugging, sending jolts of a current that I've never felt from anyone, while his hands explore every exposed inch. His hand glides from my belly to between my legs. He finds my need and his fingers work to find my release.

He rolls me onto my back, and hovers above me. "Are you sure about this?"

"Yes. Please. I've never been more sure of anything in my life before, Ben."

He smiles a breathtakingly beautiful smile, leans down, and our tongues touch while he fills me. It's like his body, and all its intricate and muscular parts, was made for mine. We move together, and we come together. And it's the most glorious night of my life, one I will for sure never recover from.

I look up at the old, tattered nylon ceiling of the tent when he rolls off of me. We are spent and satisfied as I smile to myself. I never imagined that I'd be waking up in the tent naked, wrapped in Ben's arms. I've dreamt of a night like this, not in a tent, of course. But never believed it could or would ever happen.

It did and it lived up to every expectation I've ever had.

***

Ben's arms tighten around me. He lays a light kiss on my shoulder.

"Morning," I say, even though it is still very dark. I want to roll over, but the other part of me is terrified of what will happen next. Maybe he'll say all of this was a mistake, or it was just a one-night fling. I'm not sure if I can handle either of those outcomes.

"Hi."

"This is nice. Waking up with my arms around you after an amazing night together." His voice is soft and sweet. It's not the usual way he speaks to me. His lips graze my ear. "It was perfect, Sunshine. Just like you."

I giggle. "I'm not perfect. In fact, Mr. Carmichael, some may even say I'm a little crazy."

"Nah, some would say crazy, others will say you're just passionate."

It's quiet for a moment and I feel it. The atmosphere is changing. The carefree air is turning serious. Our beautifully perfect night is about to come to an end because there's no other alternative to how this was ever going to end.

"I'm sorry that I didn't tell you sooner," he says, while placing a kiss on my shoulder.

This all seems so wrong. I'm not one to keep my opinion to myself, and I most definitely will not start now.

"You said earlier something about the timing...what is wrong with it? It seems perfect to me." I nuzzle up closer to him.

"I wish I could stay here with you, but I have to go. I have to leave."

My eyes start to burn. Tears are seconds away from pouring down my face. I don't want to hear the rest of what he has to say. I only need to know when this nightmare starts. "When are you leaving?"

"It's soon. Too soon." That's when I know it's in the morning.

We lie back down, his front to my back, arms wrapped tightly, our legs tangled together.

"Will you be here when I wake up?"

He doesn't answer.

The silence is my answer.

"Can we pretend that we will spend the day together tomorrow? What do you want to do?" I ask, knowing it is only a dream.

He squeezes me. Kisses my neck and begins to talk about our day. "We'll spend all day together. We'll eat breakfast, spend the afternoon talking, maybe watching some TV, and then I'll take you out to the movies and to dinner. You'll come to my bedroom, and we'll continue what we've started here. That would be the perfect way to spend the day with you."

After a few moments, he says, "I'm not sure when I'll be back. I've got some things I need to take care of in Vegas. I want you to find someone who is good for you, Sunshine." I catch the waver in his voice.

I don't say a word. I know that I should get upset, scream at him, shed tears over the loss. I can't tear myself away from his arms. Even if I only have one night with him. I'll cherish every second of it.

The tears I've fought so hard begin to fall, though, quietly.

This is my first—and last—night with Ben Carmichael.

And my heart may not ever recover.

6

One Year Later

At almost twenty-four, you'd think I'd have my shit together. I mean, I do in a sense; I have a great job at a hair salon, help bartend at my brother's bar on the weekends, mostly because I'm there anyway; but where I've really screwed the pooch, as Gran says, is in relationships. Yeah, I suck at those.

Trent Harrison, case in point. I just left his place this morning. He told me that he wasn't ready for anything serious as I walked out the door. I wasn't asking him to bend the knee, but some type of I won't sleep with other girls would have been nice.

I'm not really sure what I'm looking for in a boyfriend, or even if I am capable of that type of relationship. My heart was irreparably broken last year with Ben and I haven't figure out how to move on from that.

Trent is the closest I've come. He isn't exactly my dream boyfriend. If there is even such a person out there for me—or on my brother's radar—for a potential boyfriend, I haven't found him yet.

Obviously, we are a racing family. My brother and his friends are very serious about the entire sport. So are Trent and his friends. This complicates my relationship with Trent since he and my brother are competition in the racing world. Did I complicate my relationship with my brother by dating his enemy? I sure did. But I'm determined to make it work at least until I decide it isn't worth it. This is a very small town, limiting my options in the dating pool. I don't want to be known as Jake's little sister and off limits forever. One redeeming quality about Trent is that he makes me feel independent. Not that I need a man to make me feel that way, but in the relationship department, I want to be able to make my own choices without my brother's involvement. But Trent obviously can't limit his options and wants whatever track bunny that's thrown his way.

Trent doesn't care who my brother is or that my brother will make it his mission to protect me from the male species as long as he can.

Why? Oh, why, do I find the need to complicate my life more than necessary.

As I turn onto the familiar street, Matilda, my old pickup truck ever since I got my driver's license, seems to almost drive itself toward Grans. I'm not looking forward to doing the walk of shame past my grandmother. I know I'm an adult, and this isn't the first time, but I still feel like it's a disappointment to her.

I park the truck. Movement from the old Carmichael place catches my attention. A moving truck, a Harvard Remodeling truck, and a brand-new Cobra Mustang take up almost half the street.

The Carmichael house, across the street from ours, has been vacant for a few months. Even though I haven't talked to Ben or his dad, the Carmichaels have been renting out the house to a single mom with two teenagers. They were quiet neighbors who kept to themselves.

Weeks after he left, his house was rented out. I kept hoping he'd come back, but he never did.

I've tried not to think about the inhabitant of the house who broke my heart which seems like yesterday, and a lifetime ago, at the same time.

I haven't talked to Ben since he left, but Jake has kept in contact. Telling me of his races and all the wins. He even mentioned Ben has been hanging out with a new girl. I've tried to ignore the jealousy that knocks at my soul but it never works. It creeps in like some type of poisonous gas.

I never heard from him again after that night in the tent. I could never bring myself to contact him. He left me broken that night. He changed me in so many ways that I know I'll never be the same girl.

The test looks the same as the last. I've peed on like seven of these things, and they all come back positive. Pregnant. Pregnant by Benjamin Carmichael.

We used protection, but it didn't work, apparently.

Emerson holds me like only a best friend can. "Don't cry, Callie. It's going to be alright. Ben won't abandon you. I just know it," she tells me.

"He's going to hate me. He moved away. I haven't heard from him after the night we slept together. You think he's going to want to talk to me now? Play family with me?" I shake my head as more tears fall. "He's going to become a famous driver someday, and I'm not going to tie him down to a pathetic girl and a screaming baby."

"You stop that!" Her tone was harsh. "Ben isn't like that, and he wouldn't care if you were having twins. You are an amazing person. He knows it. He's damn lucky he got you pregnant. I promise there is no better person than you to be his child's mother."

"I can't tell him. He'll hate me. This isn't what either of us had planned."

"He won't hate you. And it's not like you did this alone." Her lip curls up.

"I can't tell him. I just can't."

I push the memory away. I was pregnant for only seven short weeks. A miscarriage occurred shortly after I found out. Some would say that maybe I was never even pregnant. Your period was just late. It was too early for you to be pregnant. But I was, and for a few days I was pregnant with Ben Carmichael's baby.

I glance back at the house. These new tenants seem very wealthy. There are even some kids' toys scattered on the perfectly manicured lawn. Nice cars and furniture too. The moving guys have their hands full with a very nice leather sofa.

A little girl runs out from the house, followed by a beautiful dark-haired woman. She takes the little girl's hand and jerks her toward the car. "Let's go! Daddy will be here soon!" she yells at the child.

She opens the door, roughly tugging the little girl along, then lifting her into the car until she disappears inside. I assume she's buckling the little girl in her car seat. That better be all she's doing. I stop myself from jumping out of my truck, knowing that I have a tendency to overreact to situations. Maybe I'm just sensitive to the way mothers treat their kids. Since my mom was terrible at it, I tend to have a soft spot for mistreated kids and animals.

I'm not a mom or have even had many interactions with kids, but I'd beat that bitch if I were that little girl's father. I make a silent promise to myself that I'll keep an eye out for that little girl while I can.

Once inside, Gran's at the stove. "Hey, Gran."

"Hi, dear. Are you hungry?" Gotta love Gran, always trying to feed the world.

"Not now. Maybe later." I point to the screen door. "Have you met the new family that moved into the yellow house?" I can't even say the Carmichael name out loud. I'm pathetic.

"Um... No. They have been remodeling for days. The moving trucks got here early this morning before the sun came up."

Looking at me over her glasses, I can almost see her eyes saying, "I know you weren't home to see it."

Gran takes a drink as I tell her that they have a little girl. Gran coughs, choking and sputtering her lemonade all over the table.

"Are you alright?" I stand, hurrying to pat her on the back.

"I'm fine. Just down the wrong pipe." She clears her throat a few times before she says, "It'll be nice to have a child in the neighborhood again."

"Something is off about the mom, though. She didn't seem very...motherly."

Gran's forehead crinkles. "How so?"

"She basically dragged the kid to the car and shoved her in after yelling at her. I get it, she was probably in a hurry but, I'd be pissed if someone treated my kid that way."

She pursed her lips. "I'll make sure to introduce myself and keep an eye out."

I pat her hand. "I know you will. Mama Bear to the rescue."

"Damn right, puddle."

I laugh at her silly nickname. It reminds me of Ben. I remember the time I convinced him to dig holes around the yard so that I could make my own.

Ben...I stop the memory. I have to stop going there.

I haven't thought of him that much lately. Okay—no more than usual—but seeing that new family at his house has definitely stirred up some old feelings.

I tell Gran I've got a busy day ahead of me and that I'm going to take a nap and then head to the salon in a few hours, and then to Rae's bar for my shift. Luckily, with the distraction of the new family moving in, she doesn't bring up the fact that I'm wearing the same clothes from last night.

So at least there's one blessing I can count.

7

"Yo! Callie!" My brother stands in front of me with a case of empty beer bottles, annoyed as hell, per usual.

"Good evening to you, my dearest brother."

Sarcasm dripped from the greeting I gave him while wiping the counter, giving it a little elbow grease.

"Harlow isn't coming in tonight. I need you to stay till closing. Are you okay with that?" my brother asks. His face is red with sweat dripping down his forehead.

"Sure." I nod. "What's up, you look beat and it's only seven?"

"I'm tired of her calling off. Her boyfriend is home from college, but that dude treats her like she's the bottom of his shoe. She thinks he made the sun and moon, for fuck's sake."

Somebody has a thing for Harlow, but she's with the wrong guy, and now Jake is stuck dealing with the fact he has feelings for her. It's even more of a gut punch to him because she doesn't return the sentiment.

"Fire her, then." I shrug, just feeding the fire, knowing he's not ever going to let her out of his sight if he can help it, and of course, I'd whip his ass if he ever did.

He slams the box on the bar and the rattle of the bottles shushes the whole room. I think the old country song playing even stops twanging for a moment. "How about you just pour the damn drinks." He grunts and takes his empty bottles and his happy ass to the back room.

"Jeez, just tell her you love her already," I yell at his back. His arm flings up, showing me his middle finger. I can't help but chuckle. I grab my phone from my back pocket and send her a quick text asking if she's alright.

I talked with her a few hours ago. She told me she was coming in for her shift.

It takes seconds for her to respond.

> **Harlow: Yeah, Declan apologized. We're talking through some things. Sorry to leave you with no help tonight. I'll call you tomorrow. Tell Jake thanks for being so good about me calling off.**

If she would only open her eyes, she'd see my brother wasn't okay with it, not at all.

I swipe my rag over the bar. It's a popular hangout for our small town and our customers love it. Friday nights are much slower than Saturdays, but I'll still be on my feet and busy as hell. Mindy, the other bartender, is almost forty with two teenage boys to support and a southern attitude with no patience for men hitting on her. She knows she's gorgeous and doesn't hide it. A body and curves to die for. It's like looking at Pamela Anderson in her prime. She always wears a halter top to show off her amazing abs and her big boobs that are always bouncing in front of the drooling customers' faces.

"I'm going to take a break before we really start to get busy. You okay?" Mindy asks, while throwing her tiny apron on the bar, the same one that accentuates her hips.

"I'm good. I'll take my fifteen minutes when you get back." She waves at me and leaves me all alone. I kind of like it this way. The more customers we have, the less I have to talk to them and hear their problems. I hate having to play bartender psychiatrist. I mean, if I can't figure out my relationship problems, how the hell am I supposed to figure out theirs?

I organize the booze in a familiar order for me so that it will be easily accessible as the bar gets busy. My back is turned away from the customers as I go about my happy organizing when my name is called.

"Callie Rae!" I don't turn. I know who it is. My brother's annoying friends are here. "Callie Rae-ae."

I spin to face Van and Ace. Van is my brother's other best friend. I guess they both still talk to Ben often, but I don't ask how he is anymore. I've only asked Jake about him. Where is he at? Why did he leave? What is he doing? All he ever tells me is, "He's a big boy. It was for the best that he left this town." I pushed and pushed, but never got actual answers.

I asked Jake one time when he was drunk, if he thought he was okay, and his blatantly honest answer surprised me. I thought he'd tell me he was fine and happy, but he just said, "I'm not sure if he is okay...honestly I'm not sure if he ever was."

Focusing back on Van and Ace, I say, "What'd y'all like to drink tonight?" I give them my best southern charm. Van is beyond gorgeous. Dark hair that falls beautifully around his face, tan, gorgeous eyes and a panty-dropping smile. He used to be every girl's dream, and had a bad boy reputation, but he met the love of his life in Emerson Dawson. They have been through so much. But they have managed to get through it. Ace, on the other hand, is cute in his own way, but almost too smart for me. I'm not saying I don't want my guy smart, but he's kinda boring. He talks over my head about computers, and cars, and every other subject that puts me to sleep.

Before Van can answer, Katie, the resident ex-Van groupie, creeps her way over and sits on Ace's lap. Apparently, she is now an Ace groupie?

"You know, Katie, there are these things we have here in the bar called stools, everybody gets one, it's one of the perks of drinking a beer here." I suddenly feel the need to educate her on bar etiquette, although I know it won't do any good.

She flips her dark hair over her shoulders, and rolls her eyes. "Very funny, Callie. I just want Ace to know I'm ready to have a good time with him is all."

Eww... gag me. Literally. What is this? Some stupid 90's teen drama?

Now it's my time to roll my eyes at that response, I could easily roll them so far back in my head, I could pass out. "I think everyone in town knows what your intentions are, Katie."

"Aww..." She pouts her fake outlined lips at me. "Why are you such a bitch? Is it because Trent is with Jackie?" Her baby voice makes me want to throat punch her.

I have a temper, everyone knows it. I know it. I've slugged a few gals, and even some guys, in my day, but this isn't the time. No, it's time for me to walk away before I ruin my new manicure. I slam the vodka bottle on the bar and her eyes widen. A vision of me crashing the end of it off the bar and shoving it in her face flashes through my mind.

But Gran's voice overrides the thought, "A lady never gets her hands dirty."

Ignoring her jab, I throw one of my own. "By the way, Van, any chance you know where Emerson is tonight?" I want to remind this trollop of her place. And that it isn't anywhere near Van.

"She's resting tonight. Dealing with a migraine. Ever since her injuries..." He stops, not saying more. We all know what injuries he's talking about. Her head injury from when she was married to David that caused her to have seizures and migraines.

I swallow hard, remembering when she came home with the bruises, and those were only on the surface. Mentally I can't imagine what she is feeling.

"I'm going to take a little break. Van, would you be a dear and jump back here."

He laughs. He is the easiest guy in most situations. "Of course, Cal. I'd love to play bartender. And Katie..." He stands. "Knock it off. We're all friends here. If you want to be a part of that, you need to start acting like a decent person." She starts to protest, but I don't stick around for it. I toss a glance over my shoulder to see him taking my place as bartender.

I take a pack of Jake's smokes outside with me. I don't smoke or inhale, but I like the feeling of doing something while I'm outside. Besides, if you say, "I need a smoke break," most people are like "Hey, no problem." If you just say, "I want a break to do nothing and chill," they're less likely to agree. At least my brother is, anyway.

I head out the back of the brick building, pass the bathrooms and the back office where my brother is most likely hiding before the big crowd gets here. I know he is crazy about Harlow. She's even prettier than Mindy, but in a totally different way. Since I want to own my own salon someday, hair is my thing, and Harlow's got the prettiest head of hair I've ever seen. Long, silky, and a beautiful strawberry blonde. She also has light green eyes and a body to die for, it's too bad she's with Declan.

Shutting the door behind me, I step out into the little alleyway behind the bar. Nothing out here has changed since I was a little kid. Gran used to bartend here on the side to help support me and Jake. Same old green dumpster sitting there and people still can't manage to dump all the trash in it. I bend over to pick up a few bottles and some scattered napkins that cover the ground. Gosh, people can be such pigs. As I stand, an obnoxiously loud motorcycle revs its engine, it's so loud that you can hear it over the muffled music coming from the bar.

I toss the last of the napkins in the dumpster, then check out the direction of the noise from the bike. I'm awfully nosy especially when it comes to our family bar. Gran's father owned the bar, then passed it down to her and my grandfather. When he passed, she ran it up until Jake decided to take over.

I follow the obnoxious sound as the rider shuts off the bike, lifts a leg over it, and gracefully dismounts the bike. He is blacked-out in a full-face helmet, leather jacket, jeans, and boots. I can't see who it is, but one thing's for sure, it's definitely not a girl. He's too wide and muscular. I can't move because I'm mesmerized by the sight of the man before me. Whoever he is, he's got me trapped and I'm powerless to move. I know I should just turn around and head into the bar, mind my own business, but I can't. I need to see who this mysterious rider is. Growing up in this small town, I know literally everyone. But I haven't seen this bike around here before. Not sure if it's a good or bad thing, but I know my cars and motorcycles. My brother and his friends live and breathe motors, so I had no choice but to learn a thing or two.

I somehow manage to put the cigarette up to my lips, trying to look as casual and unaffected as I can manage. He turns away from me in that moment and time stands still as he takes off his helmet. He pulls up on his helmet to reveal a ghost—the very one who knows exactly who I am and stares right back at me. His hair is shorter than I remember, but even under the dim lights of the parking lot, I can see his beautiful blue eyes sparkling like the night he kissed me for the very last time. Ben Carmichael's presence does to me what it always does—causes my heartbeat and my breathing to cease altogether.

He's not changed much, just a bit more muscular, and much more beautiful than in my dreams. A knowing smirk plays on his lips. He knows exactly who I am and the affect that he has on me. Ben takes a step forward, and like the coward I am, my feet take me straight back into the building. I slam the door behind me, almost as if I'm in a horror movie and that damn scary clown is hot on my heels.

Except Ben's no scary clown but he definitely scares the hell out of me being back in town.

8

I hightail it back behind the bar. Mindy and Van are pouring drinks as people overtake the bar. "Shit! Shit! Shit!" I say as I tie the apron around my waist. "What am I going to do?" I say to myself, forgetting I have an audience.

Van leans over and says, "What are you babbling about?"

I probably shouldn't let the cat out of the bag, maybe it wasn't him. I could be just imagining the whole thing. I've dreamt of Ben more times than I care to admit to, so maybe I just wished that it was him in front of me for some reason.

"Nothing. I just didn't want to be back there for so long." I thumb in the direction of the back alley.

"No worries." He winks.

Glancing at the back door, I'm waiting for a particular ghost to walk through it. The longer it takes, the more I talk myself into believing I made up the whole scene. There is no way he is back. There's no way my brother didn't know that he was coming back and didn't warn me. I lie to myself.

"Damn, Callie. Did your brother promise free beer or something? It seems like everyone in the world is here. He's even dropped the price of the beer. He must think it's a special occasion or something."

Mindy yells over the noise of people talking and music, grabbing another drink off the bar.

"Tell me about it. This is a madhouse." I agree, as I pour what feels like my thousandth rum and coke.

As I'm grabbing Ms. Saunders, a lonely divorcee, a beer, who insists she hates beer, Jake comes through the back door. As it swings open, he puts his fingers up to his mouth and whistles. The sharp sound causes me to raise my hands up and cover my ears. "Jake." I can't help but yell back, even though there is no way in hell he can hear me.

"Listen, you assholes!" he yells, as he cups his mouth. "Tonight an old friend has returned. You might recognize this old bastard from all the races he won, or the cop chases that he was involved in. Buy Mr. Benjamin Carmichael a beer, or twenty, to celebrate him being back in town, and have a fucking great time."

Yep, I did not imagine that at all. My brother knew he was coming back and didn't warn me. I can't lift my head, it just won't do it. Instead, my concentration stays focused on the mundane task of wiping the bar down, which is much safer than making eye contact with the very person who's just stepped back into my life.

What feels like an eternity passes. So I think it might be safe to move again. Jake has stopped talking, but the patrons' voices raise. They're all praising Ben like he's some type of hero. But he should be distracted by them all worshiping at his feet. I raise my head, with as much caution as I would lift a fragile baby bird. Then my ghost comes into full view across the bar.

He is gorgeous. It's only been a year, but I remember him skinnier, hair lighter, paler skin and where on God's green Earth did those muscles come from? He is huge. His plain black T-shirt hides nothing on his body. His muscles ripple as he does that guy hug thing where they slap each other on the back while grasping their hands together.

Ben nods, then says a few words to Doug, one of the regulars here. He is getting a ton of attention, but he's looking down. Standing behind Jake, Ben raises his head, gives a small nod to another guy whom I don't know, but blushes like a little kid at the hoots and hollers he's receiving.

I know I'm staring; I can't help it. It's been so long, yet not long enough.

"I don't know where he went, but apparently it made him even hotter than before," Mindy says slowly, giving me the vibe she may be appreciating him. I don't like it one bit. "He keeps looking at you. Maybe you should go talk to him." Mindy glances in his direction. But he isn't looking at me now. "You really should go talk to that hottie. She pauses. "It might also do you some good to get away from Trent, show him that he's not the only one in your orbit."

"Believe me, he doesn't want to see me anymore than I want to see him. Besides, Trent and I aren't in a committed relationship anyway."

Her eyes widened, "I promise, it's going to end ugly. Trust me on that." She purses her lips with her take-no-bullshit attitude.

"Neither of them matter, anyway. I've convinced myself that it's better to be single than to be attached."

"Uh...huh." She tells me, knowing I'm full of shit. I want the fairytale. I try to hide it from everyone, but I really want the happy ending.

I continue to go about my duties. Pouring drinks, grabbing beers, and washing glasses in the sink. Anything to keep me busy so I don't have to stop to acknowledge him. All while still keeping track of where he is, who he's talking to, and the closeness to me. But after checking the Budweiser neon clock above the bar, it's been over an hour, and not once has he managed to come to the bar.

I can't stop my mind from racing. Where the hell has he been? What has he been doing? He confessed how he felt about me. We spent the night together. We made a baby. Even after I found out I was pregnant, I was planning a life with him until I lost the baby. What would have happened if... I don't finish the thought. I may not recover if I do.

A lone tear trickles down my cheek. Damn it! I brush it away with the back of my hand, hoping that no one saw, but the bar is much busier than it was a half hour ago. People are in every nook and cranny. Of course, part of me would love to get out from behind this bar and find Ben. But what would be the point? He already hurt me. He can't take it back. Taking a peek for the hundredth time to see where he is, I see him pat Jake on the back and walk out the front door. Just like that, he's gone and never even said a word to me. I swallow hard, not sure what to do. Disappointment ripples through me followed by pure anger. Part of me wants to chase him down and scream, "How could you do this to me! Again!" The other part wants to run out of the bar and never look back.

I slam the rag on the bar and tell no one in particular, "I'm taking a break."

Mindy nods with no comment either way. Instead of running after Ben, I take out my phone and head to Jake's office, if you can call it that. It's mostly a supply room of boxes and a desk littered with invoices and other random papers. Above it is his apartment. It's tiny, but he uses it as his bachelor pad. He has a few ladies who tend to stay long after the bar closes.

Needing to distract myself, I realize that there is only one person who can help take my mind off of the ghost. Thumbing through my contacts, I pick a very familiar name and text Trent Harrison.

> **Me: Busy?**

A few dots appear almost immediately.

> **Trent: Only if I can get busy with u. Meet me at my place in 20.**

> **Me: See u then.**

I know I shouldn't, but I need something to take my mind off of Ben. Trent is the perfect candidate for it. He's a playboy in every sense of the word. He's in high demand, but for some reason he chooses me over the other girls, as long as I don't ask him to be exclusive. He's good with our arrangement, and I guess based on the recent booty call texts, so am I. Maybe that's why I keep coming back to him.

I get up from the stool, turning to walk out when I bump into a massive wall of muscle. The ghost's beautiful blue eyes narrow in on me, I'm sure taking in my shocked expression. He doesn't say anything, but his eyes are darting back and forth, surveying every inch of my face. I wonder if he still sees the young woman he wrecked a year ago.

I can't help but inhale the scent of him. It's different but yet the same. I can't place the new smell, cologne maybe, mixed with a musky familiar scent that I could never forget.

His lips turn up in a smirk, like he knows I'm thinking of how delicious he smells. "Hello, Sunshine. It's good to see you."

I clear my throat, pull up my big girl panties, and say, "Well, if it isn't Benjamin Carmichael? It's so good to see you. I have an actual name, if you remember. I'd love to catch up with you, see what you've been up to the last year, but I need to meet my date." I pat him twice on the shoulder as if I'm petting a dog and walk right past him. Only I don't get very far. He yanks my arm, pulling me back into his strong arms and hard chest, I'm engulfed fully against him.

"Oh no, beautiful, I haven't seen you in a year and all you can do is walk away? I don't think that's the proper way a southern girl greets an old friend." His eyebrows raise, and that stupid smirk returns. I know he thinks he's got me in his chokehold.

"You do realize that you have just spent an entire night in this bar while I was working and didn't come over to say hello. So excuse me if I'm not jumping at the chance right now to walk down memory lane with you."

"There it is, Sunshine…I've missed your feisty mouth."

"Have you, though? I mean, I haven't heard a peep from you."

His eyes soften, releasing a breath, he says, "I didn't know what to say. I saw you outside when I pulled up on my bike. Honestly, Sunshine, I didn't know what to say that you won't hate me?"

Damn him! He took away all my thunder with his honesty and sincere words. He never called. He talked to Jake, though. Jake told me a little about his new life in Vegas, about his sponsorships, and how much he was learning about racing. But something else happened, something I don't think he ever saw coming. I followed him on social media. Okay, I stalked him. He looked like he was having a great time. He had new friends. He always wore a smile in every picture. But a few months ago he stopped updating his accounts. Literally went radio silent. So I can't help but wonder why, and wonder why he's back here when everything was so great there.

"So the famous Benjamin Carmichael returns like a prodigal son. Funny." I pause and tap my chin. "I seem to recall you left without so much as a goodbye. Now, you turn up out of nowhere, obviously doing pretty good for yourself."

"Turns out Vegas was better to me than I could have ever dreamed."

"Yet here you are. If you'll excuse me, as I mentioned, I have a date that I'm late for," I add, hoping that it will hurt him.

Ben's arms fall away from me. It's as if the world has stopped turning at the loss of his touch. I pause for far too long, my throat suddenly very dry, and I know for the second time tonight, I need to walk away from Benjamin, if for nothing more than to save the remnants of what's left of my heart.

"Callie, I had to leave. I didn't want to. I knew I couldn't keep in contact with you. It was for the best."

"But you kept in touch with my brother?"

"That was different. He didn't know everything that was going on for a long time. He does now." He stares down at me.

"You know? I'm worried about you. You left because of something with your dad. I thought we had a connection that night at the lake. But you never called me. You called him and not me, but that was okay because I knew you were safe. Then Jake tells me that you're doing great racing. Getting rich and making a name for yourself. I get it...you made new connections, new friends, have a new life. But yet...you haven't once called, texted, emailed or hell, wrote a letter. So excuse me if I don't want to stay here and chit-chat with you when we have nothing to say to one another."

"What would I have said to you? Huh, Callie Rae? I literally left you after I slept with you for the first time. I abandoned you and your brother, my two best friends. You're right, things got better for me. Better than I could have ever dreamed. In the beginning it sucked. I did some things I'm not proud of, but I had a lot of great opportunities dropped in my lap. I paid off my dad's debts...and even some of my own. But not for one moment, did I ever forget about you. I could never forget about you. I made sure your brother kept me up to date on you. I know you have a great job." He smiles, trying to soften my mood. It's always been his way, but he's no longer a boy standing in front of me who doesn't know what I gave to him. I cross my arms, not leaving like I told myself I would, and listen to him. Trying to halt my heart from listening to him.

He continues, "I wasn't sure when I could come back or hell, even if I could. So it was easier to pretend that one day I'd be back, but not to let you know. To surprise you. I didn't want to tell you one thing and then not show up because that would have just made things worse."

"You got that right. You showing up was a surprise, or more like dropping an elephant from the sky."

He shakes his head. "Please, Callie. Give me a few more minutes to tell you how much I missed you and your brother? How things have changed for me, and there is some..."

I hold up my hand. "Miss me? No, you didn't. You missed hanging out with your friends. Not me, I was just your best friend's little sister, and someone you got stuck with.

"Please let me explain. You know you can at least trust me." His throat bobs, and I can't ignore the soft expression taking over his features.

I find myself saying, "I'd like to, but that person I trusted, the one I slept with before he disappeared...I don't know him anymore. Now if you'll excuse me, I need to leave." I can barely choke out the words, but I somehow manage and leave him standing there, but not before I hear him say, "I'm staying at my dad's place."

I take a few more steps until everything—literally everything—clicks into place. Like a slow tick of a clock until it hits at exactly the moment you've been waiting on. The cars, the car hauler trailer, the little girl, the beautiful, mean woman.

Is that his daughter, a wife, and a new family?

I run past the bar, past the people swaying to the music, past the guy calling out for more shots, and out the door into the night air.

Because running is the only thing I have left in me to do.

9

Thank the good Lord that my truck isn't blocked by anyone. I know I shouldn't have ran out on my brother and Mindy, but I couldn't stay there any longer knowing Ben was there. Knowing that he has a family, that I'll have to see them every day, and I'm not part of it.

Tears pierce my eyes. I want to run home, curl up in my bed, and hide away, but I don't. I do what I know will help me forget about Ben, about his family, about the time we spent making sure Emerson and Van faced their feelings for each other while we hid ours from each other.

Ben's touch is addictive, I can feel the craving beginning. I have to stop thinking of him before I can't forget his arms wrapped around me, the feel of his soft lips, the way he... Enough! Using all of my brain power, my eyes focus on the road. No more distractions.

It takes about twenty minutes to get to Trent's place, but when I do, I'm not the only one there. Jackie and a few of his racing buddies are in his garage. He stands from the ugly bright orange milk crate and gives me a shit-eating grin. "Hey, baby. I was wondering if I'd see you tonight. I was just about to give Jackie a ride home when you called."

Jackie is standing by his buddy, Todd, with knives for eyes, stabbing me. She is beautiful and smart and has a body to die for, but she's just his second choice. This isn't the first time she's been here and he's gone to his bed with me, but if I leave, she will, without a doubt, take my place, keeping his bed warm. I'm so messed up that I don't even care that I'm seeing someone who has a sloppy second.

I walk slowly over to him. My body and mind spent from seeing the ghost of my past. "Hey." I give him a small wave, not really wanting to be with him now that I'm here.

He's gorgeous, don't get me wrong. Short honey brown hair, six-feet tall, chocolate eyes and a slim body, but after having Ben touch me for only moments, I know this isn't where I want to be.

"What's up? You look like something's wrong?" Trent asks me.

"Nah, just tired. The bar was crazy tonight." I take in the red race car in the garage. Trent is a damn good street racer. The only person who ever beat him was Ben and since then, no one has outraced him. "Is the car ready for next weekend?"

He takes a puff from his cigarette, cradling it in his hand so the flame is barely visible. "Just have to check the plugs, hook it up to the computer, make sure it's making enough boost...you know, the usual."

I hear that lingo all the time and I still don't know all the technicalities. I just love to go to the races, feel the adrenaline in the air and watch those cars zoom past as the freedom fills my soul. I've even flagged races before and it was just as exhilarating.

"I'll hang out until you're done."

"I think it will be about another twenty minutes or so, you can hang out here or in the house." He thumbs over his shoulder toward the house.

"I'll go sit on your porch, if that's okay?"

"Yeah, babe." He grabs me by my T-shirt, tugging me closer, and whispers, "I'll get rid of her, I promise. Does your brother know you're here?"

"No." I tsk. "He'd kill me if he knew."

"Good girl, I hope I'm there when he finds out about us."

I roll my eyes. "Stop it, you sound like an ass. You guys are competitors. Of course, he doesn't want me hanging out with the competition." My brother knows I hang out with Trent's team. He is pissed, but I'm not sure if he knows I'm also sleeping with the enemy. I wonder if Ben cares that Trent has been in my bed, and I've been in his bed. It pisses me off that that thought even enters my mind.

"You don't think he'd care if you were dating the guy he can't beat behind the wheel of his small tire piece of shit?"

"No, I don't, but I do care that you're being an asshat about it. So you guys race each other, big deal. I'm heading to the porch. Get rid of her or I'm gone." I know I'm lying to him. My brother doesn't even want me dating his friends, let alone someone he despises. I shrug off the thought. I'm not in the mood to care right now.

He smiles, "Damn, baby, aren't we a little jealous tonight?"

"Whatever, I'm not waiting all night." Irritation doesn't even come close to how I feel right now. Seriously, of course I'm jealous. I'm here to be with him to forget someone else, but he doesn't even have the decency to hide the fact that he's hooking up with Jackie. I happen to have the grace to not flaunt the other people I'm with in front of his face. I know I'm a hypocrite and all over the place right now. We aren't in a relationship, and I need to remember that.

He holds up his hands. "Okay, fine. She's gone. I'll have Todd take her home, he's been dying to tap that," he says as he swats my ass, chuckling.

Rolling my eyes, my reaction nonchalant, because frankly darling, I don't give a damn. What I do give a damn about is my brother hating me. He will kill Trent eventually for fooling around with me. Jake hates Trent...no, loathes him, actually I don't think there is a proper word to describe his distaste for him. It's been a rivalry for longer than I can remember. It started between Ben and Trent, and after Ben left, it became my brother's problem. I know I'm playing with fire, but for some reason, I don't care...and I should. But it's not like we're going to get married and have babies.

I glance around Trent's house as I make my way to the porch. Trent's house is nothing spectacular. A small two-bedroom, ranch style with yellow siding. Typical bachelor pad; small couch, La-Z-Boy recliner, gaming chair, seventy-some inch TV hanging above the fireplace mantel, and three different gaming systems. The bedroom and kitchen have just the essentials; bed, dresser, a pot and a pan, plus some dishes. But he has an amazing back yard. It has a bar and a massive picnic table. My favorite part of his house, though, is the patio swing.

His grandfather made it for his grandmother. It's made from a tree that they had carved their initials into as kids. When the tree was struck by lightning, his grandfather cut the tree down and used the wood to make a swing, all while preserving their initials. I run my hand over the arm of the swing, feeling the RH heart NH.

It reminds me of Ben and myself. The memory of him carving our initials into the tree by the tire swing in the woods behind his house stirs something inside me, and the vision comes back like it was yesterday.

"Ben, please give me back that knife. I can do it myself." I stomp my feet like the kid I am.

"Sunshine, you can't just carve your name into a tree, 'Just because,' you have to do it with someone special or someone you love. Not with a guy ten years older than you, and especially not one in a boy band."

"But I don't have a boyfriend. I'm eleven," I snap back, handing him back the stupid red pocketknife. "Fine."

He pauses for a moment, then begins carving into the tree. His body covers my view, minutes pass as I wait, trying to maneuver myself to see around him, but it's impossible. He keeps giving me the side eye, making sure I don't see what he's carving.

What felt like an eternity passes, and he finally moves, revealing CR heart BC.

As a tear starts to fall, clomping brings me back to the present. I wipe at my face, looking up to find Jackie trying to gracefully maneuver her heels from the wooden patio to the grass.

"Christ, Jackie. What the hell do you want?" I don't even try and hide how her presence makes my skin crawl.

"I'm going to let you have Trent tonight. Todd is taking me home, and I think I have a better chance with him. For some reason, Trent has a thing for you. If you ask me..." She sits beside me like we're best friends. Her dollar-store perfume rots the air as she continues to talk as if I give a flying turd about her early-morning activities. "Well, I don't know how to say this to you."

"Just say it, you're just going to insult me or tell me how you're going to screw Trent after I leave him tonight." She pushes her feet to swing us in an aggressive manner. She must be nervous, and... I'm ready to bolt.

She runs her long hot pink fingers through her cherry red hair. Finally, after a moment, she says, "I want to be with Trent, and in order to get him, I need to share him with you. I'm totally fine with that, until he dumps you or you dump him...but what I can't figure out is why you're fine with sharing him with me." She pauses as my lips remain concrete. The bitchy redhead I've grown to hate over the years doesn't disappoint.

I don't respond. I don't have anything to protest. She's right. I can't figure out why I'm okay with it either.

She stands and takes a few steps away from me. "You know you can join us sometime. Three's never a crowd with the right people. I can share him with you. Maybe take turns." She gives me a wave.

"Threesomes are fun. Really fun," she adds in a high-pitched voice and a shoulder shrug before she turns away from me.

I wish I could see the expression on her face clearer. What would make her say that? What on Earth would make her think that I would even entertain that idea.

"Hey...Jackie? Todd's ready for you," Trent tells her as he sneaks into our view.

"My bed buddy tonight. See you later, Trent." She waves and winks, leaving it as if she didn't just promise to fuck the guy I'm sort of dating with me in the bed with them. Trent lowers his slim body beside mine. His presence doesn't excite me like it should, which makes me wish I would have never texted him or drove here.

"Damn, I'm glad she's gone. It looked like you two were having a serious conversation." He chuckles to himself. "I honestly thought I was going to walk into a bloodbath."

"Do you like me, or are you just using me to get to my brother?" The words spill from my mouth. Jackie ignited a fire inside me just now and pissed me off.

"What? Of course not. I mean, if it jacks him off, it's a bonus." I start to stand, and he tugs me back down. "Baby, I'm crazy about you. I don't think either of us are ready to settle down and have a family. We've both got shit we want to do. But I told you I'd like to be your guy."

"If I don't spend the night, are you going to sleep with Jackie?"

"Would it bother you if I did?"

"Yeah."

"Then, consider her gone."

"Really?"

He makes an X with his finger over his chest. He leans over and kisses me. It's a good kiss, but it never quite hits Benjamin Carmichael status. No one has ever hit his status. Seeing Ben tonight, knowing that he's moving back home and has a family now, it's ruining everything. I stop our kiss and pretend to grab for my phone.

He continues kissing my neck, sliding my shirt up so he can run his hands along my stomach. Something is off inside me. I can't explain it, but I'm just not feeling it tonight. I don't know if it's seeing Ben, or that it just doesn't feel right. *It isn't Ben's touch caressing me now.*

"I...um...need to go. I have to check on Gran. She says she isn't feeling well." I hold up my phone, acting as if I just got an important message from Gran. I'm lying and don't care. I need to get out of here.

He slides his arm around me, kissing my shoulder. "Come on, babe. I just kicked everyone out to spend the night with you."

I pull away, and stand. "I appreciate it, I do. But I need to go. I'll call you later, okay?"

He throws his head back, shoving his hand through his hair. "Really? You're just going to leave me with blue balls and a cold bed?"

"I'll see you soon." I don't stay to see his reaction. I get my bee-hind outta there fast. He has a temper, and even though he would never touch me, I did lead him on tonight.

Reaching my truck, I quickly shut and lock the door, while turning the key in my ignition.

The ride home doesn't take as long as it should. Instead of the twenty minutes it usually takes from Trent's place, it's only fifteen for me to get to Gran's.

When I pull up to Gran's old brick house, the craziness that was tonight has settled in the pit of my stomach, but with each step toward the house, it slowly dissipates. Gran is my calm after all the years of letdown and heartbreak, she is my rock, my constant, and tonight I need that more than ever.

    I take the side entrance instead of the main that leads to the living room. I need comfort in the form of food, and the only way to really experience that is Gran's chocolate cake with chocolate buttercream frosting. I know it's sitting on her grandmother's glass cake dish. I can picture the mixer filled with a brown batter and the heavenly chocolate aroma overpowering the kitchen.

    I turn the key, step over the threshold…

    And right into the arms of the ghost.

10

Damn it. He's here. So is Jake, with his cheek pressed against the vinyl flower tablecloth, squishing his face to form fish lips.

"He's beyond wasted. When did he start drinking so much?" Ben asks in an unfamiliar, authoritative tone.

A second ago, the moment seemed like a dream, Ben in Gran's kitchen again, but he's nothing like the boy who stood in that spot so many times before.

He's watching me, assessing my reaction, when his forehead crinkles. "Are you drunk too?" The accusation was thrown in my direction.

I begin to process his words, comprehending the situation. The fog lifting and what he's accusing me of cutting through like a knife.

"No, Benjamin Carmichael, I'm not drunk, or driving Matilda drunk. She's too pretty to get wrapped around a telephone pole."

He looks down at his wrist, a shiny silver watch wrapped around it. "It's after three, you should have been here a while ago...you left before twelve."

"And?" I fire back, the old me showing up, ready to take on this new Mr. Carmichael.

"And? It's dangerous to be out this late. You should've come straight here. We're the hell did you go? Who were you with?"

I jerk back at his words. "Excuse me? Where the hell do you get off?" I can't believe he's reprimanding me like I'm his child and he's my father.

He keeps talking, "Do you always worry Gran like this?" His frustration is evident in his serious tone.

"Not that it's any of your business...but as I told you earlier, I was on a date!"

Jake groans, mumbling with the side of his mouth still resting against the table. "Quit fucking yelling." He struggles with the last word, almost as if he's made up a version of it, but I know what he's trying to say.

Aggravated, I wing my purse onto the table with more force than a drunk Jake can tolerate because his head bolts up. "Fuck, Callie." The palm of his hand smashing into his skull. "Fuck you both. I'm crashing on the couch."

He manages to get up and stumbles through the doorway of the kitchen to the living room. Leaving me and the ghost...alone.

Walking toward the sink, I grab the sponge and start scrubbing the pan that Gran left in the sink. Must have been from dinner. I'm relieved, though. I need something to do with my hands other than wrap them around his neck.

I can feel his eyes on me, watching every movement I make. I turn the water on full strength, hoping he'll get the hint and blast away from this kitchen.

"Who were you on a date with?" he says over the gushing water.

Rolling my eyes, I know I have to face him in order to stop this confrontation—and not wake up Gran—and head back to bed. I turn off the water. "When did you become such a peckerhead?"

He purses his lips. "I'm worried about you."

"Yeah, don't waste your time, I was at a friend's house getting laid, if you must know."

He lets out a strangled noise. I'm not even sure what'd I call it, a growl, maybe? It doesn't matter because in seconds, I'm whisked away from the half-clean pan, facing him with his hands tight around my upper arms.

"Getting laid? What the fuck, Callie? I haven't been around, but I don't remember you acting like a…"

"A what?" I goad him on. What is he thinking?

He lowers his voice, his lips barely moving. "A whore."

He should know better than to talk to me like that. The rage it ignites within me is indescribable. My hand comes up, but it doesn't make it to its destination like I intended. Still holding my arms, he controls my assault on him.

"You piece of donkey shit!" I spit at him.

He smiles. The bastard actually has the nerve to smile at me. "What the hell are you smiling at, Benjamin Carmichael?"

"You. Only you would call me a piece of donkey shit. I missed that crazy mouth of yours." His face changes, his smile falters, turning rather serious. "You shouldn't spread your legs for just anyone, you know."

"Oh, that's great advice, maybe I might take it to heart coming from you, but seeing that my profession is **a whore**, I won't," I yell back. I'm so close to his face that I could stick out my tongue and lick his chin. There was a time…damn it, who am I kidding? I still would. His hold on my arms is so powerful that every time I try to wiggle out from his grasp, it only gets tighter, and we get closer.

"Callie, I'm serious. You deserve better than one-night stands."

I inch closer to his face. My finger poised in front of his face. "You're one to talk. Considering that's exactly how I'd explain the last time I saw you. I promise, you know absolutely nothing about me now." I lower my voice, gritting my teeth as I seethe the words.

The dim kitchen brightens to the point of stinging my eyes.

"What on God's green Earth is all this racket?" Gran says, entering the kitchen. Her night coat is less than flattering, making her look years older.

Ben lets go. I'm not as relieved as I should be.

"Sorry, Mrs. Rae. I was trying to tell Callie she shouldn't have come in so late. That's all."

She walks over and sits at the small kitchen table, wobbling a bit. "Ben, I don't think it's any of your business to reprimand Callie. However, I'm glad to see you again. Jake said you'd be coming back to town." She looks at me from underneath her glasses, "You can run up to bed now."

I kiss her cheek, not passing go or collecting two-hundred dollars. Wondering why Gran knows Ben was coming back but Jake didn't bother to warn me. I run up the steps as fast as my small feet will take me, and don't look back.

Closing the door when I get to my old room, I lean up against it. I can still hear Ben and Gran talking, but rather than try to hear what they are saying, I heave myself onto the bed.

He's so different from what I remember. And why does he care what time I come home? And that SOB called me a WHORE! I didn't even have sex with Trent tonight. But who is he to talk about what I do in my free time?

Since apparently, Ben is ready for the whole shebang. A daughter, a wife, the white picket fence. Everything. All I ever wanted was more from him. A life with him.

Trying to simmer down, I turn on the TV and watch reruns of *Friends*. Of course, it has to be the lobster episode. For the longest time, I thought that Ben was my Ross and I was his Rachel. Lobsters. Soulmates.

Then I grew up and realized that there is no such thing as a "lobster" when it comes to me and Ben.

11

I can't sleep. Lying in this bed is literally killing me. Knowing he is at his house with his new family. A wife. A daughter. How could I have worried about him the past year, only to find out he's been fine all along?

I wasn't.

Not for a long time after I lost the baby. Even though I wasn't very far along in the pregnancy, I was ready to be a mother to our baby. I was going to tell him. I would have gone to Las Vegas and started a new life with him, no matter what I left behind. My throat starts to swell, and I have to stop this stupid reminiscing.

Seven-twelve blazes at me from my alarm clock. I've met my limit. It's time to see what Jake knows and why in the world they both hid everything from me.

I've cried millions of tears that have been soaked up by this old mattress, and I refuse to let one more tear fall for Benjamin Carmichael. I launch the covers off of me, letting myself embrace the anger. It may be a small amount at the moment, but I allow it to fuel me to interrogate my liar-faced weasel brother.

Jake is still lying on the couch when I creep down the stairs. He must have stayed on the couch in his drunken haze. I know Ben left shortly after I went upstairs. I heard the door slam and watched from my window as he walked across the street to his new life. I didn't look long enough to see if his wife came to the door, or if his daughter threw her little arms around him and greeted him with a kiss.

I tiptoe over to the velvet flower couch that has probably been here since 1972. The local news is on the TV, so I change it to the *Housewives* station, cranking up the volume. A show mostly of women screaming at each other and screeching about their husbands, or lack of, will surely do more harm to my dear brother's head than my voice.

I sit patiently waiting until Jake grabs his head. "Christ! What the fuck is that noise?" That took longer than expected, the home shopping channel was about to be blaring in his ears.

"TV," I tell him, in a calm voice, hoping to annoy him a touch more.

He sits up, rubbing his skull. "What time is it?" His voice is gruff, sounding worse than he looks.

"Rough night?"

"Fun night, rough morning."

Fun? He was having fun with Ben, when he should be telling him to go to hell.

"Really?" I say, sarcasm lacing every letter.

Jake sits up, slowly coming back to life. "It's great to have Ben back. I missed the prick."

"You missed him?" I throw my arms in the air. "Did you miss his wife? Or his kid?"

He sits up tall at my words. "Wife? What the hell are you talking about?"

"When did he have a kid?" I fired back.

Jake groans, falling back on the couch, covering his face with an ugly knitted pink throw pillow. "It's too early for this shit."

I jump up, ripping the pillow from his face. "You knew he had a kid and a wife, and you never thought to share that information with me?" I lift the pillow higher, poised and ready to fire at his face. "Not to mention, you didn't tell me he was back. You knew it last night before work and you didn't think I needed to know that information?"

"So he kept the kid a secret until he knew it was his, what's the big deal? It's not like it's any of our business. You know he goes back and forth to race. He's been gone for like a year. He didn't want gossip to spread. You know how this stupid little town is. So what?"

But he was my business...*for one night.*

"Can we talk about it later?" He grumbles.

"No!" I hit him in the chest with the pillow.

"Damn it, Callie. Stop!" I hit him again. "Stop it!"

"Both of you stop it right now or I'll get my wooden spoon and crack it over your asses! How old are you two?" She didn't want an answer, I've played this game for years. "Not too old for a good lickin'!"

"Sorry," we say in unison.

"Now, what's so important that caused you two to be screaming at each other at seven in the morning?" Gran asked, as she sat down at the kitchen table.

"Ben..." Jake answers.

"Oh...I see." She stands, walks toward the coffee pot. "I think I'll need two cups this morning for this conversation."

I head toward her. "Did you know all about Ben? His wife? His kid?"

Her silver brows raise. "A wife? I don't know anything about a wife, but a little girl, yes, I know." She turns to look at Jake as he sits at the table. "When did Ben get married?"

He shrugs his shoulders, not committing to any answer.

"I don't know, Gran. Maybe we should all go join his new little family for breakfast and ask him." My tone is full of attitude, that as soon as I say the words, I cover my mouth. I half expect Gran's hand to fly up to my cheek.

"Callie. Please have a seat..." Gran asks calmly.

I do as she asks, even though I'm about to run out of this house and interrogate the hell out of Benjamin Carmichael.

Gran turns around and goes about making coffee and plating up muffins and donuts for breakfast. "I'll start the eggs," she says as she places the plate of goodies on the table.

"I'm not that hungry. You don't need to go through all that trouble," Jake tells her, which is surprising since he never turns down eggs, sausage, or any other food.

"Must have been a good night." Gran winks at him.

"Seems to be a really shitty morning though," Jake says, while he brings his head to meet the table. "Ow."

Gran sits, and sets her coffee down. "Now tell me what you think you know."

"What do I know?" I point to my chest, becoming more insulted by the second. "I don't know anything. That's what's going on. You two know everything and have left me out of all of this." I cross my arms, waiting for a response that will explain why they chose to leave me out of every conversation that involved Ben and his new family.

Jake lifts his head. "He isn't married to that 'see you next Tuesday.'"

Gran swats his arm "Jacob!"

"At least not that I know about. He would never marry someone like her."

"He has a daughter with her," I retort, wanting him to give me a viable explanation.

A part of me is sad for this little girl, but the other part is pissed that he got in trouble in the first place, and he's raising someone else's kid. He could have stayed behind and had a family with me...

Stop! I can't think of that whole thing right now.

Gran begins to explain. "I didn't want to tell you yesterday. You were so upset when you saw Becca and Annabella. I couldn't tell you who they were. After everything you went through with your own..." she pauses. I know what she wanted to say. She was there when I crumpled to the floor in pain and bled through my clothes as blood flowed down my leg. Gran rushed me to the hospital, holding my hand as I cried. Praying out loud that my baby would be okay. But my baby wasn't saved. Ben and I will never be parents together. "Well, I thought I'd have more time to prepare you for... the news."

"Prep me? You sound like I'm not able to handle the situation."

"You are kinda freaking out," Jake chimes in, cocking his head to the side, giving me a crinkled expression. "Which is fucked up, it's only Ben. Chill out."

Gran grabs my hand. She knows how I feel or at least felt about Ben. "He found out about a year ago. That's why he left so soon after everything happened with Emerson and Van. He had to take care of his daughter, Annabella."

"Does Ben know about her poor mothering skills?" I ignore Jake's confused reaction. I want to smack him right now, but I know it won't help get the answers I'm looking for. "I mean, her tone made our mom's voice sound angelic."

"He knows she's not going to win any mother of the year awards. But he's giving her the benefit of the doubt. He's trying to show her how to be a better mother," Gran answers, her voice soft and sincere.

"Huh..." Is all I can say. I know Ben has a big heart, but to go to the extreme to teach someone how to be a better mother is crazy. It's something that can't be taught. If anyone knows how true that is, it's me. My mother had the best motherly role model, and she can barely stand to look at me. I, apparently, ruined her life.

"We are going to be supportive." She turns her head toward me, giving me the 'that means you' look. "To all of them, including Becca. I want you to be nice. Make an effort to be friendly to her. You were raised in the south. Ben needs our help. He is part of our family." She taps the table and rises. "Now, if you'll excuse me, I need to get another cup of coffee."

Jake stands, taking a sip from his coffee cup. "I have no idea why this is any of your business. I get it you guys are friends and all, but it's not like you two dated or anything." He tosses on a ballcap that was on the table next to him. "I'm headed over to the shop. We need to get Ben's car ready for the race."

I want to know more, but I don't dare ask. I have to learn that whatever is going on with Ben, racing or family, is none of my business.

After Jake is gone, Gran sits back down.

"I know this is hard on you," she starts. "I should have told you, but you were so mad. I knew if I told you they were here, it'd be worse. I honestly thought I'd have more time to break it to you. I thought Ben would wait a while to stop by the bar."

"I guess you were wrong," I tell her, my sarcasm is inappropriately directed at her, but after the words come, I regret them immediately and apologize.

"It's okay. I will help you through this. You should try and be nice to Becca and the daughter. And Ben too." She adds, "He was a huge part of your life at one time. He only left to take care of his daughter."

"It doesn't matter." I stand, wanting this conversation to be finished. I kiss the top of her head. "I don't have to go to work until ten. I'm going to go pull weeds around the gazebo."

"Okay, dear." She pats my arm. "I'll finish cleaning up."

Normally I would offer to help, but I need some space and fresh air.

12

The gazebo is beautiful. The wood is painted white, there are two matching wooden swings facing each other, along with some potted plants and flowers adding yellows, pinks, and purples. But my favorite addition is the fairy lights. At night it feels as if magic is a real thing, and you are surrounded by it.

I go about yanking the weeds from the newer gerbera daisies I planted last week. I hate those pesky weeds that even after you pull out their roots they return double in size.

As I'm crouched on my knees, yanking away, I hear a woman yelling. "You can't leave me here all day with her. I am not going to be stuck in this stupid hillbilly town while you're out there living it up. You were at the bar. You can't race without me there, so don't even think about it." The voice fades, so that I can no longer make out the words.

Because I'm a nosy southern girl, and because I have a pretty good idea of whose voice it is, I casually grab my bucket, and walk over to the side of the house where I can get a front row seat to the shit show that is this woman Becca.

I know from past experiences that you can't easily see this part of my house from his view. I used to hide here when we played hide and seek, or if I was spying on Ben and Jake. I guess some things never change.

I put my head down and go to work on the weeds. I can hear some more yelling from her, but can't make out anything from him. "You brought me here to give me a better life?" She throws her hands up in the air. "Oh, well then, I should kiss the ground you walk on then, because what you actually brought me here for was to be a housewife. To pick up after your child and that mutt."

Not being able to help myself, I look up to see her pointing in his face like she's some sort of crazy person. I can't make out all the words, but I get the point. She doesn't want to be left at home while he's out playing with his car.

Ben places his hands on the tops of her arms. His back is to me, but I can tell he's pissed by the way her tan, too much makeup face is crinkled up at him. She isn't happy with him at all.

A few more seconds roll by, she becomes louder, I'm unable to understand what she is freaking out about. Ben is listening. Hands on his hips, shaking his head. She lets out a frustrated scream while yanking at her hair, then proceeds to push against his chest. That seems to push him to his limit. He turns, head down, and hurries over to the driver's side of the newer Mustang. This crazy girl is still yelling as he cranks the engine. It roars to life, and she steps closer, hitting the hood with her fist. I stand, unable to hide anymore. This is ridiculous. I feel bad for the spectacle they're making of themselves. I can't lie, I'm more than happy that they don't have the perfect relationship...or maybe one at all. He backs out of the driveway, and quickly down the street as she's screaming, "Fuck you!" at him, multiple times.

She spins around, giving up, I think. She slams the door, disappearing from my sight. The neighborhood is back to being quiet and boring.

I take a final peek, giving up my southern nosy ways, that is until a beautiful yellow lab catches my attention. In all the ruckus, I never noticed the beautiful creature. The cute puppy dog is sitting at the door waiting for his or her mama to let him in. I hope she's much nicer to him than she is to Ben. But then again, I can't forget how she treats her own child. I can't imagine she's any better to her dog.

Now that poor puppy dog is sitting there with its tongue hanging out, tail wagging, and staring at the door waiting for her to come rescue him. Only I already know she's not going to. Maybe I should walk over there and give her a piece of my mind, but then Gran's words flash through my head, "You be nice to her." *Blah, blah, blah.*

I go on about my business, continue over to the gazebo, and finish my gardening. I'm not sure how much time passes when I hear a jingle of metal. For a moment, I think my keys must have fallen out of my pocket, but then a stinky, slimy substance followed by panting and the cutest puppy dog eyes are staring up at me.

I fall back on my bum, and let the adorable fur-ball lick me like any normal dog-loving person would do.

"Hey, beautiful girl." I stop, taking a peek to make sure my assumption is right. Nope. It's a boy.

"Look at you, handsome. What are you doing over here? Is your mama being mean to you?" I say in a deep silly voice, while rubbing under his chin. He sits so I can reach his spot better. "Good boy." I catch a glimmer of steel from around his neck. Taking the dog bone-shaped tag in my hand, I smile at the name.

Beau Carmichael. Call 555-1212 if you think I'm lost.

I wouldn't go for lost, but abandoned definitely. Glancing over at Ben's, the door is still closed with no signs of Bitchy Becca coming to fetch the sweet boy.

I've already seen this nasty woman treat her daughter, boyfriend, or whatever, and now her dog, like they are beneath her. I think it's time to introduce her to Miss Callie Rae.

"Come on, Beau!" I shout, while slapping my hand on my leg. "Come here. I'm going to take you home." He doesn't move. I repeat and he just sits, tail wagging but not wanting to move away from his spot. I leave mine and tug him lightly by the collar. "Come."

He finally listens. I still have a hold of his collar while we cross the street.

Once I'm on the small porch, I'm pissed and saddened at the same time. I'm not sure if it's because of Becca, the dog, the little girl, or Ben—but I decide it's every last one of them.

I knock hard. I know there isn't a doorbell, so I knock again. But when I look over, I see one of those fancy doorbell cameras. I don't remember the previous tenants having it, so I'm sure Miss Bitch of Las Vegas needed protection from this small town.

I press the button. After a few seconds the door opens. I don't like her already, and the scowl she's wearing, clearly having a resting bitch face with long black curly hair that's tied up in a clip-on top of her head, doesn't help. She looks like she's just rolled out of bed. Her face is so scrunched up, I wonder if she always looks that way. What did Ben see in her?

"Oh, did that..." she motions at Beau with disgust, "bother you?"

"No. Of course not." I smile, giving her my best fake sweet version of Callie I can. I found this sweet boy in my yard, I looked at his tag and saw Ben's name. I'm an old family friend, an old neighbor," I explain, but she looks as if I've read a textbook to her. She could not care less about what I'm saying.

"Yeah, it's his. For some reason this beast won't stay in the yard."

"Maybe you should tie him out for a little bit, or even put up a run. My dog, Dixie, liked to have freedom, or even one of those collars..."

The wench places her hand up to halt me from talking. Granted, I'm rambling, but she did not just shush me. "He's fine. We know how to take care of a dog. Thanks for the suggestion." She straightens, and for the first time, I notice her killer body. She's in a crop top and shorts. She literally has a six pack. Her tan is perfect, but I can't help but wonder if her face is starting to prune, or if it is permanently fixed into a scowl.

I know what's coming. I've got a spark in me that when someone scratches the right itch, it tends to go off, so I know I need to calm down. But I can't let her get away with talking to me like that, being a bitch to her own daughter, and leaving this poor dog out with no signs of her giving a shit. So, I say in a very calming tone,

"I am sure you're a very intelligent woman, but I'm just helping an old friend out by bringing him back to Ben. Ben loves dogs as I'm sure you already know. I'd hate for something to happen to his dog if I can help it."

"Whatever." She yanks him by the collar, pulling him through the archway of the door, and kneeing him on the way through. She closes the door without a word. Stealing my thunder, I'm left standing on the porch, taking calming breaths so I don't break down the door.

Be nice, Gran said…yeah, wait till she meets this "See you next Tuesday."

13

Later that day, I'm finishing up my client, Ruth's hair. Saturdays are always so busy for me. And after this, I have a shift at the bar. I've had my cosmetology license for at least six years. Every hour I work here or at the bar gets me closer to the main goal—owning my own salon.

Harlow is drying Mrs. Hazel's hair while she tells me about my brother. "Your brother has me furious! Do you have any idea what he did to the schedule?"

I shake my head. He probably gave her a bodyguard so no one talks to her.

"He took me off nights. He said that I needed to be home with my parents studying and not slutting around for tips at his bar."

"Harlow, you knew that was coming. My brother is being absolutely ridiculous, but he does care about you. He's just making sure no one hits on you."

She is yanking on poor Hazel's hair while she towels her dry, taking out her frustrations on the eighty-year-old lady in her chair. Harlow also works some days here to pick up some extra cash. Even though her parents are wealthy, she still likes to have her own money while she attends the local college. I'm glad I get to see her at both of my jobs, though. I'm responsible for getting her both of the jobs, obviously.

"Sorry, Hazel. Bad tangle."

I stifle a laugh.

"What about you? I heard Ben was at the bar last night," she fires back. I know she hates when I bring up the fact that my brother is crazy about her.

"Yep."

"Yep. That's it? Oh no, Callie Rae. You're not getting off that easy."

"I bumped into him at the bar, then again at Gran's, and then this morning his baby mama and I had a little heart to heart over Ben's dog. So yeah, Ben was at the bar last night. That's pretty much the gist of things."

"Wow," she says slowly, her eyes wide with a what the fuck look. "I think I'm going to need more details."

By the time I explain the events of last night and this morning, Ruth and Mrs. Hazel have paid their bills, both leaving with gorgeous hair.

While we finish cleaning, Harlow listens intently while I gripe some more about the dog.

"She is truly a horrid individual for kicking the poor dog when all he wanted was to be in the house," Harlow explains.

"Horrible woman," I agree.

"What do you think Ben is going to do about her? I mean, unless Ben has changed into a horrible person, I don't think he'd want to be around a person like that."

"I don't know who he really is anymore. All I do know is he's back and I'm going to have to deal with it. Honestly, I wish things had turned out different."

Her hands fly up to her mouth, letting the broom fall. "Oh…Callie. I didn't think, I forgot. I should have known that him having a daughter might be upsetting for you. I'm so sorry." Her arms surround me in a tight hug.

I manage to break free from her Hulk-like grasp. "No, that's not what I'm talking about. I mean, that stings, I'm not going to lie, but I just wish he would have kept in touch with me. It would have made things a lot easier. Now it seems as if his whole life was some big secret that I'm now just let in on. The guy I knew is gone and replaced by this stranger."

"Maybe he doesn't have to be."

"What do you mean?"

"You have a history with him. Give him a chance. I don't think Jake was the reason he was at Gran's last night."

I shake my head. "When it comes to my brother, you really are clueless, aren't you?" I joke with her.

"Shut up!" She nudges my shoulder. "You really need to get his side of the story. A lot of things can happen in a year."

"Well, I'm not bringing it up. Besides I've moved on and so has he. I'll just try my best to ignore him. I need to calm down about it. Jake was right for once in his life... It's none of my business."

My phone chimes, halting our conversation. Answering it, Jake's voice is on the other end. "Can you bring a few of my good wrenches to Van's shop? I forgot them at Gran's the other night."

"Right now?"

"Yeah. Are you busy?"

I check my schedule just to make sure I didn't forget about anybody else. "Okay. But I'm not rushing. I'll get there when I get there."

"Fine," he says it with the disappointment of a three-year-old.

"See you soon." I don't give him a chance to add more of a guilt trip. My brother is a huge brat, but he's all I have and I know he cares about me.

"Was that Trent?"

"No." I say, while throwing my phone in my purse. "It was my brother. I have to run to Van's. Want to come and say hi to him?" Giving her a conspiratorial smile but she rolls her eyes.

"No. I have to run home." She pauses for a moment, and I know she wants to ask me something.

"What?" I nudge, wanting to get this over.

"How serious are you and Trent? I know you hang out and stuff, but are you planning on getting more serious about him?"

I shrug. "I don't know. I'm good where we are at. We like to have fun together. That's it."

"Aren't you worried about your brother, and now with Ben being back…They hate Trent. It's going to make it difficult for you to *have fun* with Trent, not to mention hurting your brother's feelings. He's going to feel betrayed."

"I'm not worried. They are big boys. It's not their business who I hang out with. Besides, he's so different from them. I think he's just the distraction that I need to help me mind my own business."

I can't ignore the pang of guilt when I think about what she's saying and the truth behind it.

"Sorry, toots. I have to disagree. He's your brother. You shouldn't be friends with the enemy."

I can't help but roll my eyes. "I'll see you later," I tell her, while slinging my purse over my shoulder.

She's right. I know she is, but what does it matter now? Ben has Becca and a kid to worry about. Jake has his bar and his cars. They both have their own lives.

I need to have my own, too, no matter who it is with…and who it will hurt.

14

Van's shop has always been like a second home. We've hung out here most nights for as long as I can remember.

I place my truck in park, and head in through the open large garage door. A semi-truck could fit through this door if it needed to.

There is a bright yellow race car I've never seen before parked in the middle. Jake, Van, and Ace are all concentrated by the front of the car, focused on something under the hood.

"Hey, boys. Got some wrenches here." I drop the old rusty red toolbox on the cement floor.

"Hey! Careful!" Jake calls to me. "Those are my babies."

"They weigh a hundred pounds and are as heavy as an elephant's ass. Not a chance that's a baby in that box." The boys all laugh at me.

"Thanks, Callie. You are a lifesaver," Van says, giving me a quick peck on the cheek.

I'm sure I blush. A girl can't help but love a little attention.

"Sure. So, who's beauty is this?" I ask as I run my hand along the driver's door frame.

"Mine," a deep voice coming out from under the car says. I already know whose voice it is, but that doesn't stop me from looking down. Ben slides out from underneath the car on a creeper. He sits up while wiping his hand with a rag. Why on Earth didn't I expect *him* to be here?

"Good to see you again."

And my heart stops. Pretty sure my mouth is hanging open like Beau's was this morning. He is stunning. His hair all mussed up, white T-shirt with splotches of grease, ripped jeans, and black workboots. Not to mention, those muscles. Seriously, where did those come from? I can only see the outline of his pecs and abs. The good Lord knows I won't be able to stand upright if he peels off that shirt.

"You okay?" he asks.

I swipe the stray hair from my face in an attempt to collect myself. "Sure. Yeah. Good." I nod, taking a few steps back from him like he's about to give me cooties or something.

He stands, moving a little closer than my brain wants him to, but my body is reacting like he needs to come quite a bit closer. "Good to see you. Sorry about what I said to you earlier. I was hoping I'd get a chance to apologize and maybe explain a few things."

I swat my hand through the air, like it's no big deal. "Oh, yeah? No need. You made yourself perfectly clear."

Jake pipes up. "Why are you apologizing to her? We were all drinking. You say dumb shit when you're drunk. Don't apologize. Besides, we all know she's hanging out with that asshole."

I must not be hiding the shock on my face because he continues, "That's right. I was told by at least two of his teammates that you've been talking to him. Am I wrong?"

"We're just friends. And I don't need an apology. All good," I say to stop this conversation.

Except it's not. Ben was rude and wanted in my business when he hasn't let me in on this past year. I want to stop time and tell myself to stop being such a puss and let the real Callie Rae loose on his ass, but

I don't. I can't let my emotions keep taking over when he's around. It's not good for either of us.

"I met your dog and your...girl...friend." Wow, that was difficult to get out of my mouth.

"Beau. He's a good boy." His forehead crinkles in confusion. "Did you stop by or something?"

"Kind of." What do I say after your baby mama stopped yelling at you and she slammed the door on the poor puppy? But there's nothing to say, so I don't. I'm playing nice, just like Gran asked me to be. "He wandered into our yard, and I walked him back over to your place. He's a beautiful boy."

Ben leans against the car with his arm up, displaying black tattoos on the skin of his biceps. I can't make out what it is because I'm too captivated by the muscles that have caught my attention. My mouth dries, and I find myself biting my lip. I have to stop my hand from reaching up to caress him.

"Beautiful," I say, not talking about the dog at all.

Ben nods. "Yeah, I thought a dog would be good for Anna. Turns out he's even better for me."

I regained my composure. The name *Anna* sobering me up a bit. And when the hell did he get a dog?

It's quiet between us for a moment, I can't stand the silence.

"I returned Beau safely to Becca. She seems...pleasant," I say, gritting my teeth together so I don't add an expletive.

"I wouldn't have used pleasant to describe her this morning. But she's trying. I'm glad she was *pleasant* with you."

I want to tell him the truth, but I don't think I have to. He lives with her. He knows the truth. Speaking of which, I say, "How long are you planning on staying in town?" There, I said it. I broke the curiosity ice block *with a sledgehammer.*

He looks down at the ground. I'm guessing he's trying to find the right words, or maybe just doesn't want to look at me. The whir of an airgun fills the silence. Like a coward, I take it as my cue to leave because even though I asked the question, I'm not sure I want to know the answer.

"Well, I got stuff to do. It was good talking to you." I cup my hands around my mouth and yell as loud as I can, "See ya, boys!"

I mean, I wanted an answer, but panicking felt like a better thing to do.

Turning around, I get myself the hell out of there before I can bring up any more topics that feel like a gut punch to my stomach and heart.

When I'm almost at my truck, the nausea starts to settle. I get in, ready to drive away, but decide I better calm myself down for a few seconds before I drive on the road with innocent people. I turn over the engine, letting some classical melodies fill the cab of my truck. For some reason the keys to a piano is what I need to hear right now.

"I'm okay. I'm good," I say to myself.

A few more seconds pass when a knock on my window startles me. I know which set of perfect blue eyes are going to be staring at me.

Ben has somehow managed to sneak up on me. "What?" I say as I push the button to let the window down.

"I wanted to see if you were okay. You've been sitting here for a while. Do you need something?" His throat bobs. In that moment, I want to reach over and just feel it for no other reason than every inch of him seems to fascinate me more than it ever has before.

I swallow back the lump in my throat. "No. I'm good. Headed out and was texting on my phone." I held it up. Thankfully I had it sitting on my lap. Not sure when I did it, but thankful that I did.

"Okay." He taps my window frame, like he's getting ready to leave, but then stops. "Look... I'm really sorry about you finding out about

Becca and Annabella this way. I wanted to come over and introduce them to you and Gran properly. Like dinner, or even having sweet tea on the porch one evening. But unfortunately, Becca has her own way of introducing herself."

"I noticed." My snarky words slip out.

"I'm sure you did." He cocks a knowing smile.

God, he's gorgeous.

"I'd like to introduce them to you properly, though. Can we come over tomorrow, maybe in the evening for some sweet tea?" he asks, almost as sweet as Gran's tea.

"Sure. I'd love to meet them," I lied.

"Good. Well, I've got to go. But…Callie, it's really good to see you. I am really sorry for the way things went down yesterday and this morning. That's not how I expected things to go. I've got a lot to tell you."

I'm taken aback by his honesty. "You don't have to tell me anything. You have… people. You're happy. I mean, we're just friends who lost touch. You don't owe me anything."

His hand finds mine on the steering wheel. "She's not my girlfriend. Things got complicated in Vegas. I want to explain it to you if you'll let me."

I pull my hand away. "It doesn't really matter now. Does it?" I make sure to give him a small smile. I want him to know nothing he has to say will change the fact that he is a father. He's raising a kid with another woman. If there is one thing I know about Ben, he is loyal.

"You're a father, Ben, and that's what takes priority." With that, Ben steps back like I wounded him in some way, and I press the button again to put up the window. I check my mirrors and back out of the parking spot, never making eye contact with him again, and head straight to Trent's.

15

Trent is waiting for me in his driveway. I texted him on my way here. It seems that after I have an interaction with Ben, Trent comes to the rescue. He opens my driver's side door.

"Scoot over."

I do only because he doesn't give me a chance to protest before he pushes my body over with his. "Let's get out of here. I need a night out—alone, with you."

I glance over at the garage, and it's filled with his friends...but most importantly, Jackie. "Kick them out. It's your house."

"It's not worth the fight. Besides, we never go out in public. Just hang here. When you called, all I could think about was being alone with you."

"Where do you want to go?" I ask, surprised because he never wants to be seen out in public with me. He doesn't want anyone to think he is taken. Which hasn't ever bothered me before, so not sure why it's bothering me now.

I should go home and stop leading Trent on, but I know Ben has a whole life that I'll ever be part of. So why not try and fall for a guy who isn't attached...and he's here and he likes me. I need to remind myself that I need to forget that I'm broken. Forget about what could have been.

"I think we should go out to dinner," he says, his voice cracking a bit.

"Are you asking me out on a date?"

"Yes. I want to stop this whole fuck buddy thing we've got going on. I like you. A lot. I don't feel like screwing anyone but you. I want us to be a thing."

"Really?" Unable to hide the surprise in my voice, I can't stop staring at him.

He takes my hand in his tattooed hand—the word 'fearless' in beautiful black calligraphy scrolling across his knuckles. I brush my finger over the word.

Seeing Ben has done weird things to my brain. Maybe what Trent is proposing isn't such a bad thing. Ben has decided on his course in life…maybe I should finally decide on mine, too. I don't want to spend my life afraid of being alone.

"You're serious about this?" I ask.

He nods. I'm not sure if this is what I want, but what I need right now is a distraction…and to get a certain Carmichael out of my head.

And Trent is just the man to do that.

***

Thinking back on the date with Trent, I realize that it was actually sweet. We had steak, baked potatoes, broccoli, and three-layer chocolate cake. It was delicious. The only problem was that it was a date…with Trent…and it was weird. Trent literally wined and dined me. So not his style. His words from earlier about me being "his girl" keep replaying in my head. Even as I lie here in his bed, after having sex, I know that being his girl isn't something I want.

He shifts, pulling me to his chest. His hand wraps around to cup my breast. "I think I could get used to waking up like this with you." His gruff morning voice vibrates against my shoulder as he kisses it. The effect making me cringe. That shouldn't be my reaction, should it? I roll over to shake the negative thoughts that's invading my pre-caffeinated brain.

Facing him, I take in his soft features...his dark eyes, straight jaw, his thin lips. He's so different from Ben. He's much thinner, taller, and covered in tattoos from head to toe. He looks like he could fit in on the stage of any rock band, only his love is cars, not music.

"Callie?"

"Yeah." Ready for him to make a snarky comment about my boobs, they seem to be his favorite subject, he surprises me even more by saying,

"I want to see where this goes." His voice sounds low, expression turns serious. "I don't want to share you with anyone. You like attention, and so do I, but I want all of your attention."

I roll onto my back, trying to stop the panic from spreading. I was just thinking of how his words earlier made me cringe, now he's thinking of me being what? Girlfriend? Exclusive? Is he kidding me right now?

"What are you saying?" *Please don't pressure me.*

He smiles. "You are going to make me fucking say it out loud, aren't you?" He sits up, the cover falling from his tattooed, shirtless, muscular chest. He takes my hand, kissing the palm. "Will you, Miss Callie Rae... will you do me the honor of being my girlfriend?"

My stomach begins to churn as I try to think of a reply quickly that won't make him angry. "What if I'm not ready for that, can we still hang out?"

He closes his eyes, bracing himself, I think. "No. I want to call you mine."

"That seems a little overboard. We started this thing between us because we didn't want a relationship, and now you're telling me that's exactly what you want, and the only thing you want."

"I thought about this…a lot. I know you want this to be casual, but my cars are my life. I need my girl to understand that. I can't keep giving up the time I could be working on making my car faster, knowing you're not in it with me. I want you to be my biggest fan. Right now, you're kind of playing for both teams."

I sit up, pulling my shirt up to cover my chest. "I am not. I'm supporting both of you. He's my brother. Of course, I have to support him. I can support both of you." I snap back, realizing what I was saying when I honestly didn't want any of this with Trent. He is frustrating the hell out of me.

"Look, I'm not willing to give up my car time for someone who isn't willing to give up her time and loyalty to me. Your brother I can handle. He is a prick, but he doesn't race enough to be a threat to me. I know he's the brains behind the tuning. It's Carmichael and Bradley I can't stomach. If you don't want to make us a thing, then I'll have to consider you an enemy because I don't think I can function knowing you're on the other side of the track with my competition."

"They're not the enemy, they're my family."

"Either way, I won't share you, not even with your brother. On race day, I want you in my pit, not theirs."

"That's not fair. He's my brother and his friends are my family. I won't turn my back on them. I'm telling you, I can support both of you."

"I can't tolerate it if you're my girl, but if I can't call you mine in public, then I'll call you my enemy, and anyone who touches you is my prey."

I can't even form a response. This conversation has gotten intense and out of control. I need to rein him in somehow.

"Can't you give me some time to think it over?" Do I need time? No, no one makes me choose when there is no choice to make.

He's silent for a few moments. The crickets are literally the only sound I hear. I'm not even sure why I'm trying to appease him with this response because I don't want anything to do with him. As the seconds tick by with an ultimatum, his dark eyes finally land on me. "I need an answer soon." And with that, he gets up, slipping on his boxers.

"So, that's it—your way or no way? You wanted this to be casual. We both decided that it was for fun, to hook up and not have to worry about the perfect relationship or the white picket fence, or the two-point-five kids."

He pounds his hand on the door frame of the bathroom before walking back toward me causing me to jump. "Fuck, Callie! Why are you making this so hard. You're here, in my fucking bed, sucking my dick, and you are acting like I'm asking you to commit a crime, rob a bank, murder a dog." His voice raises. "You were talking about being more than friends a few days ago, and now when I want that...you don't. Is there someone else you want? Is it because Carmichael is back?" he asks as he leans over me, with his hands propped on the bed. It's not in a romantic or sweet gesture. He's making my anxiety spike. The word danger flashing like a neon sign in my head over and over.

"What? No," I squeak out. "Nothing can be further from the truth. He has a girlfriend and a daughter. I have no interest in him."

"Look, this is fucked up. I wasn't expecting you to act like this" He runs his hand through his short hair, standing up. "I care about you. I want you to be my girl, if not, I'm done. We're done. I'm going to take a shower and head down to the garage to finish up some stuff. I can't fall back into bed with you after dealing with this. You can go back to bed or leave whenever you want. Give me a call when you decide, but I won't wait for long. The race is in a few days." He sounds annoyed, but his hand brushes lightly against my jaw, the harsh tone gone, replaced with his normal, soft tone. "I hope you're in my pit on race day."

When the door closes, I waste no time gathering up my clothes, getting dressed, and leaving. I don't want to deal with this bullshit. The farther I get away from his place, the more pissed I become. How dare he give me an ultimatum. We were supposed to be casual—fuck buddies—instead, he wants to be serious with me. Or what, he threatens me? Maybe my brother has been right all along...he's trouble.

16

Instead of heading home, I go do some therapy shopping for most of the day, then head to Rae's bar. I don't have to work, but I know Harlow is working tonight and I can use a drink.

The bar is busy as usual. Jake is behind the bar with Harlow. He's smiling and joking around with the customers. Of course, he is...his girl is by his side tonight. I guess that's what Trent wants, too. But just like my brother, it might not be possible. One day maybe Harlow will realize she likes him, too. With their situation, it's going to be difficult for Jake to have a future with her.

"You look like you had a rough night? Where are you coming from?"

"Trent's," I tell Harlow.

"What happened?"

I tell her all about his ultimatum and she's so astounded that she comes to sit beside me so she can hear better.

"What do you want to do? I mean, I don't think he's right for you, and I definitely don't think he should threaten you like that, but if he's what you want, I can't stop you. I can only be a shoulder to lean on."

I can't help but smile. She's so sweet. So innocent. But she's right. I shouldn't let him talk to me like that. Why am I allowing myself to be treated this way? It's not like I'm in love with him.

"I'm going to tell him to choke on a fruitcake."

Harlow laughs. "Only you would use that choice of words to tell someone to fuck off."

I tip my glass up in a toast. "To staying the fuck out of relationships."

She picks her glass of water up and clinks against mine.

The night gets better, or at least more familiar. I jump behind the bar to help out and set up for the next day. Jake offers to drive Harlow home, but of course she refuses like normal and waits for her dad to pick her up. She relies on them more than she should, but I think she's afraid of being on her own. Harlow just recently found out she was pregnant and so did I. Her asshole baby daddy isn't supportive. He wanted her to get an abortion. Not because she wanted to, but because he doesn't want to ruin his football career. She has only told her parents. I've been sworn to secrecy and I'm going to support her anyway I can. She still doesn't look pregnant. I can't help but wonder how things will change once the baby comes.

She's the first to leave. Jake decided to let me close tonight since the bar is empty. "I'm headed out. Let me walk you out to your truck."

We headed out to the parking lot together. He tells me he'll see me at Gran's, and he's gone. I started up my truck, only to notice I forgot my other uniform t-shirt to wash for my next shift. "Seriously?" I huff out. "Only me."

I get out, scanning the parking lot for anything suspicious. I don't know why, but the hair on the back of my neck raises, I'm not comfortable being here alone, so I turn back to my truck. When I leave the parking lot, I see a car similar to Trent's parked across the street. Yellow, with identical wheels. Is that him? Is he watching me? Waiting for me? His words echo in my head. I'm his enemy.

At a closer glance, it looks like a woman. Relief washes over me. Deciding I don't have the energy, I ignore the earlier unease that seemed to settle into my bones.

When I get home. Jake's car is in the driveway. Relief washes over me. He's home safe. I've never really worried about him before, but the unease I felt at the bar calmed at the sight of his car.

I head up to my bedroom and get ready for bed when I catch a light out of the corner of my eye, shining through my bedroom window.

Ben's porch light is on and he's outside watching his dog while he does his business, I assume. Not being able to help myself, I keep my eyes glued to him. He really has changed, but obviously my feelings for him haven't.

I'm still watching him. I want to bring up that night. I want to tell him about the baby we made, if only for a short time, but I can't bring myself to do that because he's got a new life, one that doesn't involve me. A life I know nothing about. I could ask Gran or Jake what they know, but I want Ben to tell me. I want his truth of how his family happened.

All I can see is his broad back facing me. He's holding onto a leash while Beau sniffs the ground. Ben moves with his dog, letting him take the lead and sniffing anywhere he wants. Beau takes him over to the road, and then Beau looks up at me. Causing me to step back from the window. Surely, he didn't see me. Sneaking back to the window, but careful not to be seen, I peek out and see that Ben is staring up at my window. He bobs his head towards the ground, then up to my window with an empty stare. He mouths something that I can't hear or make out. He tugs on Beau's leash, and they head into the house.

It is at this moment that I long to go over to him. Ask him why is he with this horrible woman instead of me? Why did she get to have his baby and not me? Why is she spending her life with him instead of me when she doesn't even appreciate what she has?

17

The next day starts as normal. Breakfast with Gran and Jake, and four clients at the salon. When I arrive home, Gran is busy with pots and pans on the stove. The kitchen smells of turkey and stuffing.

"Is it Thanksgiving and no one bothered to tell me?" I tease.

"Oh, honey." Gran spins to kiss me on the cheek. "I'm glad you're here. I need a hand with the dessert. Can you finish icing the cake?"

She doesn't let me respond before she's thrusting a butter knife in my face.

"Is the President coming to dinner?"

"No," she says calmly. Not even laughing at my little joke.

Weird, normally I'd get a little chuckle from that. "Aren't you silly?" she'd respond, or something along those lines.

I hesitate, then ask, "Who's coming to dinner, or is it just us?"

She sets down her towel and looks at the counter, as if she's bracing herself for some not so happy information she's getting ready to tell me.

"Benjamin, Annabella, and his friend are coming over for dinner." She lifts her head, waiting for my reaction.

"Oh!" I let out a puff of air. I should have known.

"I promised him a home-cooked meal, and tonight seemed like as good a night as any. I hope you can put the past behind you and be nice to everyone at my table this evening. I know it seems complicated, but it's been a while. You've both moved on with your lives."

I flinch, that stung a bit. We just talked about how this made me feel, and now she wants me to put it all behind me, bottle it up in a jar and forget. I know she's right, though. I need to let him lead his life and I should lead mine.

I stand up a little taller and agree. "It will be a nice evening, Gran. Thank you for working so hard on a delicious meal."

Gran and I work side by side to prepare a turkey dinner that we've done hundreds of times. For some reason, I want it to be the best meal that they've ever eaten. For a moment, I let myself wonder what the night will be like. Will Becca be nice? Will Annabella like me? Will Ben feel comfortable? As I let all the what-ifs run through my head, Jake comes through the door.

"It smells dee-licious!" He sounds as if he should be on the *Dukes of Hazzard* by the emphasis on his southern accent. "Ben said he and the family are stopping by tonight. I'm glad you're doing this for him. He doesn't seem like himself." He tilts his head, as if he's thinking hard about something. Seeming uncharacteristically concerned. "I know things are different now, but something is definitely off with him. I guess it's probably coming back home with a new family."

I can't help but listen to his words a little more carefully. He's different, that's for sure. To me, of course but for him to be different with Jake, it seems odd.

I'm just pulling the rolls out of the oven when the doorbell chimes.

Gran rips off her apron. "Wonderful. They're here," She almost sings with excitement.

I inhale, hoping my lungs will fill with her enthusiasm. Because right now I want to be anywhere but here.

Jake opens the kitchen door, and it's as if everything is right with the world when Ben's large frame enters the kitchen. A flash of hope washes over me, as if he's here just to see me. But as always, reality strikes and Becca walks through the door next. A polite smile graces her stunning features. She looks much better with a smile instead of a scowl. Plus, she is dressed like she just got off the runway in a tight pair of black pants, white silk button shirt, and black stilettos. I'm all for gorgeous shoes, but this gives me another reason for the green monster to resurface.

"Hello," she says so sweetly that it makes me be the one to scowl instead of returning her smile. Ben's smile, on the other hand, is good-natured, like he's genuinely happy to be here. There is a small little girl with her head buried in his chest. This must be Annabella. "Thanks for inviting us."

"Come on in and we'll head into the living room while Gran finishes dinner," Jake tells him, motioning toward the couches.

Jake then tries to get Annabella's attention by tickling her arm. She just shakes her head and buries it farther into Ben's chest.

This poor baby is shy. You can see it all by the way she attaches herself to Ben.

Becca speaks up, "It's nice of you to invite us over. Ben has said some wonderful things about you all. Especially that you are a wonderful cook." Her voice is as sickeningly sweet as a bowl full of sugary cereal.

Gran flourishes under the praise. Her hand comes up to her chest. "Thank you, dear. I'm just happy I can cook Ben a good home-cooked meal. I hear in Vegas those are far from normal."

"Well, I do prefer vegan and juicing. My health is so important to me," She pauses for a beat. "Is there going to be anything with carbs?"

Gran runs through the list of delicious food: turkey, mashed potatoes, stuffing, corn, rolls, and of course, cake. Turkey seems to be her only option. Right on cue, Gran apologizes for having made the wrong dinner for her.

Ben chimes right in. "Becca, it's only one dinner. It will be fine."

"Sure, if you call twenty pounds fine." She nods and looks at Gran. "I'll just have some turkey." Hmm... Sickeningly sweet to severely health conscious. This is getting ridiculous with each second. "That's fine, dear, whatever you like. I'll never force anyone to eat my food." Gran gives her a polite smile, trying to remain a nice host, but I can even see her patience crack. "Callie, why don't you get everyone drinks. Go ahead and slip into the living room and get that precious baby settled." She nods to Jake, patting him on the back as he walks by her. "Go on now."

Becca walks past me without even a sideways glance. That's fine. I'll add it to her list of wonderful characteristics. Her poor daughter hasn't asked for her yet. I find that odd. I'm sure it's not uncommon for a child to favor one parent over the other, but I always thought a girl would want her mama in situations like this. What do I know though? I don't even know where my mom is right now or has been for the last five months.

I know the sweet side of Becca is all an act, and she is officially an ungrateful bitch posing as a polite monster. Their muffled voices can be heard from the kitchen. I steel my nerves and continue to fill the glasses of Gran's famous sweet tea. Maybe I should put a little rum in it to loosen her up. Like Gran has taught me, I place the drinks on a tray so I can deliver her the tea properly.

I straighten my shoulders, preparing myself to enter the line of fire.

18

Entering the room, Annabella sits on Ben's lap. I'm finally able to see her adorable face. Big blue eyes, the same shade of blue as Ben's. A cute button nose, pouty full lips, and dark ringlets create the cutest toddler I've ever laid eyes on. The only feature that mirrors her mother is her shade of hair color.

Jake and Ben are talking about the race that's coming up. Becca is looking at her fingernails, no doubt bored out of her mind. She doesn't look like the type of girl to know what they're even talking about. I doubt she's even been to one of his races.

I've been to races what feels like hundreds of times. I love hanging out in the pits while the cars are getting prepped and ready to race. There are always a handful of racers I can cheer for. Van hasn't raced in a while. He's usually everyone's 'go-to mechanic'. My brother is the tuner, making the call about what tune the car will need. More power or less. More nitrous or back it down. My other favorite part of racing is the street. The drag strip.

Cars are lined up side by side. Most of the people involved are behind the race cars. Watching from that position gives you a great vantage point.

How would I even choose who to support between my family and Trent? I'd always choose family.

"The race is in two weeks. We will have new shocks and tires by then." Jake's smile widens as he finishes a conversation that I just walked in on. "It's so good to have you back," he says as he pats his shoulder.

Annabella's smile brightens as she looks up at her daddy. "My daddy goes fwast."

"I bet he does," I say without thinking. I didn't want to pay him a compliment, but how can I not agree with this cute as a button princess. Ben gives us an unsure smile.

And I... I feel like someone has sucked the air from my chest. This little girl just called Ben daddy. Wow. Reality just smacked the shit out of me.

Ben directs my attention back to him. He's holding his daughter on his lap, her head still secure against his chest. He's gently brushing her hair from her face and soothing her at the same time. My ovaries turn into a gif with hearts. I'm on a rollercoaster of emotions, and I just want to get the fuck off.

It's a normal gesture between a parent and child, but I've never seen Ben this way. The last time I saw him in this light, he broke my heart.

I set the tray of iced tea on the coffee table, offering glasses to Becca first, then to Ben. Jake is on the La-Z-Boy chair with a content look on his face. It's easy to tell he likes having his old friend back.

"She's not used to being around new people," Ben tells us.

Jake shakes his head and says, "A kid? I can't believe it. I knew you just found out about her recently, but to see you with her. It's crazy."

They all made me feel as if the jokes were on me and I'm the dumbest person ever. Everyone knew he was a dad...everyone but me.

Ben must miss my Callie attitude, or is used to it because he is unfazed. "I just never thought we'd be sitting here talking about kids.

It's crazy to believe I've got responsibilities now." He turns to Becca. "Becca has had more time to get used to it than I have."

It is crazy to believe he is taking on the responsibility of a father, and I guess he hasn't known for that long? Was there a paternity test? I have so many questions and no one to ask without making myself sound jealous. She seems to be attached to him, maybe even more than her mother. I guess I would know the answer to all of my questions if I'd let him talk. But do I even want to know?

"Being a single parent is awful," she sighs. "I've had to deal with a lot of bullshit. But Benny is back in my life, and things are so much easier now." She smiles lovingly at him, kissing him on the cheek. *Ugh.*

Ben flinches at her touch, taking me by surprise. Ben did say they weren't together, but Becca has a different agenda it seems. I really want to act like a teenage brat and make a gagging sound, but Gran isn't far away and would kick my backside if she saw me. Instead, I respond, "That's great that the two of you have each other to depend on."

Ben's eyes widen while Becca squeezes his thigh. "He's the best."

Thank goodness Gran saves me and calls us for dinner. I know I can't handle any more of the fake words being slung around this room.

Ben stands, whispering something into Annabella's ear. I wish I could hear what he said to her, because whatever it was caused her to lift her head and smile in my direction with familiar blue eyes, chubby rosy cheeks, and curly black hair.

As if he read my mind, he explains, "I told her I saw a chocolate cake on the counter and that maybe it is for dessert."

"I love cake, too." My words were only directed to her. "But I like mine with ice cream the best."

Her eyes light up, she shifts pulling slightly away from her dad. This is the farthest she's been away from him.

"Me, too," she says softly. My heart melts. All of a sudden, I'm overcome with a strange protectiveness over this sweet angel. My arms itch to reach out and touch her. I have to hold them tightly at my side so they don't betray me. Instead, I ask, "Would you like ice cream with the cake after we eat? I have chocolate or vanilla."

Annabella cups her little hand to whisper in her dad's ear. "Chocolate, her favorite in the whole world," Ben answers for her.

It's so odd to hear his voice in a stoic, calm manner, rather than the cold, matter-of-fact voice that he's given me so often.

We head into the kitchen. Gran says a prayer as we hold hands. Thinking I'm safe, I peek one eye open to see Becca rolling her eyes as Gran prays.

Becca locks eyes with me and scowls. I shut my eyes, holding my lips shut before I snicker. This is the real Becca, the one I originally saw in Ben's front yard. More than anything else, I want to let everyone at this table know she's not who she seems, but that would only make me look like an ass. I refuse to be made into an ass for her.

Once Gran finishes, the plate passing begins. Ben has Annabella on his lap, and Becca sits beside them across from me.

I have to tell myself to concentrate on my own plate. I can't help but wonder if he still keeps his food separate. He hated when his turkey touched the stuffing, or the corn made its way into the mashed potatoes. Or if he refills his tea when he still has half a glass full. He only likes it full during dinner. All the little things that I used to watch, and notice are suddenly flooding my mind.

"So…Becca, tell us about yourself? Will you be looking for work while you are here?" Gran asks. Instead of looking at Becca, I concentrate on her daughter. Annabella is so much more fascinating than her mother could ever be. Her little finger pokes at the mound of mashed potatoes.

She sits up in her seat, shoulders back, and says proudly, "I was in customer service."

Ben clears his throat as he wipes his mouth with a cloth napkin. He swallows. "She used to work in her father's casino in Vegas. Now she's going to stay home with Annabella for a while."

Becca rolls her eyes. "I told him, we'll see. I'm not the kind of woman to stay home all day with a kid. I mean, I haven't done it for the whole three years she's been alive. That's just not me."

For the first time, Ben doesn't seem to be hiding behind a hard, fake smile.

Gran jumps in. "That's alright. Plenty of women feel like you. As parents we sometimes lose ourselves. Working gives us purpose." Gran reassures her that her choice is admirable. Admirable for most women, but for her, I don't think that's the case. "I was a barmaid for years, and just recently handed over the bar business to Jake."

"I'd really like to start my own business. I'm very competent. I can manage people well. You know, get them to do what they are supposed to. There just aren't capable people left in the world nowadays." She leans in and winks at us as if she's telling us the world's most important secret as she completely ignores Gran's words.

Ben takes a large gulp of tea. I watch Annabella and wonder how this sweet baby girl could be related to this piece of work in front of me. But then I smile because that same sweet girl launches a piece of turkey at her mother.

Becca gasps, and practically growls in disgust. "Anna!" She shrieks. "Why do you have to be such a..."

Ben intervenes immediately, placing an arm on her to quiet whatever ludicrous words were ready to spill out of her mouth. "Bec... She's three. Let it go." Ben, who has been quiet, has reminded me of the old Ben. I can't help but cheer on the inside that he doesn't let her get away with treating Annabella poorly. My only concern is that she treats Anna like this when he isn't around, and what she has been treating her like for the last few years.

Becca acts as if it's not a big deal that he scolded her in front of people she just met because she continues on with the conversation, while wiping at the stain left by the flying turkey.

"I used to work at my father's casino in Vegas, that's true." She rolls her eyes. "But really, I was overseeing the whole place. I like dealing with gamblers and restaurants. I told everyone what they should be doing. They all answered to me."

I try to fix my face from the horrified expression that I know I'm wearing. How can the Ben I've known since I was eight years old even be friends with this woman, let alone have a child with her?

Ben doesn't seem to notice and keeps his attention on his baby mama. "Her father and I thought it would be good for Becca to move here. Start fresh and spend more time with Anna."

Once again Becca rolls her eyes. "Yes, we'll see. I've never lived in a small town. It's taking some getting used to."

She talks so casually about her daughter, her career, if you can call it that, seems more important to her than her own flesh and blood. I can't for the life of me see what Ben sees in her. The Ben I know wouldn't have even set foot near her. He hated girls like this. She is a superficial bully he would have put in her place and not thought twice about it.

She continues to make small talk, mostly about herself and how amazing Vegas is, and how I should definitely stop by her father's hotel sometime in a perfect Valley Girl voice. After a few more excruciating moments, I stand, clearing the empty plates. Becca must take it as her clue to leave, probably afraid I would ask for a hand.

"I think I'm going to head out." She faces Ben, placing a hand on his arm. "You can put her to bed. Don't wait for me. I've got a headache."

She stands. Ben's expression is tense. He's clenching his jaw like he's stopping himself from expressing his opinion. She doesn't care that she is in a room full of people she barely knows. People who have manners and respect for others, as well as the utmost respect for their family. All of which I'm convinced she isn't capable of possessing. This girl is an embarrassment to herself and to Ben.

He stands, placing his napkin on his plate. "Will you please excuse us?"

His voice is lower than earlier, and much more serious. I've been on the receiving end of that voice, so I have an idea of what is ahead of her. Ben follows her out the door.

Becca turns to face us. She plasters a fake smile on her face, and in her most high-pitched squeaky voice, says, "Thanks for dinner. It was…nice."

Gran is ever so polite and answers her. "You're most welcome, dear. I'm glad you enjoyed yourself. It was a pleasure having you." She looks toward Ben. "You can hand over precious Annabella to me while you escort Becca back to the house."

"You don't have to do that."

"Hush now, son. I've known you since you were little. I love this little girl already and would love to spend some time with her. You kids go on now." Ben picks up Anna and hands her over to Gran, who doesn't waste a second before she kisses her cheek. Who can blame her, this kid is adorable?

Gran takes a piece of cake on her fork and feeds Annabella. The screen door crashes behind us, followed by whispers. I try to block them out so I can concentrate on the cutie pie in front of me. Her chubby cheeks puff out, they then form a smile that melts my heart.

"Is that yummy?" I ask her in my best childish voice. As she answers, "Mmm," some of the cake squishes out the side of her mouth. I giggle at her, which makes her let out more cake. Before I know it, the whole table is laughing.

I wipe her mouth with a nearby napkin. "Thanks."

"You're so polite." I'm gifted with her radiant smile.

Ben enters, frowning, with irritation radiating off of him.

Jake asks, "Everything good, brother?"

He lets out a breath. "Not sure."

"If you want to go with her, I'd be happy to keep an eye on Annabella," Gran offers.

"I appreciate the offer, but it's probably best if I stay at home tonight."

"Anytime you want to go out for the night, I'm more than happy to spend the evening with this precious little lady." Gran's smile is infectious as she admires Annabella.

My phone chimes in my pocket. I excuse myself to take a look. Trent's name flashes on the screen. I stupidly drop it on the table, and of course, it lands face up, displaying Trent's name to the whole table.

Gran scowls. And within seconds she lets me know about it. "That boy is trouble." Her voice is low. I don't know if she doesn't want anyone to hear us, or if it is only emphasizing her point.

I swipe the phone up without looking to see what it says. Hopefully it wasn't inappropriate.

"He's just a friend. We've been over this. I'm headed out, too." I glance at Ben, then to Annabella. I kneel down so I can be level with her face. "It was nice to meet you, sweet girl."

Before anyone can ask any more questions, I say a quick goodbye. Jake yells, "He's an asshole," as I leave the house.

I'm not even going to see him. I texted him that I had other plans. He left me on "read." Instead of going to Trent's, working off my anxiety by passing out beers and wiping down tables seems like a much better solution.

19

Once I walk into the bar, the night is in full swing. Part of the swinging, to my surprise, is being done by Becca. Her hips are swaying to the beat of the music while she's dancing on the bar. She's got two guys gunning for her attention, cheering her on. I don't recognize them. Not bad looking guys, of course, because as much as I hate to admit it, she is gorgeous.

She's giggling and drinking a fruity drink through a straw, but the liquid is spilling out the sides.

"Dear God, why?" I say out loud as I slam my purse on the bar. Mindy must read the look on my face. "This one is a real trip." She nods in Becca's direction. "The loudmouth hasn't stopped talking about what a dive this place is, how she can run it better, and how this hick town could use her skills." She air quotes skills. "Not sure what *Coyote Ugly* bar she came from in Vegas, but this town ain't it."

I grab the apron Mindy has in her hand for me. I toss my blonde hair over my shoulder, bracing myself for a long ass night ahead.

Tying the apron around my waist, I realize that the bar is packed. I'm talking wall to wall, and most of the eyes are glued to the dark-haired beauty dancing on the bar. I pull out my phone, text Jake about how busy it is, how I'll be helping out, and that Becca is now the center of the show at Rae's Bar.

She was supposed to be home with a headache.

Becca happens to be in the spot on the bar where the draft beer taps are. The spot where I'll most likely be spending most of the night, and the very place I will make my tips.

She's laughing, while she moves to a kneeling position, and one of the guys picks her up and sets her on the stool. She's touching this guy as if she doesn't have Ben waiting at home for her. An ache forms in my chest out of nowhere. I would give anything to go home to Ben with a sweet girl waiting for me. *Where did that come from?* It takes me a moment to compose myself. But the dreams of him and our child come back in full force, whether I want to acknowledge them or not.

I grind my jaw, bracing myself to drag her ass out of here. She needs to go home and take care of her daughter.

"Becca!" I call out, saying her name like a swear word.

"Hey." She waves and smiles, then looks confused. "Do I know you?"

Are you kidding me? She was just at my house. What was it like, an hour ago?

"Callie, remember?"

Clarity dawns on her face. "Oh yeah, the neighbor girl, right?"

"Yeah." I want to say, "Correct, *dumbass.*" But I don't.

She winds her long black strand of hair around her finger, then tosses it over her shoulder. "I met her tonight." She explains to her new boy toy. "She is...average, right?"

"I don't think that's the right word for her?" He gives me a wink. "But will she give us free drinks?" He looks down at my shirt, or my tits, or both, with appreciation written all over his face.

"No, but you can pay the ten dollars and seventy-five cents it takes for me to refill yours." I wink, hoping he'll get the point.

The flavor of the night throws a twenty on the bar, then leans in to say something into her ear. Of course, she lets out a cackle-ish giggle.

"Oh geez!"

I decide that I'm not going to help out this situation by having a rational conversation with her and turn my attention back to work, asking the next customer what they want to drink.

After a few more customers, a familiar face sits down in front of me. "Hey, Cals. Can I get a beer?" His usual relaxed demeanor is gone tonight.

"You look a little tense tonight. Is something bothering you?"

Van answers, "Spoken like a true bartender."

"That's what I'm trained to do." I wink at the panty-dropping stud in front of me. If he wasn't like a brother to me, before he got with Emerson, I would have been highly tempted for some fun with him. Who am I kidding, I've already got issues with Trent, I certainly don't need any more with Van. Plus, a certain other guy has held my attention for much longer, and I can't seem to shake him. "So what's bugging you?"

"I'm just worried about Ems. Her headaches are getting worse. She also had a seizure last night."

"Van... I'm sorry. I know it is awful to see her like that. But she is strong. She'll be better soon."

Did I know that? No. But if anyone could beat her sickness, it was Emerson. She had a fight in her unlike anything I had ever seen.

I shove the beer across the bar. "This one's on the house."

"Thanks." Van takes a long pull, draining the bottle, and slamming it down on the bar.

"Another?"

"Yep. Keep 'em coming."

"Anything I can do?"

"Ems is at home. She made me come here tonight. I think she's annoyed that I keep watching her. I just want to help her. You know?"

"I know what you mean."

"Tell me some good gossip or a joke, anything to get my mind off of her being home alone."

"Have you met that piece of work over there?" He shakes his head no, and tosses back another drink from the bottle. As we continue talking about Em's new medicine that could potentially stop her headaches and seizures, an obnoxious cackle interrupts his monologue. Becca is getting louder and more animated with her hands, especially where she's placing them on a certain man's body.

"Who's she?" Van nods towards Becca.

Placing my hands on my hips, smiling at my opportunity to introduce Van to the new pain in my ass. "You haven't met Ben's baby mama yet?"

The beer that was in Van's mouth has now been spit onto my bar and thankfully missed me.

He swipes at his mouth with his flannel-covered arm and apologizes. "Sorry. That's Becca?" He leans in. "Why the fuck is she here with that guy when I know for a fact that Ben is at home with their kid? I texted him to come out tonight. He said he had the kid."

"Yep, she's here slutting it up, and he's at home taking care of their daughter."

"Do you know anything about her?"

"I didn't know anything about the whole situation until he showed back up. So let's just say I'm the last to know anything about Ben's life, let alone his baby mama or whatever she is."

"Sore subject, huh?" he says and I nod.

"Fair enough. Tequila, please."

I pour two shots of Patrón, pushing one over toward him. He raises his glass. "To fucked-up situations." We clink, liquor burning down my throat, but it quenches the aggravation that the thoughts of Becca and Ben bring.

As is if on cue, she shouts. "This is my song." In her too-short red skirt and sky-high heels, she manages to clamber onto the bar again. Getting into a standing position, she gives her best "Woo-Hoo!"

She must have changed after our nice little family dinner.

"Damn it!" Slamming my towel on the table, I move to where she's dancing. As I glance up, I get a disgusting view of her girly bits. "No one wants to see that," I yell.

"I do!" Some guy yells back to me.

"Come on, Becca. You can't be on my bar, dancing and exposing yourself. You're a mom, for God's sake," I scream up at her.

She squats down in the most unladylike fashion. Great, her crotch is now in Van's line of sight, and unfortunately mine as well.

"Ummm... It's time for me to get the hell out of here. My days of partying are over. I need to go home to my girl," Van says as he takes one final drink.

"Do you have a ride?"

He rubs his hand down his face. "Yeah. Ace is here somewhere."

"I'll go find him. I don't need any more problems than I already have."

Just as I say the words, Ace raises his hand up for Van to see. Relief washes over me. I know he'll get home safe. I haven't served Ace tonight, and I noticed he was drinking water.

Van drops a twenty and I quickly swipe it up, taking my payment and feeling like it's for me dealing with this whole shit storm named Becca in front of me.

Becca has fluctuated from the bar, to a stool, then back up to the bar. I've lost track of how many times she's done this in the past twenty minutes. I need to have her bounced out of here...but there's no bouncer on duty tonight.

I give myself a quick pep talk. "Ben is a friend, or was a friend when you were young. You'd do it for anyone else." I inhale and stomp over to her.

"Hey, Becca. Did you have a good time tonight?" I say loudly so I can get her attention.

Her eyes raise, but in the way she is trying to hold them open and not like she's acknowledging what I said. I wave my arm in front of her face. She blinks and her head bobs like one of those bobbleheads.

"I think it's time for you to go. Why don't you call Ben, he'll come and get you."

She straightens with a jump, like I just stabbed her. "I'm fine. Besides, he only wants to talk to you. Callie this...and Callie that. Well, you can have him. He's keeping me locked up in his house like some kind of animal...no, prisoner is more like it. Rapunzel! That's it!" Her voice shrills in my ear.

She's acting like a spoiled teenager, and part of me is doing a little happy dance inside. If he's talking about me, then maybe he still thinks about me. *Stop it!*

Trying to stand, she stumbles, and Mr. Polo catches her. "You alright, babe?" Acting like he gives two shits if she's okay.

I answer instead. "She's fine. Let's be honest, she's too messed up to help you out tonight. I'm going to call her *boyfriend* to come get her. You can move along now and pick up some other hussy."

Even though Ben said he isn't her boyfriend. She's still living in his house, with their child. Playing family. So there has to be some feeling there.

"He's not my boyfriend. He just knocked me up. That's all." She stomps her foot like a child only to get her off balance. Catching her before she knocks me over, it takes me a moment to process her words. *Maybe they aren't a thing.*

"Come on, sit down and I'll go call him." Okay, her little tirade might have made sense, but it doesn't calm the nagging feeling in the pit of my stomach.

Struggling with her body weight, somehow I manage to lift her onto the stool. "Stop. I don't want you to call him." She orders with a stern tone.

"Fine, I'll take you home then."

"Oh, let's share him." She slurs, slaughtering the English language, giggling at the same time.

The polo guy moves between us, taking the chance to look me up and down. Geez, what a pig. "Seriously?" I question, crossing my arms, completely fed up with his crap. "Go find someone else to prey on tonight."

I'm seconds away from leaving her on her own. I should wash my hands of this mess and Ben. But I wouldn't want anyone to leave me all alone with some guy who only has one thing on his agenda tonight. That's a violation of girl code. Of course, the other violation is that we have a thing for the same guy, only she's winning right now because she lives with him and birthed his baby. I grumble at my thoughts. This is none of my business, he is none of my business. Dear God, I'm giving myself whiplash over Mr. Benjamin Carmichael.

I compose myself for a second, a flash of pretty blue eyes and dark curls enter my mind. Annabella. I don't like Becca, but I don't want anything to happen to her, for Annabella's sake.

I try to tamp down the little voice that is trying to bring up a memory that I've tried to suffocate for years but the soft voice manages, *"You were once Annabella. This was once your mom."*

"Fine," I grit out but promise myself if she won't listen, then I'm done. Call this my last attempt.

"Becca, I'm taking you home. It's late, and I'm sure your baby girl wants her mama to tuck her in."

She huffs, crossing her arm, pushing up her tits. "You're just trying to make me feel bad. Fuck you, Sunshine."

How does she know his nickname for me?

I compose myself, securing my fist at my side, because it really wants to jump up right now and pummel her ugly mug. There must be some divine intervention that makes me turn to her Polo flavor of the night. I make sure to look him in the eye, glaring at him so he doesn't get distracted. "Listen here, asshole. You're not getting any tonight. From either of us." I lighten my tone a little. "I mean, I guess you can, but she just tested positive for that. What is it?" I bring my finger up to my chin, tapping. "An tsd, nsd, Oh wait, STD. Yeah, she has an STD?" I frown, making sure he heard the letters clearly.

His eyes widen, deer in the headlights kinda look. He stumbles back a few steps, like he could catch it right now standing next to her.

"Ahh...thanks for the beer." He looks down at his watch. "It's getting late, I really need to go."

Becca reaches for his arm. Thankfully her reflexes are too slow, and he moves pretty quick. He's across the room before I know it. Her Polo boy's fast movement causing her to fall off the stool, again, landing flat on her ass. She looks pretty comical except for the fact she's not wearing underwear, and this is the third time tonight I've accidentally seen her lady bits. *Gross.*

My God, the shit I get myself into.

20

Bending down, I slide my arms under her armpits, and pull her up. Damn, she's dead weight. But somehow I manage to get her out of the bar and into the parking lot. She stumbles and leans on me, but at least she's up on her feet.

Her sky-high heels make it even more difficult. Her ankle keeps giving out. It would be funny if I were watching the scene unfold from my truck, but unfortunately, I'm not.

We end up stopping three times on the way to my truck for her to puke. Each time, she accuses me of being a horrible person and a prude and my favorite —boyfriend stealer—like we're in third grade or something, for taking away her Polo boy. She has no clue what his name was.

Once she figures out how to hoist herself into the truck, with my assistance, of course, I slam the door right in her ugly mug. I've had more than my share of this ratchet bitch. The amount of horse shit I stepped into tonight has got to be a new record. I can feel my patience long gone, and heat flowing through my body.

Once I start up the engine, she's already snoring. But not softly like you would expect from her now serene face, nope, it's like a Harley motorcycle is revving its engine right in the cab of my truck. I laugh, praising Jesus that at least she isn't talking.

We are a few streets away from freedom, when Becca starts to mumble. After a few words it becomes audible. "Callie, Callie, Callie Rae." Her head sways like she's following along to a song. "I never heard about you. Ever. Then we come to this hick town and Callie, Callie, Callie. His Callie Rae. Sunshine." She air quotes the last word.

"What are you rambling about?" I understand her, I just can't believe it.

"Are you deaf?" Her high heels land on my dash with a thud.

"I'm not his perfect Callie Rae." She chuckles and looks at me. "But then again, maybe you're not either."

As I pull into the Carmichael driveway, I feel a bit shaken. I've dealt with plenty of bitches and drunks, but I've never dealt with someone who also has feelings for Ben. I pull beside his souped-up Ford Mustang. Black with flat black stripes, even distinguishable in the dark of night. The wheels are custom made...at least I haven't seen those before. Trent would kill for a ride like this. I wonder what happened to Betty, his original Mustang and the one I backed into.

Just the thought of Trent invokes guilt and makes my stomach turn. I have to give him an answer. I know I'm betraying my brother and my friends by being with him. I want to be on their side, not his. So I just have to tell him.

Trying to push those thoughts aside, and deal with the mess I've got going on in front of me, I contemplate my next move.

I could just wake her ass up, pushing her out the door and leaving her on the front lawn. I mean, if she can make it to the porch, there is a cozy bench. That's more hospitality than she gave to the poor dog.

I take a moment to examine her. Maybe I've missed something about her that makes her a good person, or at least seem genuine.

Her long dark hair is straight, but no extensions, which surprises me. Even with her head tilted it's almost to her waist. Her lashes are definitely fake, as one of them has gone askew. Her eyeliner and mascara have melted together and have run a race down her face, leaving streaks in its wake.

Becca's lips have been injected too. Being in the beauty industry, even in a small town, I can tell that her lips have been stuck and filled to the max. The snoring coming from her puffy lips and red smeared lipstick are doing nothing for the sexy look she's trying so hard to achieve. I stop myself from glancing farther down at her assets before I start comparing apples to oranges or fake to real.

But I can't help but feel the sting of jealousy, even though I can take solace in the fact that she's a mess now, I've seen her put together earlier tonight and she is stunning.

Taking my attention away from her, I place it on the brick house in front of me, only to see the man whom I've never been able to get out of my mind walking toward me and the mother of his daughter.

Opening the driver's side door, uneasiness washes over me. Unsure of how this is going to go. I jump down, closing the door. Becca can probably step down with ease, her long legs meeting the ground fluidly while mine drop like a sack of potatoes but taking some solace in that she's too drunk to manage that task tonight.

I wave at him. It's awkward, because I'm stopped by the sight of him in sweatpants and a plain white T-shirt. His hair clearly skewed, probably from falling asleep on the couch waiting for Becca.

He frowns as he gets closer. "She's out cold." It's not a question, more of a statement.

Ben doesn't even hide his aggravation. "You should have called, she can be handful when she's like this." He gestures at her, then leans against the front grill of my truck. His arms cross and he looks down at his feet.

"Does this happen often?" I ask, as gently as I can manage.

He looks up at me, frowns, then says, "Enough."

He turns to open her door. While he gathers her into his arms, she moans. "Where are you taking me? I wanna have fun!" She shouts the last word, wiggling in his arms, trying to fist pump the air.

"I'll get her bag and shoes."

He mutters thanks.

Ben waits as I gather her belongings, rushing to get the door for him.

As he passes by, he has to wrangle her in his arms. She's a sloppy drunk, that's for sure.

The house looks nothing like I remember. Besides the gorgeous new furniture that looks straight out of an interior design magazine, there are little girls' stuffed animals and dolls scattered on the floor and on the couch.

The wall that once separated the kitchen from the living room is gone. Now the once dull wood cabinets have been replaced by bright white cabinets. Marble countertops, updated appliances, and a small table with benches. Even though everything is crisp, clean, and new, it still has a very homey feel.

"I'll be right back. Make yourself at home," he says as Becca makes a movement that causes him to visibly struggle from dropping her on her ass. I can't say I wouldn't watch that and enjoy the show.

"I'll head out." The sooner I get out of here the better.

"Just hang out for a sec." I go to open my mouth to answer, but he speaks before I can. "Please." The sincerity in his voice stops me. Once again, he asks and I can't refuse.

Beau is at my feet, pawing at my leg. I've been so entranced by Ben, I haven't even noticed the sweet dog.

Bending down, I give him the attention he needs. Petting his soft fur while he licks my cheek.

A few moments later, Ben returns. "I'm sorry about her. You should have called me, so you didn't have to deal with this." He cocks his head toward the door.

"She was having fun, at least." I shrug.

"Too much fun it looks like."

He pats the spot next to him on the couch. "Have a seat." And just like that, I feel eighteen. Ben asks me to do something, and I do without question.

"You've been good to her. I don't think most guys would be as patient."

"I do it for Annabella. She is my daughter and I'd do anything in this world for her."

"As you should."

"I want to explain it to you, but first I need to apologize."

"No, you don't have to. Life happens," I shrug my shoulders, as if it's no big deal. I still feel the need to avoid this conversation, even though I'm dying to know what's going on in that head of his.

"I'm sorry about everything. About the way I left. Not talking to you. But when I left, my life was falling apart. She and Anna are part of the new life I found out there."

"What did you do in Vegas?"

"Do you have all night, and the next few months, for me to explain?"

"At least tell me how you and Becca met?" Seems like a safe question, and I can't help but wonder how he ended up with her.

"She had a very different upbringing than you or I. She grew up in a casino. Which means she spent her childhood running around a hotel, seeing show girls as role models, gambling addicts coming and going. Becca is having a rough time adjusting to the simplicity of motherhood."

"And you just recently found out about Annabella?"

"Yeah. I fucking missed everything. The pregnancy, the sonograms, her first steps...fucking everything."

"I'm sorry." My throat tightens. Tears threatening to show because I want to tell him that he missed both of those things—twice—with Becca and with me.

He shrugs. "Becca's parents and staff have been mostly taking care of Anna. But when they decided they wanted to have more of a life, and not have so many strangers involved in raising her, they called me. Finally." His head falls into his hands, threading his fingers through the strands as if he's holding himself together. "They tried to give her more responsibility, but it didn't go well for any of them. Her dad made her tell him who the father was, but in true Becca fashion, she had several options to choose from. After testing six guys, I was number seven and found out that I had a daughter."

"Wow, I can't imagine how you felt?" I swallow down the guilt because the secrecy from telling him he was going to be a father was eerily similar. I kept the same secret from him, and the distress on his face isn't helping. Keeping the secret now seems like the wrong thing to do but how do I tell him and would it even matter?

"You have no idea." He leans away from me, resting his back against the couch. Seeming to relax a bit. "Becca and I were together for maybe three months before I found out she likes a variety of guys to choose from." He pauses, looking intensely at me, eyes searching, expression serious, waiting for some kind of reaction. I don't give him one. I want him to keep talking, telling me what he has been doing since he left, why the mystery? Why wasn't I important enough for him to stay?

He turns his head, breaking the trance.

"I knew she was pregnant. I just didn't think it was mine. We used a condom. I knew better than to trust her with taking her pill on time. She didn't even stay in Vegas during her pregnancy. She came back right before she had the baby. Her parents never said anything to anyone about who the father was or gave away any other details. I just figured it wasn't me."

"You know her family well then?"

"Too well. They are why my father had to go to Vegas in the first place."

"He owed them money," I say quietly. Because that's what racing is all about. The betting. It's starting to click into place. Of course his father led him down this dangerous path.

He just nods. "Anyway…Annabella is my life now. That's why we're here. To give her a normal life."

"She is absolutely adorable."

His face brightens. "She is, isn't she?"

"You are in so much trouble in about ten years." I lean my leg close to his and give him a playful nudge.

"Don't I know it. But no little girl can be as much trouble as you were."

"Me?" I bring my hand to my chest to feign innocence.

"Yeah…you. I can't imagine Annabella taking her Gran's car keys at the age of eleven, with the intention of driving to her friend's house a half an hour away. Thank God she caught you on the main road."

"I wasn't going to really drive all that way. I made my point."

"Which was?"

"I'd find a way to get what I want. It was to get to the mall—not to my friend's."

"What was so important that you needed to steal your grandmother's car at eleven years old?"

I knew exactly what—or who—the gift at the mall was so important for. And he was sitting right beside me.

"A video game."

"Must have been a good one to risk getting in all the trouble."

"It was worth it." He was worth it since it was his thirteenth birthday. "I did end up getting the game, by the way."

He met my eyes, my heart sped up, my nerves hit new levels of alert. With each second he didn't respond, I wish he'd figure it out, remember the gift I gave him all those years ago, but my hope is squashed when Becca comes stumbling out of the doorway. "What is she doing here?"

"She dropped your ass off. Let's get you back in the bedroom." Ben walks over to her, he takes her hand and gently places his arm around her waist, as if she might break.

It stings to see him take care of her like this, but yet when I needed him to take care of me, he wasn't there.

I swallow the hurt and turn to the door. "I'll see you around. Take care."

I use all my strength not to turn back around and torture myself anymore.

21

Gran and I are sitting down at breakfast. Quietly eating our eggs, when she slams her fork down. "Dear. If you do not tell me what happened last night, I'm going to spank your bottom like you are five years old.

I saw you bring Becca home last night. So tell me what happened."

I reply vaguely, "I did."

She quirks her head. "Spill it, puddles."

I roll my eyes, here we go.

"Becca was hammered, dancing on the bar, and getting ready to go home with some strange guy, so I stepped in, told him she had an STD, and brought her home. Girl code and all," I explain casually, as if it was no big deal. "I was also being friendly, just like you asked," I add poignantly, glancing in her direction.

"I promise you that that no-good lush doesn't need your help anymore. She's just looking for a way to get out of here."

I spit out the second mouthful of scrambled eggs I just put in my mouth.

I apologize, wiping my face with a napkin before saying,

"I can't believe you called her that! What happened to what you told me about her, the benefit of the doubt and all?"

"From what I've seen, she's not a good person. Do I feel bad for her? Yes. Do I know she's in trouble? Yes. But Ben can't fix her by bringing her here. Just because she's left Vegas doesn't mean her problems stayed back there."

"I hope she isn't as bad as I think she may be to Annabella."

"Me too. I understand needing to let loose and have fun. I've been around long enough to know she isn't on the right path. You and I both know how this story ends." She takes my hand, her face softening with compassion. She doesn't have to say it. I already know. She's talking about my mama.

I push down the emotions that try and creep up whenever I think of her. The way she left, the way she only talks to me if she needs something. The way she seems to be everyone's favorite person, and how I'm never hers. I steer the conversation away from me.

"She was all over this guy. I had to lie to him to get him off of her. He probably would have had sex with her if she would have let him."

"I don't think Ben bringing her here is going to be good for him or his daughter. Some women just aren't meant to be mothers." She pauses, her face turns solemn. "I love your mother very much, but she was not capable of being a mother. She is horrible for the way she treated you and your brother. She doesn't have it in her to be there for her children, but my darling girl, you do."

My throat dries. I've never heard her admit that before. She's always said my mother loved us and that she needed to do other things in life, but this is the first honest conversation we've had about the woman who birthed me. I know she was just trying to protect my feelings. Protect me from the truth and maybe protect herself from the guilt.

Gran pats my hand, then clears her throat. I know she's done with the conversation, at least anything that has to do with my mother.

"So, what plans do you have for the day?"

I swallow back the emotion, grateful for attempting to change the subject. "Oh, you know, the normal...work at the salon, pick up some drinks for the lake, go skinny dipping. The usual."

Grans shakes her head. "No skinny dipping. Never let the boys see your goodies, they'll think they can have them all the time."

***

The salon was busy as usual, but in-between clients, Harlow showed me the new line of wigs. I couldn't pass up the chance at trying out a shorter hairstyle for the night. I felt like Reese Witherspoon's character in *Sweet Home Alabama*. I can't tell you how many times I watched that movie. The short blonde bob is so much different than what I am used to wearing.

Instead of donning the new wig, I fluff my normal, long blonde hair as Harlow and I walk down the path to the lake. Our sandals crunch along the gravel. "Thank goodness I know better than to wear heels," Harlow says.

"Even though I love my heels, a girl's got to know the right occasion. Preferably when she's in a skintight dress, wrapped around someone special."

"Oh my...you are ridiculous sometimes."

"My brother wishes you'd wear heels, you know?" I wink and she gives me a shove. "Come on. Let's have some fun tonight."

Once we see familiar faces, I scream. "Hey, y'all!" as loud as I can manage.

Someone screams back, "Callie's here, now the party has started." And it makes me laugh.

Ben, Jake, Ace, Van, and Emerson are gathered around the fire.

Emerson is stunning as usual. Classy, well dressed in jeans and a casual navy suit jacket, not the attire for a night around a bonfire at the lake. Will my girl ever learn?

"Wow," Harlow exclaims. "She is stunning. Pure elegance."

I run up and give her a huge hug. Squeezing her with all my might. "I have missed you. How are you feeling?"

"I'm good. Just a little run down. My headaches have been just awful."

I really have missed her. That sonofabitch ex-husband of hers has been nothing but pure evil. Thankfully, things have turned out good for her now, but the road she took was nothing short of hell.

Van pulls her closer to his body. "We have a doctor's appointment to see what's really going on." Kissing the top of her head, she kisses him back and somehow escapes his grasp. Giving him a quick peck on the lips.

"You hang here with the guys. I'm going to talk with the girls," she tells him.

"You look really tired." Sometimes it would be nice if my brain would filter itself before the words come out of my mouth.

"I am. But Van has been wonderful. He literally hasn't let me lift a finger. But I've been working a few days a week on my business as well as his. I'm taking a little break, though. Just enjoying life."

'You deserve it," Harlow and I say at the same time.

"A little birdie told me that Ben is back and has a daughter and a baby mama. How are you?" Her eyes widened when her question was obviously directed at me.

"She's awful. Don't let her fool you. And Trent... don't even get me started," Harlow opens her big fat mouth. I haven't wanted to burden Emerson with my problems. Mine are minor compared to what she had to endure.

"I'm fine. I mean, it sucks. We had a little thing. Didn't hear from him. But that was to be expected. It's what he does. Races, comes home, races, comes home, and the cycle just continues. I mean, so what if he left for longer than usual. He has a kid. He's acting responsibly and taking care of her. And Becca—I don't think she's going to win mother of the year, but she's in his life forever. Moving on is the only option."

Emerson's eyes widened. "I cannot believe you. Callie Rae, you kick and scream your way through life. You cannot just roll over like a dead dog and not fight for him."

I straight up laugh in her face. "Have I rubbed off on you? Dead dog?"

"Fine, maybe you have. But you cannot give up on Ben. I know how you really feel. And this Trent guy is bad news. Granted, he is your brother's competitor, and he hates him. So does Ben and Van. I've overheard their conversations about him. The way he purposely wrecked into Ben last year. I mean, you are asking for trouble."

"Emerson, it's fine. It's just a little fling." The guilt rises in my throat. She is the last person I should lie to, but I don't want her to worry. I've got it under control.

She nods and doesn't say more. We talk about some of the local gossip, and how she has a new perfume in the works. But after a bit she says her head is hurting and Van comes to her side. They decide to leave early.

Honestly, I'm relieved to talk with her. Getting it all out to the one person who won't judge me. I'm not fooling her in the least.

After a few minutes, Ben walks over to me and Harlow.

How does he even look gorgeous in the dark? He's wearing a button-down flannel, jeans, black boots. His blond hair looks dark. His blue eyes twinkle in the fire light.

"Hey, ladies. Harlow, do you mind if I have a second alone with Callie?"

Before I can answer, he pulls me away from Harlow, who wiggles her fingers at me, giving me a "have fun" wave.

"Let's go sit down by the log bench."

We walk over to the large mass of trees that are a bit away from everyone else and the fire.

Ben gestures for me to sit first.

"Where is Anna and Becca tonight?" I can't help but ask. A vision of Becca lurking in the woods and ready to jump out at me dance in my mind... a girl needs to prepare.

"They are at home. Becca has a headache, and I put Anna to bed before I came here. They should have an easy night."

Silence fills the air.

He opens his mouth to say something, then shuts it.

"What?" I say goading him. Wondering what speech he's going to give me.

"You know...I could never forget you or what a great friendship we had."

The word friendship isn't exactly what I want to hear from him.

"I just want to apologize for Becca's behavior last night. She told me that some guy was harassing the two of you and that you stood up for her, but she already had too many drinks and couldn't remember how she acted toward you. I'm sorry you had to deal with that asshole guy."

I bite the inside of my cheek. Is she trying to say she was innocent last night? She doesn't remember offering herself up on a platter to that asshole?

She's trying to get away with it. Should I let her?

No, I shouldn't, but maybe he wants to be with her? Make it work for their daughter? I need to know, so I can let this thing between us go.

I face him. His beautiful blue eyes, shimmering even in the dim light. It's now or never. I'll let his answer make my decision.

"Let me ask you a question?"

"Shoot."

"Are you with Becca because you love her?" I swallow down the poison of the word love, "Or because you have a kid with her? We were always honest with each other. I'd like us to be that way again."

He reaches for my hand. "Things have been...awkward since I've been back, but I need to tell you the whole story of what happened while I was away."

A gut-wrenching feeling whips around in my stomach. He's finally going to tell me, and I'm not sure I'm prepared for whatever his reasons may be.

"You don't have to explain," I say the words quickly, almost willing him not to explain. He didn't say he *didn't* love her, and that gives me pause.

He rubs his thumb along my knuckles. *Oh please, don't do that.* He's making it hard to stay mad at him, or care about him, or admit I still never got over him.

"I was living the life." He laughs. I keep my eyes trained on our joined hands. I don't think I could bear to look into his eyes right now. "I raced some big names, won against them, and made bank. I'm talking about setting myself up financially for a long time. Becca's father was the one who got me into those races."

He lifts my chin with his free hand. "Please look at me. I need you to help me get through all of this. I know you were hurt, too, even if you don't want to admit it."

I see the softness of his normally serious face, the glint in his eyes, and I listen with my full attention. "One night, I won big—over one hundred grand." He has a far-off look in his eyes, the moon light catching the sparkle dancing in them. "That night we got so wasted." He shakes his head, but he looks down at his watch. "I didn't even remember that I had slept with her until the memory came flooding back when she told me I was the father. It's an asshole thing to sleep with someone and not remember it, but that's the truth. Just a one-night stand. We used protection, I know that for sure. So no, I do not love her and never have."

Relief washes over me. He doesn't love her but... My already delicate stomach takes another ride on the Ben Carmichael rollercoaster. A flashback of our night comes back to me, and I wonder if he remembers our night, or was it just a fling? Did our night together mean nothing to him like theirs did?

"It was a rough night. My memory is foggy. I remember her hitting on me like crazy. But I knew if I touched her like that, her father would kill me, and she wasn't the kind of girl you brought home." He pauses, glancing at me.

"I guess not," I reply with an awkward chuckle.

"I woke up in her bed. She was in even rougher shape than I was that morning. I didn't think there was a shot in hell that I touched her, though. I just thought we fell asleep at her place. We both had our underwear on, and she said we just fooled around a bit." He lets out a breath. "That day, the night I was with you. She showed up with her daughter, our daughter. I laughed in her face, told her she was crazy. That she was making up another Becca story."

"She came here to tell you?"

"To say my worlds collided that day would be an understatement. I never wanted the stuff I was doing in Las Vegas to follow me here. I was just racing there to make money. I was going to come home and race for fun. Finally tell you that I wanted to be with you. Only you."

I ignore his last comment. I don't know how to even begin to process his words. But I know they are the most memorable words he's ever said to me.

"You don't race for fun now? Because the Benjamin Carmichael I know gets the biggest smile on his face when he's behind the wheel."

"Maybe a little." He playfully bumps my shoulder.

"I did the paternity test right away. Only took a few days to find out I was her daddy."

If only I could tell him that he was already a daddy. We made a baby together. Would he have been happy, or would he have stayed? Even after I lost the baby? Swallowing back the lump in my throat, I tried to stop the voice in my head.

"She's beautiful." I can't help but say my purest thought.

"I'm a lucky sonofabitch. I came back to give her a good life. Not a life of living in a casino with a mother who can't stay…"

A cracking sound followed by crunching footsteps interrupts his words. I'm relieved, but still curious what he was going to say.

My brother comes into view. He's huffing and puffing, out of breath and furious.

Ben jerks his hand away from mine. I'm not sure if Jake catches it or not. "There you are. You okay?" he asks, the confusion written all over Jake's face.

"Yeah, just talking."

He stands like a soldier with his hands on his hips, still catching his breath. "Your boy." He nods at me. "Trent, he's here. Asking for you. Said you invited him and his boys here. If that's true, I'm going to make sure you explain to him that you had a major lapse in judgment. You better get them out of here before I throw his ass in the fire!"

Ben places a hand on my arm to stop me from getting up. "I'll handle them. You stay."

Ben glares at Jake. "We can handle them."

I shrug him off, as his hand falls away, I stand. "No, I got it."

On the short trek over to Trent and *his boys*, I start to fume. Why in the hell would he think it was okay to come to our lake party? It's not a big secret that they are never invited.

Ben yanks at my arm, scolding me. "Why would you tell him to come here?"

"I didn't," I snap back, pushing my feet to go faster. It wouldn't do any good for Ben and Jake to get there before me.

By the time we get there, Trent and Todd have made themselves comfortable with beers in hand and casually sitting in folding chairs.

"There's my girl!" Trent smiles wide and yells loud enough for everyone to hear.

My girl? Is he crazy? No, he's drunk.

I trudge up in front of him. "You need to go. Come on!" I take a piece of his shirt, trying to budge him, but of course, it doesn't do a thing.

"Oh, come on, I'm here for the party. You always say you have so much fun, blah, blah, blah...I wanted to see where the fun happens. Besides, I wanted to welcome Ben back. He's going to be racing soon, and I just wanted to wish him luck." Trent slips his arm around my waist.

I try to push him away. "You're trashed, and you and your friends don't belong here. Don't you want to get along with these guys if you want to be with me?" I ask. Of course, I'm lying, I definitely don't want this, but it seems like it's easier to play his game right now.

"Ah...babe. Look at you. So beautiful tonight. I wanted to show your brother I can play nice. He should know that I'm going to be in your life from now on, so we need to get along." He nods his bottle in Jake's direction.

"Well, I don't want to get along with you or your boys. So get your drunk ass out of here before I throw you out." Jake practically snarls, if I had any doubt that I could make it work with Trent, it's gone now. My brother may kill him all by himself.

"Come on. Let's go talk over here." I yank his shirt again, and with God's good grace, he follows without a fight. I'll take his eye roll and the beer bottle he throws to the ground in defiance any day. I risk a glance at Ben, whose arms are crossed over his chest and has his eyes trained on me. His hawk eyes are the least of my problems.

Once we're far enough away from prying ears and eyes, Trent starts in before I get a chance to. "I'm not going anywhere. I told you I wanted to be with you, and I got nothing from you. I'm here for an answer."

There it is, the words I've been waiting to hear from him for a few weeks now, but now that it's here, it doesn't make me feel good. The last few minutes have confirmed that he'll never fit into my life, and I know that he's not what I want. I'm aggravated with myself for being such a brat. Wanting to defy my brother and his friends, to do something they wouldn't. To be friends with people they wouldn't. Being with Trent has been a fun and rebellious act on my part, but I need to put the big girl panties on and end this *friends with benefits* situation that has seriously gone off the rails. Ben isn't mine...but neither is Trent.

Taking a breath, calming myself so I can speak gently to him.

I can feel Ben and Jake's glare torching my back.

"What's it going to be...my pit or theirs? I told you that you don't want to make an enemy out of me." His voice has changed from calm to ferocious in an instant.

"Are you raising your voice at my sister? You better fucking watch your mouth when you speak to her. In fact, get your ass out of here and never talk to her again!"

Jake is at my side within seconds.

"She has a choice to make. I came here to get my answer. So..." Trent shrugs.

Jake cuts Trent's words short. "You want my fucking blessing?"

"I want her to pick." Trent is rigid and his words are coming through clenched teeth. "And if she doesn't pick me, then we have to come to a different understanding."

"Trent..." I say, hoping to stop their confrontation, but I'm quickly losing control.

"No." Jake puts his hand on my shoulder. "He's right." Jake admonishes. "Let me help him come to an understanding." He tugs me behind him. "My sister is a pain in my ass. She wanted to make new friends. I just never imagined it would be you. She's my responsibility. If I don't let any of my friends touch her, what in the hell makes you think I'd let her get anywhere near you again?"

"You don't have a choice. She'll be in my pit...not yours!"

His words are deafening, not in volume but in meaning. This has nothing to do with him caring for me. This is just another race, a prize at the end of the finish line.

"Did you Neanderthals really forget I was standing right here?! I can make up my own mind." I shove against Trent's hard chest. "I don't need my brother or his friends to scare off boys from his baby sister. And I don't need any men making decisions for me." I grab Trent's hand. "I'm sorry, but I don't think it's going to work between us. I wanted to tell you in private and at a different time but..." I look back at both Jake and Ben, who just so happen to be ready to pounce.

Anger flares in Trent's eyes, his face tightens, his expression hardens. Gone is the casual, fun Trent I've grown to know. He leans in close to my ear so only I can hear. The words are low, but full of meaning and hate. "You better watch yourself. Like I told you, you're my enemy now."

Trent steps away from me, lifts his head toward my brother. "You can have the whore, she wasn't any good..."

Out of nowhere, with no notice, I'm pushed and stumble to the ground on my knees. I look up to see two bodies on the ground in front of me. Trent on the bottom and Ben on top of him. Fists flying. Bones crunching. Blood spurting.

Ben gets in another bone-crunching hit before he is yanked off by Jake and Todd. Both of their faces are covered in blood, although I think it's mostly Trent's.

Ben pushes away from my brother. Moving to stand above Trent. "You ever come near her again, you motherfucker, I'll kill you!"

Jake stands next to him, a wall of force and threats to back up Jake's words.

Trent is on his feet now. "Don't worry." He spits blood to the ground. "I don't want any piece of that whore. You can have her."

And with that Ben punches his lights out.

22

Ben is pacing back and forth in front of the fire and hasn't really said anything. Trent and Todd finally left after Trent came to. Jake is talking to Harlow and I can't really make out what they are saying. They look to be in deep conversation. I'm not surprised. She's probably trying to calm him down.

I'm still in shock. I knew hanging out with Trent was a bad idea, but I didn't really think he'd be interested in anything but friends or sex. I have to admit, I'm flattered the way Ben acted, but also appalled. I can handle myself, especially when it comes to Trent. I think his threats are just that...threats. It's not like he would hurt me.

Checking my phone, it's after two in the morning. I've had enough fun for one night.

"I need to head home."

Jake ignores my comment, chiming in with, "I can't wait until you hand him his ass in the race." Jake moves his attention from Harlow to Ben. "He raced you before you went to Vegas and got some more experience. You beat him then and you'll beat him now. Matter of fact, he shouldn't even be on the same street as you." Jake takes a drink from his beer.

"Can one of you please tell me why that was necessary. I had it handled with Trent." Harlow looks nervously between all three of us. She knows that mine or Jake's temper is coming to the end of the line.

But it's Ben who answers, but with a question of his own. "Does he always talk to you like that?" he asks calmly, but my body turns to ice at his tone.

Instead of feeling relieved, I'm furious. Why does he even care? He has done more harm to me than Trent ever could.

"None of your business. My life, who I'm with or who I'm not with is none of your business."

He stops pacing, turns and charges toward me, quickly halting in front of me. "You are always my business." He grits through his clenched jaw. Icy blue eyes lock to mine.

"Knock it off, you two. He's just trying to protect you. You're like a little sister to him. Harlow, are you ready?" Jake tells us.

I roll my eyes. He's never noticed the connection I have with Ben and right now, maybe I've been wrong all along.

"Aren't you riding home with me?" I ask her. "You did ride with me, Harlow."

I sound like a brat. I don't care though. I do not want to have to be alone with Ben right now, especially not since he had a death glare on me a few moments ago.

"Jake offered. Besides, you're both going to the same place." She shrugs her shoulders. I'm not sure what game she is playing or what she intends to do with my brother. Her boyfriend is still very much a part of the picture. At the moment, not so much, but he's still there in the background, waiting patiently.

I want to slap that grin off of her beautiful face. Not only does she like spending time with my brother, but won't admit it to me, she also likes being right.

"Come on," Jake says, taking her hand, leading her away from us.

I throw my hands in the air. "Thanks for asking," I yell at both of them. Jake sticks his middle finger up in the air at me while guiding Harlow to his truck.

Once they are gone. Ben and I sit in silence. I hate silence. But I refuse to be the one to talk first. He was the one acting like a caveman moments ago, not me.

"The fire is dying down. We can probably go," he says from beside me, not affected by the awkwardness of the silence, or my brother and Harlow's antics.

"I never offered you a ride home. Harlow did."

"You're right, but I think you owe me more than a ride home. Don't you?"

"No. What on God's green Earth are you talking about?"

"Exactly what I said. I can recall bringing your drunk teenage ass home a few times." Tossing some sand on the fire with a shovel that has been here longer than I can remember, he looks at me for confirmation.

"I'm not a little girl anymore, and I'd appreciate it if you'd stop treating me like it. Trent and my relationship is none of your business."

He leans the shovel against the log to face me. "It's just smoldering now. Let's get out of here. You can yell at me all you want on the way home." He shakes his head. "Damn, girl. You are exhausting."

"Well...if I'm exhausting, you're infuriating."

When we reach the truck, the awkward silence returns. If I'm exhausting him, I guess I'll remain mute.

Ben turns on his phone in the cab of the truck. His phone lights up like he's the President of the United States and has to stop some nuclear event.

"Christ...what the...damn it!" He slams his hand on the dash.

"What the heck was that for?"

"Anna. Becca did it again! Let me drive."

"I don't really think that's a good idea. You seem pretty upset."

"Callie Rae." His voice is stern and threatening. It's not the time to argue. I pull off and we trade seats. He pulls out onto the road, screeching the tires as he goes. I hold on to the side of the seat, bracing myself. If there is anyone behind the wheel that I trust to drive at this speed, it's him.

"She thinks that she can do whatever the hell she wants. Leaving a three-year-old all alone. Thank God your Gran is the nosiest woman on Earth." He lets out a nervous chuckle. I'm not sure if it's relief or just nerves.

"I'm going to kill her for leaving Anna alone."

"What?"

It's almost two in the morning and she's left a three-year-old at home.

"Exactly what I said. I can't make this shit up...no one can. That's Becca, a real piece of work."

The ride is torture. What I thought would be me telling him off about Trent has turned into a heartbreaking experience. I know Gran is taking good care of Anna, but this is so inconceivable.

What seems like hours later, we pull into Ben's driveway. He wastes no time getting out of the truck and running into the house. I follow quickly behind, but can barely keep up with him. When I reach the inside, Gran is sitting with Anna in her arms. Anna's eyes are closed while Gran shushes her.

"Thank you, Gran. I'll put her to bed."

Ben bends down, lifting his sweet, sleepy baby girl in his arms, cradling her close to his chest. He kisses the top of her head. I can feel the relief wash over him.

I sit next to Gran. Not really sure if I should talk or stay or go. But as always, she knows exactly what to do. Placing her hand on my knee, she says, "She's okay, darling. Just a little scared, but I was able to calm her down pretty quick."

"What happened? How'd you know?"

But before she can answer, Ben comes back into the room, but he passes us by without a word, making his way into the kitchen. I hear the water faucet. When he returns there is a glass of water in his hand. He stops before he reaches the hallway. "Don't go yet. I need to talk to both of you."

He's mad. That much is obvious. All the manners ingrained in him are long gone. Gran pats my arm. "He's upset, and more than anything, scared. He'll hold that baby girl for a few minutes and calm down."

We sit in silence, holding hands. Unspoken understanding passes between us. Gran has been on the other end of this exact thing. Only I was Anna. My mother would leave us alone all the time. She had men to pursue, and children got in the way of that.

I've seen Ben upset before, but tonight there was sheer panic on his face, radiating off his body. My heart aches at the sight of him holding Anna in his arms. From the way his eyes can't leave Anna's door, he couldn't bear to be apart from her.

Lost in my own thoughts, it takes me a moment to register that Ben has quietly entered the room. He turns on the lamp sitting on the end table next to me.

"Tell me exactly what happened. Leave nothing out." His voice is quiet, yet full of authority. I've never heard him talk to an adult like that, let alone Gran.

"I was sitting out on the porch. You know how I like a glass of sweet tea in the evening." Ben cocks his head to the side in warning. He knows her better than anyone. "I'm sorry, but I was snooping. I saw her leave while I was at the kitchen window. I never saw a car or person come to the house to maybe take care of Anna. So…I thought I'd sit out on the porch, wait and make sure everything was alright. I had that same feeling I used to get with their mama." She gestures towards me. "My daughter made me feel the same way—anxious. That Becca reminds me so much of her."

Speaking of anxiety, Ben's knee is vigorously bouncing while he waits for her to get to the point.

Gran lets out a breath, making more room in her lungs for the rest of the story. "Well, I didn't see any lights after fifteen minutes. I figured I had overreacted, but as I grabbed the doorknob to go back inside, I heard crying. The closer I got to your house, the louder and more heartbreaking those cries got. I knew I had to get in. I knocked and knocked…and nothing."

"How'd you get in?" I asked, regretting how inappropriate that must sound. As if I'm not listening to a story about someone I know.

"I had a key. I always make sure to get a key from the new tenant. You know, just in case. I once had a neighbor…"

Ben interrupts, losing his patience. He cuts her words, "It's fine, so you got to Anna, where was she?" "Locked in her bedroom." He stands, bringing his palm to his forehead as if he's got a headache. He does…a big one and her name is Becca. Gran continues while I hold my breath. "Thankfully I learned how to pick those types of locks when I was a child. Good thing you didn't replace that old lock."

I rein Gran in before Ben loses his mind. "Was she alright when you got to her?"

"Poor darling, she had tears streaming down her puffy cheeks, beet red, hoarse screams, but all in all just scared. I grabbed her up outta that bed. Thankfully after I hushed her, and rocked her for a bit, she calmed down."

Ben's biting his lip when I chanced a glance at him. Within seconds, he's up. Ben's fist pounds the wall. Not reacting a bit to the fact that he just left a massive hole in the plaster, or the blood trailing down his fist to his elbow.

I want to jump up, wrap him in my arms, but I know it's the last thing he needs right now.

"Ben...Anna is okay. Just concentrate on her right now," Gran tells him. Always the voice of reason.

"She never thinks of anyone but herself. She is a mother, for fuck's sake. Isn't that a natural thing, aren't women born with that instinct?"

We don't have the chance to say anything when Anna walks back into the room. Her little voice asks, "Daddy?"

Ben softens his face for his little girl. "Hey, sweetie. What are you doing up?"

Anna rubs her eyes. Her dark curls are a wild mess, as if she was wrestling a tiger in her sleep, but she couldn't be more beautiful.

"I heard a loud boom. Where's Mommy?"

Ben lifts her in his arms, once again holding her close to his chest, protecting her from the world.

"She's not here right now. But you remember my friends. It was nice of Gran to come and watch you, wasn't it?"

Anna shakes her head. "Can you read me a story?"

"I think it's time for you to get some sleep."

She wrinkles her nose. "I can't go to sleep without a story. Do you think Miss Callie will read to me?"

My heart melts into a pile of mush.

"I can," I say eagerly, clearing my throat of all emotion. "I like to read."

Ben passes Anna to me. When he does, her little arms wrap around my neck like we've known each other forever. Something changes with her touch. I'm not sure what it is, but my heart breaks for her. An overwhelming need washes over me to protect her.

We enter her bedroom. It's everything I imagined for a three-year-old little princess. This is absolutely perfect.

A small toddler bed in the far corner of the room. A white sheer canopy hangs above, draping down around her bed. Elegant white dressers, pink and white polka dot chair—just her size—and a fluffy white bean bag chair near the bookshelf made to look like a castle. Each shelf is filled with books. Setting Anna on her bed, I ask which one is her favorite. "I love *Cinderella*. Because I love pretty shoes."

"You, sweetheart, are a girl after my own heart."

I open the book and begin to read. After a few pages she yawns. "Thanks for reading to me." Her voice is soft and adorable. Barely pronouncing words correctly, but I understand her. "My mommy hates to read books. But my daddy loves to read to me."

"Lie back, sweetie." I swipe her hair away from her face. She smiles contently, while I adjust the comforter around her. "Close your eyes, and I'll keep reading."

After two more pages, precious Anna yawns, I continue to read, unable to pull myself away from this room. I finish the book and she's out like a light. An unexpected urge takes over, I lean over and kiss her on the forehead. How has this little girl, who isn't my child, whom I've only known for a few days, taken over my heart so quickly.

As I stand, Ben's voice as he talks on the phone carries loudly. I take one last glance at Anna, and put my ear to the door.

"Vince. I'm done."

Then a pause as he listens to something being said.

"No. Do you hear me, no!"

Opening the door a smidge, I'm careful not to jiggle the handle to give myself away.

"I told you I would bring her here. But she left my daughter all alone tonight. She doesn't want to be here. I'm not making her stay, but my daughter stays. Do you understand me? Anna is mine." Ben is quiet, I can only assume he's listening.

"She is on the next flight to you as soon as I find her."

Followed by more silence. I think he may have hung up, so I open the door and walk down the hallway but stop as his voice deepens. "You will take her back. If you ever want to see Anna again. I have done unspeakable things for you over the last five years—the gambling, the illegal racing, the fighting, for what? You kept Anna from me. I have every right to be her father. I have to protect her from your daughter, who is a sorry excuse for a mother. I will not continue to live this lie. I don't love your daughter, I never have. Anna and I will be better off without her."

Ben throws the phone. The noise of it shattering is piercing. I look back at Anna, hoping she didn't hear. She hasn't moved. I hurry back over to the stool I was sitting on earlier, pick up the book, and say, "And they all lived happily ever after," I whisper, feeling his presence.

"Thank you," Ben says from the doorway. His face is still red, and his breathing is heavy.

I set the book on the nightstand. "She is the sweetest. I enjoyed every second."

He smiles. After hearing him lose his temper, there is no doubt in my mind how much he loves her. "Come on," he says, nodding to the hallway. In this moment, after everything that has happened tonight, all these years apart have only deepened my longing for him. He is still the sexiest sight after all this time.

The living room has pieces of his broken phone. Glancing at the ground, he tells me, "Be careful."

I bend down to pick up the pieces, but he beats me by taking my hand. "Don't...it's my mess. Please sit for a minute."

"I'm sorry about Becca. I hope she is safe." I'm not sure if that is the truth, but for Anna's sake, I hope so.

"I'm sorry about this whole night. I was hoping to explain everything. I haven't been the man I need to be around you. I've learned a lot about life since I left. This is not how I want to live my life." He places his hand on my knee. "You are great with her, by the way."

"She is amazing. It's hard to believe she's yours." I knock my knee with his.

"Me, too."

"Probably because I haven't grown up yet."

With a smirk, he says, "You've definitely grown up." My face flames, I know because it feels as if it is on fire. Before I can say anything, the door opens and the mother of the year comes stumbling over the threshold.

"Hey, look." She slurs. "It's Benny boo and Callie too! Haha...that rhymes." She barely makes it to the couch, falling with an oof. "I am so drunk." She exaggerates each word, letting out a cackle.

"Callie, I'm sorry, but I think it's time for you to go. I'll talk to you tomorrow." Ben's face is sterner than I have ever seen. I'm almost afraid to leave Becca with him. I know he'd never hurt her no matter what she did, but tonight a line was crossed.

I'm relieved I didn't have to be the one to make an excuse to go. I have no idea what is going to happen, but I don't think I want to stick around for it. As much as I don't like Becca right now, or want to let her know what a horrible person she is, it isn't my place. I'm not sure I can keep calm without disturbing Anna in the next room.

"Sure. I'll see you later."

"You don't have to go. We can all have some fun. Together." She's trying to sound seductive, but it's just a drunk mumble.

"Becca, enough!"

I let myself out. Wondering with each step what tomorrow will bring and what him sending Becca back to her father will mean for us.

23

I'm startled awake. Glancing at the clock, it's six thirty-four in the morning. I can hear yelling coming from outside. "What in the world?" Grabbing the pillow beside me, I smother my face so the noise goes away. I'm not ready to wake up. But as my brain slowly starts to catch up with the world, I recognize her voice. It's Becca.

Rushing over to the window, I spy a large SUV in Ben's driveway, along with three men in dark suits. The sun is barely shining, and so far it's a gray, cloudy morning.

I lift my window so I can hear better.

"You bastard. I'm not leaving without my daughter. I came here because you made me."

A few more moments pass. Becca's voice is growing louder. "It's awful here, Daddy."

She blabs about something else, but I can't make out what it is. Instead of hiding, I throw on some sweatpants, and a sweatshirt. I know this isn't my business, but whatever is going on, I need to find out.

An overwhelming need to protect this innocent little girl washes over me. I'm going to guard Anna from her own mother. It sounded crazy in my head, but I was protected by my Gran. Maybe a little too late in some ways, but others just in time. I want to be the one who is just in time for Anna.

I race out the door, down the steps, slipping on a pair of slippers as I go. Before I do something I'll regret, I peek out the window. The three men are toe to toe with Ben. Anxiety blooms in my chest. Are they here to hurt him and take Anna?

Stepping out onto the porch, Jake is sitting on the steps, stopping me in my tracks. He looks up, giving me a knowing look. The same look he'd give me when our mom would come home drunk, or with a bastard boyfriend. He wants me to sit quietly and let him handle it. I think we both know Ben needs our support right now, but we can't get in the middle of this.

"Should we go over there?" I ask, but I already know his answer and I'm hoping I'm wrong.

"No. If he needs me, I'll be there. You shouldn't get in the middle of this. It's not our business." Jake chuckles, but it's a nervous chuckle. "I never would have thought he'd air his dirty laundry in the neighborhood."

"I don't think he has a choice," I tell him.

Becca rips her shoulder from the older man's grasp. She steps close to Ben, shoving him in the chest. Ben's body moves back, but I don't think it's by the force of her strength. She leans in, telling him something we can't hear. She turns away from him, while another man helps her in the SUV. Once she's inside, he places suitcases in the back.

She's leaving?

Ben and the older man are in a tense conversation.

"Who is that?" I can't stand sitting here, not doing anything.

My brother says, "Her father. He and Ben are on the same page when it comes to Becca. Anna I'm not sure. He might be in for a tough fight over her."

Ben is giving Becca's father a stone-faced glare. Becca's father buttons his suit jacket, nods at Ben, and gets in the vehicle. While the last goon gets in the passenger seat.

Once they've left the driveway, I stand. Jake grabs my arm to stop me. "You don't want to get in the middle of this. I know you want to help, but now is not the time to be a nosy southern girl."

He really doesn't get it. He has no clue how much that isn't true. He is part of our family. And this nosy southern girl takes care of family, even if he isn't mine.

"I'm going to check on both of them. He needs a friend right now. Are you coming?"

"No. He's a big boy. I think he'll be fine. I'm going inside, back to bed. You should, too."

"Yeah, you're right," I agree, but he should know I never do as I'm told.

He leaves me on the porch. I know he's right. I should leave him, he may need space. I'm sure he doesn't want me to badger him with questions, but I can't stop myself.

I move before I can rationalize that this is not a good idea. Ben sees me before I make it to the door. "Go home, Callie." His tone reminds me of when we were kids, and he didn't want me to follow him to the races. It sparks annoyance, which spurs my mission further.

"Is Anna alright? Is Becca gone for good?"

Ben doesn't answer. He goes into the house but doesn't close the door. So I take that as an invitation. Once inside, the kitchen is destroyed. Plates, glasses all in pieces on the floor and counters. Various kitchen items strewn about, including a huge stand mixer that is shattered. I didn't know those could even break. I freeze. Did he do this? Where is Anna? Did she wake up, scared?

"Careful..." he scolds as I take a step toward him.

"Is Anna okay?"

"She's fine. I told her it was the TV. This isn't the first time her mother has done this. It's why we left in the first place. You shouldn't be here."

"Too bad. I'm involved now."

"Involved. No, you don't want to be involved in this clusterfuck I call my life."

"I'm worried about you, the both of you."

"You met her five minutes ago, you don't care about her. Her own mother can't even be bothered with her. Look at what she did while her baby was asleep in the next room."

He rests his hands on the counter, holding himself up, bowing his head. Unable to stop myself, the pain is radiating off of him. I carefully come to stand beside him, touching his shoulder. "Anna will be okay. She has you."

Ben jumps back from me just as a little voice enters the room.

Our moment is gone.

"Hey, sweetie." He scoops her up before she steps on any broken glass. "Why are you up? It's early."

"I'm hungry." I can tell Ben is hiding her from the mess in the kitchen by shielding her with his body.

"I'll make you breakfast in a little bit. I was going to make you pancakes, but I dropped the mixer, and it made a shelf break. Silly daddy, huh?"

My heart shatters and melts at the same time. How is that even possible?

"Silly daddy." She leans away from him, her big beautiful blue eyes, much like her fathers, fall on me. "Daddy, is Miss Callie staying for breakfast, too?"

He smiles. "I think so."

"Yes, I'll help clean up Daddy's mess."

He takes her hand and leads her back to her room.

Becca must have thrown one hell of a temper tantrum. I know he was involved with a group of people I know nothing about, but this is out of my league.

I kneel down, picking up bowls, silverware, and shards of glass.

There is so much I don't know about Ben. What has he been through? Becca, Anna, even Beau. In all these years, he's never mentioned any of them. Speaking of him, I wonder where the cute pup is? He must have him in the basement. I'm sure he wouldn't want his paws to get cut. Geez, no one is safe from this woman.

As moments pass, the room is starting to look a little better. Ben finally comes out of Anna's room.

"Is she really alright?"

"Yeah, it's so messed up. She can't even count on her mom. I'm so glad I'm in her life now. I won't ever forgive Becca from keeping her from me. I thought maybe I could get past it, but the closer I get to Anna, the more I realize what I've missed out on."

That pang of guilt returns. Would he be upset when he finds out about our pregnancy? That I kept a secret from him?

"She's with you now. I'm glad you have her." I smile.

He smiles back, but then it falters. "I'm a single dad. Who would have thought?" he tells me as he grabs a broom.

"I have to admit the whole thing is a huge surprise to me. You've been living the racer life. Racing in all kinds of cities. Living this whole other life outside of our small town." I pause, working myself up to get the courage to say the one question I've been meaning to get to the bottom of. "So why have you been so secretive about everything?"

He stops sweeping and leans his weight against the broom. "To protect you and everyone I care about. The people I'm tangled with in Las Vegas are different from anyone in this small town."

"I don't understand?"

"Becca's dad runs an elite racing syndicate. So that's why over the years I've only stayed here for a short while and then go. But Anna is changing all of that."

"And what about Becca?"

"Her father funds the underground drag racing syndicate. My dad got wrapped up in gambling with his guys. Then when my dad told him I could pay his debts with my racing skills. Life changed."

"What is going to happen now? Are you going to vanish again?"

"I want a normal life for Anna, a preschool class to go to everyday, healthy snacks, dinner on the table. But how do I do that while I prepare to get behind the wheel every week with my car prepped and ready to go. It seems like a lot to figure out."

"You sound like you've grown up quite a bit, Benjamin Carmichael."

He comes to stand in front of me, my breath picking up as I look up at him. "Have you?" The seductive tone in his voice is almost wilting my legs. "I think you still have some feistiness in you."

"That will never change." My body heats at his sexy tone. He's flirting, I think, and I'm definitely returning the favor.

"Let me make you some breakfast, then I have to deal with the rest of this mess."

Ben made a small breakfast for just the three of us. We talked about our favorite foods and how when we were kids we'd always have cereal taste testing.

"Do you remember when we convinced Gran to buy different cereals at least once a month to do a taste test? I think Raisin Bran waged war against my taste buds." He laughed about the memory.

"We had so much fun. Gran would pick one horrible cereal, and then she'd pick something amazing like Cap'n Crunch. The worst part is she wouldn't buy another cereal until we finished the whole box." I stick out my tongue in disgust as I can almost remember having to choke down the horrific tasting cereals she chose.

"I specifically remember the time you tried to throw away the whole box of that raisin cereal and took out the trash. She actually stopped the garbage man before he threw the trash bag in the truck. She made you go through the bag and find that cereal box. You had to eat at least one bowl." He laughs.

"Thank God there was nothing gross in that bag."

"I know. I probably would have thrown up."

We laughed and enjoyed the morning. Anna and I played with her dolls while Ben did the dishes.

As he put the last plate in the drying rack, his phone rang.

He listened for a long moment. His face rigid as he rubbed his forehead.

"Yes. I can. Immediately." He spoke into the phone.

My stomach dropped. Who is he talking to?

"I'll give you a call back with the details."

As he hangs up, he looks over at me and Anna. His once tight face contorts into a smile.

"Everything okay?" I manage to somehow choke out.

"Yep. All good. Are you planning on leaving soon?"

"Yes, I have to be at the salon in about an hour."

"Perfect, that'll give us more time to hang out and get to know each other a little better."

We continue our morning, almost like a family with him and Anna involving me in their day to day, each of us blissfully unaware of the changes that were to come.

24

After leaving Ben's house, I went to work and haven't talked to him since yesterday. I've been hanging out with Emerson, so she has taken my mind off of his weird reaction to that phone call.

Today is race day. I know he was busy testing his car. Van, Jake, Ace, and Ben put their racing minds together to see how fast Ben's car will run. They used computers to tune the car just right. It's such a long, detailed process. I've been around it for a long time, but was never really interested in all of that. I love to just watch it all play out.

There are tons of people wandering around trying to get a glimpse of the cars and drivers.

Ems and I walk up to the car haulers. There are at least fifteen racers today. Most of them are from other cities. Ben and Trent are the only ones from our town here today.

Em's eyes widen when she spots the familiar race car. "I never get tired of seeing all these people here to watch this."

People are lining the street in anticipation of the race. The rickety wooden bleachers built before I was born are filled shoulder to shoulder with spectators, but that's not where we will be. No, we will be right at the starting line.

Although street racing is illegal, and the cops have broken up races in the past, even impounding cars and issuing high-dollar citations, this spot is safe from the cops. It's been a tradition for years. The cops respect our tradition as long as we are respectful of them.

I yank Emerson by her shirt. "Come on. Let's see how the boys are. I'm anxious to see how the car does."

"Hey, boys!" we say in unison. It only takes a split second for my eyes to find Ben. He's got a rag in his hand, wiping grease off of it.

"Callie. Ems. Glad you can make it," Jake speaks first. Ben watches me without saying a word. His gaze is intense, almost making me feel as if I'm in trouble for something.

"Can I talk to you for a minute?" Ben is asking, but his tone is non-negotiable.

"Me?"

"Yes, you," he states firmly.

I nod, already frustrated by whatever he could possibly have to say to me.

I stride past him, out of the trailer.

"Good luck today, by the way."

"Thanks." His hands are on his hips, with his head down. "I need to know something before I go out there today. I need to race with a clear head." He pauses, drawing in a sharp breath. "I couldn't sleep well last night. It wasn't because of Becca or Anna. It was all because of you, Sunshine.

"Okay...shoot." I twist my ring, unsure of what he's going to ask.

"Are you lying to me?" His forehead wrinkles.

"What would I lie to you about?" My voice cracks. I don't think I've lied to him about anything.

He lifts his head; he's chewing on his lip waiting for my answer. I could tell him yes, aggravate him, but that wouldn't be right, especially not before a race.

"Trent. He mentioned you were his biggest fan, and that you would be in his pit today. So, what's the deal with him?"

"The deal?" I huff. "There is no deal. You were there when I told him I don't want to be with him. Don't you remember punching him?"

Shaking his head, he says, "He was pretty convinced you were his."

I take a step toward him. I don't care how much bigger he is than me, I don't like his tone.

"Why do you care, anyway?" It comes out brattier than I intended.

"I care because you said you aren't with him. He sure seems to think you are still a couple."

Frustration fills my core. "Why can't you boys listen to me? He's delusional if he thinks we're anything. He wants a different kind of relationship...one I want no part of."

Ben leans in closer, backing me up against the trailer. His broad chest brushing against mine. His hands resting on the trailer. Lowering his voice in the way that sets me on fire, he says, "And what kind of relationship do you want?"

It's hard to think when he's so close. He's messing with my mental stability.

"I..I..." Stuttering is not good.

"Come on, Callie...is he who you want?"

"No..." I breathe out.

"Then don't pretend to be his friend or whatever he wants." Ben stares me down. He takes a step back, giving me a second to clear the haze of lust from his closeness. "He's impulsive. We've seen it on the track."

"What do you mean?"

"Never mind. Just stay away from him," he mutters.

"Look...I appreciate the big brother thing you have going on, but I think you are the last person to be giving me relationship advice. Besides, there isn't one."

His nostrils flare, eyes narrow on me. "You would see it that way."

"What other way should I see it?"

"Never mind. Maybe you're the delusional one, Sunshine." He shoves away from the trailer and walks away from our conversation.

Well, that went a different way than I anticipated.

***

When I see Van and Ems in their own private conversation, I head over to the starting line to calm my nerves. What was that about? Where did all that come from?

This is the first race of the season, and I'd be lying if I didn't say the majority of me is thrilled to see Ben behind the wheel of a race car. Even though right now he isn't my favorite person. Even pissed at him, I have to admit there is nothing like it. His race helmet sits on his hip as he walks around the car, checking that it's ready to go. Once inside, he puts his helmet on, the seat belt locked in place, and last were his black leather gloves. In the past, before every race I'd run up to his car and wish him luck.

He'd always say, "I don't need luck. I have you, Sunshine."

Jackie comes up to stand beside me, interrupting my memory. Great, just great. Her tits are up to her chin, and her makeup is caked on.

"I'm on my way to visit Trent's pit."

"Good for you."

"I'll be waiting for him at the finish line."

"First of all, you should be waiting for him at the starting line because that's where most people greet the winner, and second, I don't care."

She continues, as if I just didn't give her valuable street racing advice. If she's going to be his back-up girl, she should at least know the rules. I mean, her main job is to wear a sexy, revealing outfit, while guiding the race car backward to the starting line after the driver does his burnout before the flag goes down.

"You know, Trent is planning on winning and he'll do *everything* he can to win."

I don't like her tone. It's like I'm not in on some big secret.

My death glare takes shape easily enough. I usually have to envision her kicking a puppy or something, but looking at her ugly mug does the trick.

"What is that supposed to mean?"

"Trent isn't going to back down. He'll do whatever it takes to win."

"Every race car driver feels that way. It's not a secret."

"Let's just say that you should come to our pit, it will be much safer over there." She winks, leaving my stomach in a knot.

What the hell does that mean?

When it's time for Ben to take his car to the starting line, I can barely hear myself think. God, I love it.

Cars and trailers line both sides of the road. Spectators and race crews scatter in every nook and cranny. People are sitting on car hoods, on the pavement, or popping a squat on the curb. But the best place to be is behind the starting line. There is a mountain of us, waiting to see who takes the lead.

One thing we all have in common is the adrenaline rush that comes with the sport. When the flagger waves their arm or flicks on the flashlight, everyone's heart stops until the few seconds it takes for the winner to be announced.

Ems and I are at the starting line along with Van, Jake, Ace, and a few of the other racing guys.

Tonight, two miles are blocked off for the adrenaline spike we all crave.

As Ben's car comes up to the starting line, my heart picks up speed. The rumble of the engine makes you want to plug your ears and turn up the volume at the same time. You can feel the vibrations from the ground tracing its way through your toes and up to your racing heartbeat.

"This is crazy," Ems yells from beside me. "How does this never get old?"

Trent pulls up beside Ben's yellow Mustang. It's not the same car off the lot, it's been altered to get the most power and speed. There have been countless hours of tuning, and programs and test runs put into his car. Looking at Trent unsettles my nerves. Even with his helmet on, his eyes are only focused on the road ahead of him. He's tense—hands glued to the steering wheel. Where Trent is all fired up, Ben is at ease, calm. Smiling and talking with Van. I'm sure going over the final details. I know this because this is their routine.

The starting line clears everyone but the racers, and the very attractive female flagger. I've never seen her before, and I'm sure she has everyone's attention. She's got a skintight leather romper on with a black-and-white-checkered race flag pattern on it. Patent leather black boots up to her knees. They've already done their respective burnouts to help their tires stick to the road better, so they are ready to go.

Once the flag waves, they are off. The cars are loud, roaring down the track. The crowd has gotten even louder. They are neck and neck, straight as an arrow. All of a sudden, Trent's red car crosses the white line, and slams into Ben's passenger side. Watching in horror as Trent's car sideswipes Ben's car, metal screeching in my ears. Trent loses control, spinning out. Ben somehow manages to keep it on the road, but not for long until it stops in the grass.

Before I can register what I'm doing, my feet are carrying me to him. There are other people running beside me. All I can think of is Ben. Is he hurt? With a racing heart, I pick up the pace.

Reaching the wreckage, my questions are answered.

Ben is out of the race car that is now in the grass. He slams his helmet to the ground and Trent walks up to him, casually, as if he didn't just try to kill him. I was so focused on Ben, I never even looked to see if Trent was out of his car.

"What the hell was that about?" Ben screams.

"Callie." Trent wastes no time, shoving Ben back a few steps. Before Ben can say anything or shove him back, several people intervene, and push them away from each other.

I can't move, frozen in place at the sound of my name. Trent smiles in my direction. The smile screams at me. Ben is right. Something is wrong with Trent.

Trent stalks over to me, helmet in his hands. "You're in the wrong pit, baby girl. I told you you'd be the enemy, and the game just started."

Jake runs in my direction, but when he reaches me, Trent is safely far enough away from me.

"What'd he say to you?"

"Nothing."

"That's fucking it! You stay away from him. Do you understand me? If he comes near you again, I'm going to kill him."

For the first time in forever, I don't feel the need to argue with him. He's right.

I want to run to Ben. I need to know he's alright. Did he get hurt at all? Did he injure his neck? Did he bump his head? But I decide against it, and slowly make my way back to Emerson.

***

When Ems and I reach the shop after we've stopped to have a bite to eat, the guys are replaying the events of the race over and over again. Trying to figure it out. I'm not really in the mood to relive what happened. I just want to escape all of this. The guys know everything about me. They are always wanting to protect me. And that's the problem, maybe the reason why I gravitated to Trent. I need space from these guys, these people I've known forever. I need to find my own way.

Ben approaches me. He's got a cut on his lip. I can't help myself, reaching up, I brush my thumb over the cut, but pull away quickly. I think in that second, I see his eyes shut.

"You've been quiet ever since you got here." His tone is flat, almost annoyed.

"You didn't have to make the comment about me and Trent. He's a jerk. He's making that point very clear. You and Jake are right about him. Is that what you want to hear?"

"No. I don't want to hear anything about him. Especially anything that has to do with you." I roll my eyes. "Let's forget about the race for tonight. Are you alright?"

"Me? Why?" I ask, unsure why he'd care about me. He was the one in the wreck.

"Because your dad died behind the wheel of a race car."

"I was a baby. It's not like I was there," I snap at him. I shouldn't do it, but I don't like to talk about my dad. I'm very good at pushing the hurt down and away. I've done it enough over the years. Dreaming of what it would have been like to have a loving father. A protector. Someone to be proud of me. Someone I could count on. Because that's what people say he was. He was one of the good ones.

He got behind the wheel of a car, raced another car while drunk. He lost and wrecked into the other car. The other driver survived, but was severely injured, and thankfully, recovered. My father was turned into the villain in that race. It wasn't even a street race. No, he was on a busy road and lost control of his car.

He made one mistake that cost him everything. From what was said about him from those who loved him and knew him best, it was out of character for him. He would never have gotten behind the wheel if he were drinking. But he did. My mother was never the same after that, Gran told me. I'm sure that is why she couldn't be a good mother to me or to Jake.

Jake remembers our father, I don't.

"I didn't know him. It doesn't bother me at all." I'm lying, he knows I am. I've confided in him how that's my biggest fear for Jake. Dying while racing his car.

"Okay. Sunshine. I'm glad then."

There is an uncomfortable silence between us.

"How's Anna?"

"Good. Gran's watching her today. I did hire a babysitter, but Gran said that she wouldn't hear of it." He laughs.

"I can't imagine you would have won that argument."

"Definitely not. Hey, ummm…I think I've had enough of these guys for the night. Do you think you could give me a ride back?"

"Yeah…sure thing, Ben."

***

We left the shop. Our ride to his house is quiet and I try to stop my mind from wandering to the conversation about my father. I didn't know him. I only grew up around my mother. That subject isn't good to think about either.

We pull in his driveway and Gran is sitting on the couch, reading a book, when we walk inside his house.

"You look comfy," I say with sarcasm.

"How could I not be cozy? This place is a dream. Ben, you've really outdone yourself with the remodeling of this place. I didn't really pay much attention...you know, the last time I was here, I had a more pressing issue. But this place is something." Gran's eyes are glinting with excitement.

"I'm glad you like it, Gran," Ben tells her. I can hear pride in his voice.

"I do." She stands, wobbles a bit. Ben doesn't miss a beat, his arm reaches out, steadying her by the elbow. "I'm good, dear." She pats him on the cheek. "I'm headed home now. Anna and I had a lot of fun for today, but this old bird is cooked for the day."

"Thanks, Gran," Ben says. He still takes her by the elbow and guides her to the door.

"Could you walk me home, dear?"

"I'll do it, Gran," I offer.

"I'd like a big strong man to walk me home. You stay here and watch Anna. Then you can come home later." She doesn't allow me to argue. I've never seen the old bird walk out the door so fast. I know all too well she is fine to walk next door on her own two legs.

I laugh to myself. She's up to something.

I lean down to pet Beau, who is patiently looking out the glass door at his master walking away. I laugh a little to myself. Gran can talk anyone into anything.

After I say my hellos to Beau, I go in search of Anna. She is playing Barbies, and explains to me that Barbie must drive the car instead of Ken, there is a knock at the door. Maybe Ben forgot his key?

When the door opens, a short, dark-haired teenager that I recognize with thick cat-eye eyeliner is standing there with a smile on her face. Lindsey Potter. I think she may be sixteen or so.

"Lindsey, what are you doing here?".

"Ben gave me a call about babysitting tonight. I need the cash, and Mrs. Rae told me this morning about Mr. Carmichael needing a babysitter." She smiles up at me.

25

When Ben and I come out to the driveway, I recognize the bike from the night I saw him at the bar.

"You want me to get on that...with you?"

"Doesn't Trent also have a bike? You've never been on the back of his?" He seems surprised.

"I've never ridden on the back of any bike. I'm a little scared, to be honest with you. And if I'm really being honest, I don't trust Trent. He drives like a maniac, whether with two wheels or four, apparently."

He opens a backpack attached to the back of his bike, removing a helmet. "Here, this is Becca's. It should fit you though."

I hesitate, unable to push the jealousy back as I think to myself that she probably wouldn't be happy about that.

"She only wore it once," he answers as if I had spoken the wayward thoughts out loud. "Listen, I tried to make it work with her. I tried to make her part of my life. It wasn't ever going to work. Maybe just like you and Trent, ya know."

He hands me the helmet, I take it, letting his words soak in. He's right. Trent and I don't fit into each other's worlds, and it's obvious that Becca doesn't fit into his.

Ben lifts his leg over, kicks the stand, and balances the bike between his legs. He extends his hand to me. "Step on the foot peg to lift yourself, then swing your leg over."

I do as he says, not sure what to hold on to, so I grab his shoulder.

"Are you ready?"

"What do I hold on to?" I ask, feeling like an idiot.

"Wrap your arms around me."

Oh my God. Why does this feel more intimate than the night in the tent that I spent with him? He takes my left hand and places it on his belt. "Grab my belt if you feel like you might fall off. I promise you won't, but it will make you feel more secure."

I wrap my fingers around his belt, pulling myself even closer to him. My front is against his back. He smells good and manly and I'm having trouble concentrating. So I hold on tighter.

He slips on his own helmet. The bike rumbles between my legs. A jolt of excitement courses through me. "Wow," I say out loud.

"You ready, Sunshine?"

"I think so."

The next thing I know, we are moving. He starts out slow, navigating the road. "Relax. Act like you're a sack of potatoes sitting on the seat. Just hold on to me and move with me."

I'm not exactly sure what he's talking about until we take our first turn out onto the paved road. His speed increases. "Ahh!"

I can't help it. I don't mean to scream, but I'm not sure what else to do. The wind whips around us. I feel like we're going straight into a windstorm, but it feels amazing. The night air is crisp and cool. I tighten my hand around his belt when he takes another turn.

"Are you alright?"

"Yes."

We rode for another ten minutes or so. I'm not sure where we are headed because in my entire life, I can't ever remember being on this narrow road.

"Where are we going?" I yell over the loud exhaust of the motorcycle.

"It's just another half mile or so," he yells back over his shoulder.

I find myself relaxing against his back, wanting the ride to be much longer. I'm not sure if it's because this is fun and freeing, or because I know I don't want to let him go. He's home to me. I've never felt more at home than right now riding on the back of a motorcycle having no idea where I am, only that I know I'm with the person I most want to be with.

When I glance up, there is nothing but a two-lane empty road ahead. There are no trees, houses, or any sign of life. For the life of me, I can't figure out where we are.

He accelerates, and the wind takes my breath away. If I wasn't so scared, I'd let go, rip my helmet off, throw my hands up in the air, close my eyes, and tilt my head to the sky. I can just imagine the feeling of complete freedom and peace.

The wind lessons as he slows. A large storage facility comes into view.

"What is this?"

He doesn't answer. The bike slows as we get closer to the building. There has to be at least a dozen garage doors.

He stops the bike in front of the door marked with the number nine.

Ben takes his helmet off, he runs his hand through his hair and my breath stops. God, I love how sexy he is, the way he makes such a little motion so hot.

"Have you ever been here?"

"No, not this particular storage unit."

He gets off the bike and I follow suit but feel as if my head is about to topple over. I try to take the helmet off, but I can't get the buckle to release. Ben must notice the awkward struggle, and he smiles, and gets to work, his fingers brushing against my chin as he frees me.

"There." He places the helmet on the seat. "What did you think of your fist motorcycle ride?"

"I loved it. It was so fun and freeing."

"I'm glad." He leans in, placing a light kiss on my cheek. The spot catches fire from his touch.

It takes me a moment to get my breathing under control—from the motorcycle ride and that kiss—but I follow him over to the storage unit. It's not the typical storage unit. It's a lot bigger and I tell him so.

"It's an airplane hangar. In the fifties, this was the site of a small airport, but after a tragic plane wreck, it was turned into a hangar and an airplane graveyard. But most of all, it makes an awesome track to test race cars."

Ben opens the door, and his old race car appears. The race car from his childhood, the race car that I watched him work on for hours while I fell in love with him.

"You recognize her?"

"Of course, I do. I'm so glad you kept it. Do you still race it?"

"Haven't for a long time. I do want to show you something else." He takes my hand. I can't hide the smile on my face. It is in that moment that I know that this is where I want to be. Not with Trent or even someone else I might meet in the future. It's clear that he is my future.

We walk hand in hand until we reach a sight that I've never seen. In the distance, an old single engine plane with a broken wing and crinkled metal with scrape marks along its side. Sadness washes over me, catching in my throat. "What happened?"

"Years ago, before we were even born, a young man wrecked this plane. It had a rough landing, even scraped a hillside." As if he can read the expression on my face, he puts me out of my misery. "He survived."

My hand goes to my chest in relief. "Oh...thank goodness."

"He never flew again. At least, that is what I was told by him."

"You met him?"

"Right before I left, when I put my car in the storage garage. He was standing here, staring at the plane. He told me that he was so grateful that he survived, and the next day he proposed to his wife. He said there is no point in waiting for your life to begin when you can start it right now."

"That makes me happy. I'm glad. I was worried that maybe you were going to tell me a sad story."

He brings my hand up to his lips and places a kiss on the top of my hand. "I like happy endings too. That's why I wanted to bring you here. Show you a place that is special to me. That brings me peace."

"Let me show you something else."

We walk back to where the old Mustang, named Betty, I backed into last year sits. Thankfully the dent wasn't too serious, and he forgave me for hurting this car.

"I'm glad you forgave me for that," I say, pointing to where I remember my little oops.

He steps closer, causing the back of my knees to touch the front bumper of the car.

"Oh, I definitely forgave you for that. I just wanted to show you that we can move on from the past."

His warmth envelops me. There is excitement and the memory of his touch. He makes me feel cared for and calm. Ben leans in closer. His mouth is just inches from mine, and my body comes to life.

"Mr. Carmichael, are you trying to kiss me?"

"I'm not trying to, I'm going to…and I'm going to do much more to you."

"Yes," I whisper, barely able to speak.

"Callie, I've missed you so much; I want to be with you. I've fucked this up between us, but I want to make it right. Will you let me fix us?"

Nodding in response. His lips crash to mine. We devour each other. His tongue mingles with mine. He's sweet and minty.

Before I can stop him, and make this last forever, he pulls away, but then those same lips are on my neck. Moving torturously slowly down to my chest. His hands move down my sides.

"Mr. Carmichael, are you going to take me back to your house, or are we going to make a pit stop here?"

"Sunshine, I'll never make it home," he murmurs against my sensitive skin.

He slowly, teasingly removes my jacket, then lifts my shirt above my head and tosses it to the ground. Exposing my black bra to the night.

"Oh no, you can't remove mine without removing yours." He complies, taking his leather jacket off, laying it on the hood of the car. Then he reaches up above his head and around the back of his neck, tugging up as he removes his t-shirt.

"Oh, Sunshine, I had to do something to keep my mind off of running back to you."

His lips devour mine again. And I never want him to stop. But when he does, his hands reach my bra. With his finger he ever so gently tugs the cup down and places his mouth on my breast. Tugging and nipping with his teeth.

I claw at his shoulders, unable to stop my body's response. He moves down to my belly while his hands find the button of my jeans. He tugs them down while my back falls to the hood of the car. The cold leather of the jacket bites my back.

I look up into his heart-stopping beautiful eyes. Glinting off the moonlight.

"Do you understand how much I wanted this to happen again? I'm so sorry I…"

I slip my hand over his lips. "Shh… we are here now. Let's not worry about the past. I'm tired of thinking of then. Let's do now."

"How did I get so lucky?" He murmurs against my neck, my skin reacting to the gentle touch of the swipe of his tongue. My body demands so much more.

His mouth finds mine again. And it's as if something in me takes over. I want him, I can barely contain myself.

He pushes me back, the back of my knees hitting the front bumper until I'm lying on his coat. "I'm going to taste every inch of you, Sunshine." His voice is breathy and low. His hands wander down my thighs as he pushes them apart. Lowering his head. My back arches, my head follows. My panties are long gone. The crisp air changes to warmth.

"Oh…" I mewl, as his tongue brushes against my clit. He sucks and nips and tugs until I can't hold back. My hands go to his silky strands, tugging as the pleasure mounts. His arm reaches up, grabbing my breast. He's suffocating every inch of air around me and I need more of him. The gentle glide of his tongue, hitting my most intimate spots. I move for him. I couldn't stop my body's reaction if I wanted to. I feel the release building and it's close.

"I could do that all night." He raises his head. His lips glistening as the moon shines brightly in the sky.

"I want you so much. Please." I beg. I'm not a beggar, ever. But I want him. His strong arms wrapped around me, lifting my torso close to him. His hard, chiseled chest against my breasts. His mouth finds my neck again, the vibration of his mouth releasing an inferno throughout my body. I barely notice his movement as he reaches behind him, never breaking our contact.

He takes a condom out of his pocket, rips the tab with his teeth. "I want so much more time with you, but I can't stop myself." I tug him by the neck, letting him know I need more.

"Don't stop." I pant. He leans over me.

"I'm crazy about you, Sunshine. I promise, I'm yours." His voice is barely a whisper, gazing up at me through incredibly long lashes. His eyes are trained on mine as he pushes inside me and lets out a gasp. "Oh, Sunshine. You're perfect."

I can't help but succumb to his body, his soul. He is everything I've ever wanted and so much more. I want to stay in this paradise and have this feeling last forever.

26

I've been at the salon all day. It's getting late but I have one more haircut and I'm ready for this day to be over with. As I'm returning from the bathroom, Trent is here, at the salon, waiting in my chair. My gut fills with dread.

"I'm not cutting that mop on your head," I tell him, trying to sound confident.

"I'm on your schedule."

I peek at my notebook, and there his name stares back at me. My stomach sinks. Shit! How did his name get on my book and I didn't notice.

"I just need a buzz. It won't take long." He rubs his hand over the top of his head.

"I think you should go somewhere else. After the last time I saw you, I figure this is the last place I'd find you."

"No. I'm not moving. We need to talk." His tattooed arms cross while a dark smirk covers his face. "Did you enjoy the race?"

I grab the scissors. Acting as if I'm going to trim his hair, but part of me feels that it wouldn't hurt to have a backup plan that involves a weapon, and nothing better than a sharp pair of scissors. It's not as if I'd hurt him, but I'm not sure I can say the same for him.

"It's late. We close at nine. That's in ten minutes and no, I didn't. It was bullshit on your part. You threw the race."

"I didn't throw the race. I told you that you didn't want to make an enemy of me. But the truth is, I'd rather mess with Ben and not you. I still think we can be together, babe, or at least work something out."

My usually sturdy hand is shaking. Placing the scissors at my side for a moment to make it stop, hoping he doesn't notice, I can't even formulate a reply. It's getting late and I'm the only one here. Dread fills my stomach. My gut instincts are telling me something is off. I can't believe I even considered starting a relationship with this lunatic.

At that moment, I spin the chair to face the mirror. At least if I have the scissors in my hand, and he decides to hurt me, I'll have some protection.

I clear my throat. "I appreciate your honesty, but I'm just not sure we are meant to be." I do my best to sound casual.

Trent startles me, grabbing my hand. It's so quick, I can't even think about what my next movement will be. Holding it tight, I glance at his face in the mirror. His expression is hard, eyes piercing. I can't look away, even though every ounce of my body is telling me to run.

"My honesty. You haven't even given us a shot. I threw out every other girl for you because you asked. You made me think you wanted me, but instead, Carmichael came back and he took you from me. He thinks he's better than me with his money and his connections in the mob. He's nothing. Not a mobster. Not a race car driver. He's nothing!" Trent's hand squeezes even hard.

"Ow...please, stop. You're hurting me," I plead.

His teeth grit together as he tells me, "I'm sorry." His features soften, and he lets go of me. "I'm jealous, okay?" He lets out a breath and my nerves calm. "I never felt this way about someone before. You're gorgeous, sexy as fuck, and you make me feel things that—fuck!" He braces his hands against his forehead, then yanks at his hair. He startles me by jumping from the chair, then coming closer and his hands gripping around my waist.

"Trent. Please, just calm down. I'm not in a relationship with Ben or anyone. He has a daughter and…" I stop myself before I tell Trent anymore of Ben's business. I'm not sure where this conversation is going, and I don't want to give Trent anymore leverage over Ben. Even though Ben and I made it official with each other, I don't need to fuel the fire.

He rests his forehead against mine. "Please, just give me a shot. I know I'm a lot to handle, but I would never hurt you. I want you to be mine."

His grip loosens, and I'm able to pull away.

My mouth opens to respond, but nothing comes out.

His finger softly brushes over my lip, "Just think about it. About us."

I'm still speechless as I watch him walk out the door.

I might have considered this before, but last night with Ben changed all of this. Trent may have feelings for me. He may even care for me. However, his temper is something that I can't ignore. He intentionally crashed into Ben. Our worlds will never come together.

After a few moments, my limbs regain feeling. I get up and rush to the door, locking it so he can't come back inside.

My phone pings with a text.

Relief like I've never known floods my veins as I see Ben's name on the screen.

> **Ben:** Sunshine. What are you doing tomorrow morning? I got plans for us.

> **Me:** Now, Mr. Carmichael, what makes you think I want to spend tomorrow with you?

> **Ben:** Because I can barely stand not driving over to that salon and ripping you away from whatever you are doing there and dragging you into my bed.

> **Me:** You have a little girl you can't wake up. She needs her beauty sleep.

> **Ben:** I'd be so very quiet.

I can't help the smile that spreads across my face. It's a vast contrast to the feeling Trent had on me just a few moments ago.

> **Me:** I'd love to spend the day with you.

> **Ben:** Good. See you soon. Anna and I will be there at 7am. She likes to start the day early.

I smile. It's amazing how hearing from him washes away any notion of Trent and his visit. I'm not going mention it to Ben. It will just fuel the fire between them. Although it isn't solving the problem of Trent proclaiming he wants to be with me. I'm hoping this is his final attempt.

***

I've had my shower and put on a yellow sundress with the prettiest red flower print. I think they might be pansies. I'm not sure and I don't care because the happy little flowers reflect exactly how I'm feeling right now. It reminds me of sunshine, and I want to live up to his nickname for me.

Walking across the street, I am barely to his front porch when his door opens. He's holding Anna by his side. He lifts her a bit so she's level to his chest. Her smile widens as he points to me. Did my heart just leap through my chest and land a big fat kiss to her cheek?

Ben has an equally large smile on his face. I can't tell you what that does to me. His blond hair is growing out, so today it's parted to the side. His sharp blue eyes scan my dress and end at my lips as I approach him.

"Hey, beautiful," he says.

"Hi," I respond, not being able to come up with a witty reply with the gigantic smile on my face.

"Hello, Sunshine," he says, while pulling me to his chest. Anna's leg scrunches against my chest.

"Daddy, ouch!"

"Sorry, peanut," he says, but before he finishes, she leaps into my arms. "Miss Callie"

"Hey, baby girl. Don't you look pretty."

She's wearing a baby pink dress with little gems dotted throughout. Her hair is adorable in pigtails, and her shoes are as sparkly as her dress. But the crown on top of her head is what gets me in. Isn't that the most precious thing in the world? I've always considered myself a tough girl, but when I was little, I always wanted to wear a crown.

"I thought we could go to the racetrack. I want to show Annabella a little bit of what her daddy does when he's not with her. I'd like to share that with you too."

"I'd love that." And off we go.

***

We make a right off of the main highway. It's nothing like it is on a race night. The road is quiet. No cars in sight. An empty back road with trees covering both sides. This road leads to a deserted field which makes it perfect for when the cars get to flying and the asphalt ends, they skid right into a large field.

Ben opens the car door to his everyday car—his black Mustang. I can't help but wonder if he's going to get a minivan or something more suitable than the three cars he has now. His two Mustangs and one race car. Getting Anna out of her car seat, she giggles as he kisses her on the cheek. *So adorable.*

I follow their lead. He sets her down on the road. "This is where I come to race my car. On race night, only two cars..." He shakes his head and reaches in his pocket, pulling two Matchbox cars from there. "Okay, I'll show you with these toys. Here is where the cars go."

He places both cars side by side. Then he tells Anna to stand behind the black Matchbox car and he stands behind the yellow one. There is a white line drawn across the road. I know that this line is for the real race cars and is where they line up. He explains that much to her. He hands me a flashlight. "Now, Callie here is going to flag the race. She has done this before, so she is a professional." He winks in my direction. "You push your car as fast as you can when Callie presses on the flashlight. Then we'll see which car goes the fastest."

Annabella's pigtails bounce up and down while she jumps. "Yes, Daddy! I'm going to go the fastest."

She's so excited, it brings a smile to my face.

"Okay, put everybody into position," Ben orders.

We all eagerly take our spots. I count three, two, one and turn on the light. Surprisingly both cars take off and make it past my feet. Just like she said, Anna's car wins. She jumps up and down even faster than before. Clapping her hands excitedly. Ben yanks her in his arms and spins around with her. I stand here, unable to peel my eyes off of this man whom I have loved since I was eight. Seeing him with his daughter only makes my heart grow bigger for him.

"Callie! I won." He lets her down and she runs into my arms. Sweeping her up, I kiss her cheek. "You sure did, pretty girl."

"I'm going to drive fast cars like Daddy!"

"And you will win like he does," I tell her. "Let's try to beat him again." We take turns racing each other. Most of the time the cars don't make it very far, but I thought this was a great way for Anna to understand what her dad is doing without being scared of the cars and the loud noises—and the potential wrecks—in person. It really can be very intimidating for an adult. I'd imagine she would be scared her first few times at a race.

The rest of the afternoon feels like a family movie. We stop and get lunch. Then stop at Build a Dolly store where Anna picks out a long, dark-haired doll with curls. She picks out three pink dresses and lots of bows for her hair. By the time we buckle her in her carseat, she's wiped out. Clutching her doll with heavy eyelids.

As Ben pulls out of the mall parking lot, he grabs my hand and places the other on the steering wheel. "Thank you for today. We had a lot of fun. I know you didn't sign up to hang out with me and my kid, but I hope you had fun too." His eyes remain trained on the road. I can't help but stifle a smile.

"I had a great day. I'm glad you asked me to come along."

"Me, too." He turns his head finally at my admission and gives me a bashful smile.

A twinge of guilt nags at me. It is a perfect day. The only thing that could ruin it would be to mention Trent's visit. Pushing the guilt down, the thought of Trent is erased from my mind, replaced with Ben's smile.

27

We reached his house well after Anna's bedtime. She passed out after the pizza and ice cream sundae she had for dinner. He lays her in bed, covering her without so much as a sigh from her.

"Are you going to change her?" I whisper.

"Are you crazy? Not a chance I'm risking her waking up." He whispers so low that I barely hear him and ever so gently closes the door behind us.

Once we make it to the hallway, he guides me to his bedroom. His intentions are inherently obvious. I realize that I haven't been in this bedroom before. I inappropriately wonder where Becca slept. As if he reads my mind, he says, "She never slept here. She slept in my old bedroom."

Relief floods my soul. "I'm sorry. I couldn't help but wonder."

"It was all over your face. I don't want you wondering anymore." He picks me up, his hands cupping my ass, supporting me. His blazing blue eyes, straight nose, plump lips, are inches from my gaze. "I never slept with her after the night I got her pregnant. I never, ever had feelings for her. I promise. It was only because of Annabella that I made her part of my world."

My fingers hold on to his silky strands. "Thank you for telling me."

"I want you to feel comfortable in my bed. I want you here, with me, always."

He lowers us onto the bed and kisses my lips, sending every kind of tingle up my spine. Electrifying every inch of me. We fall into each other and only come up for breath long enough to wrap our arms around each other and drift off to sleep after the most amazing night of sex I've ever had.

***

Last night was beyond anything I could have imagined with Ben. Making love to him knowing that this was it, this was our time. That he wasn't going anywhere...that feeling of him not leaving me before the sun rises is the best feeling in the world to wake up to.

I stayed cuddled in his arms until about seven in the morning. We decided last night that we didn't want Anna to wake up and see me in his bed just yet. Her mom just left, and we both didn't want her to feel like I was replacing her.

I got dressed and headed home before she woke up, but not before stealing some kisses from Ben.

Packing up the chocolate cupcakes with light pink frosting, I'm careful not to leave any of the frosting behind. I painstakingly place the white pearl sprinkles for Anna to enjoy. I know that Becca is not the kind of parent who bakes. I'm sure Ben would buy her the biggest cupcake in the world if she asked him, but there is something to be said for a homemade baked good made with love. Anna mentioned to me that she loves cupcakes. She even said that if I made her real homemade cupcakes, I'd get a big hug from her. Who am I to deny a child?

Knowing that Ben had some errands to run. I spent my afternoon baking and hanging out with Gran. She spent most of the time playing games and surfing Facebook. She insists on staying on top of technology. She claims it'll help her live longer and her mind stay stronger.

Gran is sitting at the table playing Wordle on her iPad. "I cannot for the life of me figure out today's word. Damn electronics. Are you headed to see the neighbors?"

"I am." I feel like I'm ready break out into a song. This southern girl is in love. Holding up the plate, "I think since dinner time has passed, she won't ruin her appetite with dessert."

I tell her goodbye, taking the steps to his house. Knocking with anticipation, while juggling the cupcakes, I wait. And knock.

And wait.

And knock.

Again, and again.

Taking out my phone, I pull up his name to text, only there is a text from him that for some reason I didn't see.

From six minutes ago. *How did I miss it?*

> **Ben: I'm so sorry. I have to go. I'll be back in a few weeks. I know I promised not to go, but there is nothing I can do to avoid this. I will call you later to explain. I'm just boarding my plane. I promise I WILL BE BACK AS SOON AS I AM ABLE. I WILL MISS YOU EVERY SECOND I'M GONE.**

What in the world?! No. No, this can't be.

He said he wouldn't leave.

He promised. It's only been a few days.

The air around me vanishes, replaced with a wave of pain that washes over me. It's so powerful that it brings me to my knees. Barely noticing the concrete scratching my legs. Unable to find my breath, I try focusing on the sight in front of me, only it doesn't help. Cupcakes are littered around me. Reaching for one I squish it between my fingers. Grounding myself with the feel of destroying something, anything. Just like my heart feels right now.

Ben has been the only person to ever inflict incomprehensible pain on my heart.

He's gone.

Again.

***

Emerson sits across from me on the couch with a mug in hand. Taking a sip from it and watching my every movement, she says, "You don't have to watch me. I'm fine."

"I know you are, but..." I swallow, not wanting to say the words out loud. "You almost died, Ems. If Van hadn't come to find you at the chapel, David would have..." Tears well up in my eyes every time I think of her beaten and frail in her bed at David's parents' mansion.

She holds out her hand, touching my arm. "I'm fine, really. The headaches are getting better. Let's talk about you."

"I'm good." I swallow, even though I hear my high-pitched answer.

"Haven't heard from Ben?"

"I've heard from him. I just haven't answered."

It's been a week since he left.

"Why not?"

"I don't know what to say. I'm so confused. I don't think I fit in his life right now. He has to worry about Anna and Becca, and I think it's best if I give him his space. It's not like we were anything." Such a lie, because I thought we were everything and more. He lied to me and said we were. "Sure, he said he had feelings for me, but he left me so easily. He repeats the same old pattern. Just when he finally admits he wants me, he's gone. Someone else is always a priority." I look at her, even after everything she's been through, she's so put together. "I'm such a blubbering mess. We should be talking about you and how working with Van is going." I sniffle.

She sets down her mug, leaning back on the couch. She reaches the side table for a tissue, then hands it to me. "It's been wonderful. I literally went through hell to find him. And that's how I know that things will work out with you and Ben. You just have to get through the hard part. And have faith he'll be back in your arms soon."

I sniffle again. "I'm not sure I can wait for him."

She leans forward, giving me a hug. "I promise, it will all work out either way. It's your choice if he's worth the wait."

"I honestly don't know anymore. He keeps breaking my heart, Ems. Shattering it, really."

Her silence is enough to tell me that she understands.

A few moments of quiet pass before she states, "Let's go do something fun."

"Let's go shopping."

The mood lightens as we do some important shoe shopping. Her positive attitude and high spirits are wearing off on me. She makes me think that maybe I should give Ben a call and let him explain. I shut the optimism down. I'm mad. I'm hurt. Most of all, I'm scared of the power he has over me.

***

The next few days are quiet and mundane. I welcome the monotony. From dealing with Trent to the chaos of my relationship with Ben, the peaceful and routine time I've spent alone in my room, at the salon, and even at the bar have been just what I've needed.

The last customer of the night has left the salon. Good old Mrs. Wayne. I permed her hair, talked about the new mayor, and what hairstyles she used to wear in the 1960s.

I'm just finishing up when my phone pings with a text.

> **Ben: I'm missing you. Please call me. I have so much to tell you. Please don't do this to us.**

I toss my phone on the chair in front of me. Part of me wants to melt at his words, but how can I act as if he hasn't hurt me. That he hasn't left me with no explanation…again.

How does he expect me to respond to that?

I shake my head, annoyed and frustrated.

Taking the empty hair color bowls over to the sink. I begin scrubbing them, with each thought of Ben, I scrub harder until my fingernails are scraping against the bowl.

"Damn it!" I yell to absolutely no one.

I glance at the wall clock. Shit. It's after ten and very dark outside. I'm done. I can't concentrate on cleaning, and decide tomorrow is another day. I'll take myself home, eat a gallon of ice cream, and try my best not to text Ben back.

Once the door is locked, I head to my car.

It's a warm evening, so I leave my windows down. My favorite song comes on the radio, reminding me of the days when life was simple. Uncomplicated. Easy.

As I settle into my seat, and embrace the wind blowing around me, enjoying a good song, headlights flash in my rearview mirror, blinding me momentarily. I'm able to make out something dangling from the rearview mirror. I can't tell what it is, just that it's long.

"Ugh...jerk. Turn off your bright lights, damn it!"

I adjust the mirror to relieve my eyes. "Jeez, crazy ass."

The bright lights from the car disappears and the driver pulls ups beside me.

I try to ignore it because I'm not in the mood tonight.

Then the car horn blows next to me.

I allow myself a quick glance. I don't recognize the car. Speeding up, I try to get away. It doesn't work and the car catches up to my truck. I slow down, hoping the driver will give up and realize that I'm not wanting to race.

People are used to street racing around town. It's normal for someone to challenge you to a drag race at red lights and stop signs. They honk, pull up beside you, and you race. Only this feels different, unsafe even.

I can't make out who is driving and I keep my hands tight on the wheel, sitting up straight, my body alert.

My brain goes into panic mode. I'm not stopping. I have no idea who this is or what they want. All I know is that I need to get away from them. I need to get to the bar, or even the police station, so that this idiot fucks off.

I speed up again, knowing that the bar is another good five minutes or so. We are coming up on Hell's Bend. I slow down, hoping the car beside me will do the same. There is no way we both can make the turn.

I lift my foot off the gas, tapping the brakes, only I don't get the chance to bring the truck to a stop. The car beside me swipes into the side of my door. Before I know anything else, my body is jostled, tossed like a rag doll around the cab of my truck. My seatbelt slams into my chest with the force of the impact, pain slices my head. It only takes seconds, but I feel as if I'm in slow motion. I can't help but notice my purse contents spilling out around me. The cries of the metal bending and twisting eventually came to a halt. When it does, the truck gives one final groan.

Opening my eyes, I realize I'm hanging upside down by my seatbelt. It's eerily quiet now. My wits come back slowly. I've been run off the road. I push my hair from my face, realizing that it's wet. That's strange. As I lower my hands to my line of vision, they are stained red.

"I'm bleeding. Oh my God, I'm bleeding. I've got to get out of here." I feel my heart in my throat

Adrenaline mixed chaotically with panic kicks in. I reach for the keys to turn off the car. Maybe it works but I don't care. The first thought that comes to mind is the truck catching on fire with me stuck inside.

I reach for the seatbelt, and thankfully it releases me, falling onto the roof of my car. Stretching out my arms, I'm unsure of what I'm touching. I can't see anything because it's too dark.

Scouting around, trying to decipher what I'm touching. Thank God, I find the smooth metal of the door handle. Yanking it, and by the grace of God it works. I sink to the ground. Something isn't right. Water. I'm in water. I inhale a mouth full of water. I can't breathe.

My hands lower to the ground. Mud gushes between my fingers. it takes a moment to decipher I'm not on dry land.

It dawns on me that the truck has rolled into a pond or creek. No, this can't be happening. I'm not going to drown after being run off the road. Finding strength to survive. I move my arms and legs until I break the surface, letting air fill my lungs.

"Come on, Callie, move those arms and legs." A flash of Gran teaching me how to swim comes to mind.

Chopping my hands through the water, I feel for anything to grab on while I swim. My hand scrapes against something, and I grab for whatever it is. I'm unable to see much, but by the light of the moon I can tell it seems to be a branch. I hang on for dear life. Taking a moment, I inhale a breath. A long, deep lifesaving breath. God, it feels great.

The water is bobbing up and down around me. I need to get to land.

Feeling the panic start to creep in. "Don't think about it. Go. Just go," I say out loud. Willing myself to keep moving.

My shoulder scrapes up against something sharp causing a jolt of pain. I keep a hold of the branch. Using my other arm, I reach out. I think I'm at the edge of the water because my feet are touching the bottom of something. I'm no longer bobbing at least. I claw my way up the dirt and rocks, until my whole body is finally out of the water. I roll over onto my back, breathing so heavy but so damn glad to be on land.

The sky above me is dark, but filled with the brightest, biggest moon I've ever seen. Stars sparkle brighter than I have ever noticed before, as if they are shining for me. Telling me you are going to be okay. We are keeping the sky lit for you.

I'm tired, oh so tired. What happened? Where am I?

Nothing's making sense. But the exhaustion is taking over and I think to myself that I'll just close my eyes for a minute.

***

Opening my eyes, the sunlight shines too bright. I can't make anything out for a few moments. Trying to sit up, I realize that my body isn't following my brain's instructions. I'm wet... and so damn cold.

I roll to my side, breathing through the pain. My leg hurts and I'm too scared to look at the reason why. Taking a deep breath, I try to move my right leg. Nothing but searing pain. As if someone has stuck a knife straight through it, rummaging around in it. Stabbing, throbbing pain.

"Ahh..." I scream. "Help!" I repeat over and over. I don't know how long or if anyone can even hear me. My voice becomes hoarse. My throat aches. I'm so damn thirsty.

How long have I been here? It was dark when I closed my eyes. It is daylight now, but I can't tell what time it is.

I roll back onto my back. I can't just lie here until someone comes along. But what do I do?

Closing my eyes, my mind drifts back to the accident. A car, going so fast, side swiping into me. They tried to kill me but I'm not going to stay here and die.

No, I can't be weak. I have to try and find a way out of this situation. I pull myself up to a sitting position. The pain is almost bearable now or maybe I'm used to it, or even numb to it.

Taking a good look around, I'm not that far from the creek. Out in the distance, I see that my truck is surrounded by large rocks, a crap ton of water, and is laying on its roof. "My poor Betsy," I say.

I scoot to get a closer look. Okay, this scooting thing isn't so bad. Maybe I can get somewhere by doing this, or maybe I can make my way up the hillside. From where I'm positioned, I can see where my truck broke through the guardrail and tumbled down the hillside, landing in the stream.

I chuckle to myself as I realize that the stream isn't that deep. It wasn't like I was in the ocean. In my panicked state, it only felt like it. Probably a couple feet of water at the deepest point. Panic sets in again as I survey the damage to my truck. Anxiety blooms in my chest as I think to myself how am I going to get myself out of this mess?

Can I scoot all the way up the hillside so I can make it up to the road? Can I make it across the stream with a messed-up leg? Maybe someone would see me?

I swipe the hair from my face. My hands are bloodied and scratched up, but nothing horrible. I touch my chest, rooting around my torso. No ribs seem to be broken. I'm just bruised and sore.

My jeans are ripped on both legs, revealing bloodied skin. My right leg is worse because I can see deep into the muscle of my leg. My stomach churns looking at the mixture of skin, muscle, and bone that form into something that looks nothing like my normal leg. Gagging at the sight before me, bile rises in my throat. Lightheaded and nauseated, I vomit into the grass beside me.

"Ew..." I dry heave a few more times. Lying back, I catch my breath. I'm starting to realize that I may not be able to get myself out of this mess. Scouting across the grass to get out of here, seems almost impossible now.

I'm wearing a flannel shirt, although it's wet. I cover up my leg with it so I don't hurl again because looking at it is worse than the actual pain at this point. I need something to support my leg if I'm going to be scooting for any distance. I crawl to where a large branch is, thinking it'll make a good splint. I remove my shirt to tie the arms of it around my leg to keep the branch from moving. This probably only took a few moments, but it felt like it took an hour and zapped all of my strength.

I have to rest and plan a way to get across the creek and up the hill to the road. "Did you just hear yourself think? You want to cross the creek and then haul your ass up the hill with a leg injury and exposed muscle and God knows what else."

I lie back and close my eyes. Thinking of Gran. She is probably so worried about me. I wonder if she has the whole town looking for me.

I wonder if anyone called Ben and told him that I'm missing. Maybe no one realizes I haven't even come home.

My back is so sore from the ground beneath me that's comprised of jagged rocks. All I want to do is curl up in my bed and sleep. It doesn't help that the air is getting warmer, and I know it's getting late. How much longer can I lie here?

Off in the distance, a noise catches my attention. A faint sound of a lawnmower or chainsaw or something with a small motor sends shockwaves of excitement throughout my body. I can do this, I can get to that noise as long as it keeps making a sound. Someone is close by, I know it. I won't think about the fact that sound travels far and is pretty loud in the woods, though.

Sitting up again, I face to my right, in the direction of the noise.

It's the most beautiful sound I've ever heard. It means I'm not alone. Someone is going to find me. But I use my voice instead. Calling out to them, "Hello! Help!" Over and over, I yell until three very familiar faces appear. Ones whom I don't expect to see, walking side by side forming a perfect line.

Jake and Officer Alex.

And Trent.

28

"She's over here!" Jake yells.

Moments later there is a gang of people. Cops, firemen, and even familiar faces. Before I know it, I'm swept up in my brother's arms, Trent close beside him.

"Oh, thank God, we found you," Jake says, his voice weak, but full of relief.

"I'm okay. My leg is messed up, though. But other than that, I'm okay. I can't put any weight on it."

Trent stands behind Jake, arms crossed, his thumb pressed against his lips. He's watching me intently. Eyes scanning my body. "You've got a nasty cut on your head. Please lie back," he says, his voice shaking, as Jake lets go of me, backing away.

"Yeah, you do. Denny!" Jake yells, and within seconds, a fireman is at my side.

The fireman asks me a gazillion questions, all of them I answer the same, "Yeah, it hurts." Even with all that is going on around me, Trent's eyes never leave me.

"We are waiting for a board. Should be here in a few minutes. The firemen are going to hike you back to the rig. Only about a quarter of a mile. Thankfully, Trent saw your truck from the road. We've been looking for you since about four this morning." Jake tells me.

"What time is it now?" I ask.

The fireman, Denny, looks down at his watch. "It's about ten. You've been out here for a bit. Let's get you to the hospital. They'll make everything better."

What feels like an eternity, another group of firemen surround me, this time, with my new ride—a board.

I don't miss that Trent is standing in the shadows, quietly, and hasn't approached me yet. Jake is giving him straight-out mean looks, I almost think he's going to growl at him. I know he doesn't like him, but he obviously found me, and for that I owe him everything.

"Trent!" I call, holding out my hand for him. I'm not sure what the sudden tug is, but I feel like I should thank him.

He takes a few steps over to me, while the men finish strapping me to the board. My head is in some contraption where I can't move, so I can barely see him. "Trent, thank you." My voice is hoarse.

He peeks over a fireman's shoulder. "You're welcome, babe. I'll see you soon." A moment of unease comes over me, but then the pain sears through to my leg.

Jake doesn't let him in my line of sight for more than one second. "The fuck you will," Jake tells him.

I tell him to stop it. But don't get much more than that out before I'm hoisted in the air.

By the time we make it to the ambulance, I've been jostled, shook, and am in so much pain that the tumble down the embankment felt like a kiddie ride.

The hospital isn't much better, but at least I'm in a warm bed. The doctors and nurses give me some medicine, and before I know it, I'm in dreamland.

***

Sometime later, when I wake up, Gran is at my side.

"Oh dear, you scared the ever-living shit out of me!" She throws her head back and slaps her leg in true southern theatrics.

"Gran!" I try to yell back, or at least try, but it comes out more like a whisper.

"Hush, darling. I can say anything I want after a day like yesterday. You've been resting for quite a while. Jake, Van, Emerson, Harlow—to name just a few—are all in the waiting area. You scared us all half to death."

"Sorry, Gran. I don't really remember everything that happened. I was driving, and then before I knew it, the truck was in the creek. It's all a blur."

"Darling, we are all a little shaken. Don't worry, everything is going to be alright. Your leg got mangled and you have stitches and staples to put it back together. The doctor spit out some fancy words, but you also have a concussion, bruised ribs, and multiple cuts and scratches. But you are going to be just fine."

"I'm so grateful that Jake found me." Trying hard to remember what made me crash the truck. There is blackness in my mind that I can't push through. Ben's smile flashes in my mind.

"Has Ben? Does Ben know?" My voice trembles even more as I speak his name.

Her face softens with a sad smile. "No. I didn't think it was my business to tell. Besides, my only concern is you. Do you want me call him now that you're on the mend?"

"No."

The look of pure love mixed with compassion and sympathy makes a tear trickle down my cheek.

"Did anyone else get hurt?" I ask, hoping the memory of just my truck in the creek is correct.

"Only you. When we get you out of this hospital bed, I'm going to have to keep you on a short leash for a few days." She brushes a few strands of hair away from my face. "My sweet, precious girl. What would I have done if something worse would have happened to you?"

A lump forms in my throat. I don't replay the memory because I don't want to think anymore. One thing is for sure, her smile is all I need to see to know that I'm going to be just fine.

29

A few days later, I'm released from the hospital and I'm back at Gran's. The rest of my hospital stay was luckily uneventful. Ribs are sore, but other than that I was able to be stitched up and given a walking boot with crutches. My mobility is minimal, though. But Gran was made for mothering the injured. So I'm in good hands.

I'm having nightmares about the accident, though. Something about that night nags at me, like there was something that I need to remember, something that I should have noticed. Something that isn't quite right. Obviously, the whole experience is unsettling, but there is something else that I can't put my finger on.

"Callie, do you want something to eat? We're about to make breakfast," Jake mentions from the doorway separating the living room from the kitchen. He has also been a shining example of a loving brother since the accident.

"Sure," I say as he walks over to me. Jake smiles at me and leans down to help me stand. My crutches are against the couch and he grabs them, making sure I have them for support. It's great to see him helping Gran out and being here for us. I sometimes forget how much I need my big brother and am so thankful for my family. He's even helped me up the stairs for bed and back down the stairs in the mornings, making my life easier rather than struggling.

Once I'm at the table, we eat a hearty breakfast of eggs, bacon, and toast.

"I can't wait until you are cleared by the doctors to get back to work. I need some help. Harlow has called out three times this week," Jake whines, shoveling food into his mouth.

Gran hits him on the shoulder. "Hush now. You can see Callie can barely get from the couch to here by herself. You'll just have to hire someone new if Harlow can't work."

There is a knock at the door and Jake puts down his fork begrudgingly and goes to answer.

I look past Jake, noticing Trent at the door, holding flowers and a box.

"Hey, look, it's Trent fucking Harrison. I didn't know you and I were such good friends." Jake places a finger on his chin, like he's in deep thought or something, then he says, "Nope. We're not motherfucking friends. So what the fuck do you think you're doing at my house?"

"Jake. That's enough. Like it or not, he is a friend of Callie, and *he* did help us find her."

Trent isn't even fazed by Jake and sidesteps him. Setting the items in his hand on the side table.

"Hey, darling. How are you feeling today?" Trent struts into the kitchen like he owns it. I can't help but notice the grimace on Gran's face. I know she appreciates what he did, but that doesn't mean she likes him. I'm certainly undecided about my own feelings for him, but he did help find me. I'll forever be thankful for that.

"Fine. Feeling better." I smile at him. He reaches for my hand and instinctively I pull away.

"I want to apologize for the way I was acting toward you. I just want to be here for you through this." He takes my hand again in his. This time I let him. "Can you forgive me?" he pleads. His face softens with an apology and a smile.

I smile back. He must have noticed my unease, too. "Sure. I know things got a little crazy. How can I be mad at you, you helped save me, after all," I tell him, squeezing his hand back.

"I'm so glad I did."

Gran drops something in the sink, then raises her voice. "I think you should probably go upstairs and rest, Callie. Trent, maybe you should visit another time?" she says in her sweetest southern accent.

"Gran, I'm feeling good today. We'll sit on the couch and visit for a bit."

"I brought her some flowers and candy. I can't leave until I know she eats some of her favorite chocolates," Trent says with a charismatic wink. He's putting it on for Gran. He knows she doesn't like him but she is being equally as polite and fake as she can without telling him to get the hell out of her house. I get it. They aren't fans, but I wouldn't be here without him.

Trent is finally giving me the attention I have always wanted—only I never thought Ben would have come back into town, ready to give me the same attention, and make me question my feelings toward Trent. With a kiss on the cheek, I smile back at him.

"So I've got some big news." Trent's excitement is coming off of him in waves.

"Oh, yeah?"

"I won the race last night. Took first in three races. I'm number one on the leaderboard," he says with more enthusiasm than I have ever heard from him before.

"That's great. Tell me all about it." I need a distraction. Trent is all too eager to tell me how he was able to keep his car straight, how his tires gripped the road, and how fast he was able to fly down to the finish line.

In what seems like a half an hour later, he finishes.

"I'm so glad you did well," I tell him, realizing I'd zoned out about halfway through.

"Well, none of it would mean anything if you weren't here. I'm so glad you are okay." It's the first sincere thing he has said to me.

"Me, too. I owe you so much."

He swallows, giving me a weird look, almost weary.

"We looked all night for you. I think I was just lucky that I was the one to see you." He stands. "So, do you want to get out of here for a bit? I can help you with walking. We can stop by my place. A bunch of people are coming over to hang out."

"Thanks, but I'm really tired. I'm still recovering and all. But I'll take a raincheck."

"Right. Right. I'll just hang here for a little bit. We can watch Netflix while you get some sleep." He seems jittery.

Trent helps me get situated on the couch. Just as we decide on a movie, Jake busts into the living room and sits on the other side of me. "What are we watching? I have to make sure everything stays PG." His big brother's protective eyes glare at Trent.

"Calm down, you big oaf. Trent is my friend, and I can have whoever I want over. " I snap back, even though it's only at Jake.

I take Trent's hand off my lap, turning to face him. *When did his hand get there?* "I'm sorry, but maybe you should go. I'm tired and I don't have the energy to deal with my brother right now."

Trent stands.

Jake stands, too, widening his stance, and puffing out his chest. "Oh, for heaven's sake, Jake. Knock it off, he's leaving."

"I'll call you later. Let me know if you change your mind about coming over later." He leans down and gives me a kiss on the cheek. "Jake. Always a pleasure." His tone is full of obvious sarcasm.

As Trent opens the door, Ben is there, standing in the doorway. Scowling, anger dripping from his beautiful features. His eyes are narrowed on Trent.

"What the hell are you doing here?" Ben roars.

"I was on my way out, but interestingly enough, I think I've changed my mind."

Ben's eyes drift over to me. His gaze softens but his jaw still tics. "Can I come in?"

He knows I don't want to see him. My silence to him texting and calling spoke volumes, I'm sure. But none of his messages asked how I was or what happened. I find it strange; I thought it strange that the news hasn't gotten to him yet. But since he seems to be good at disappearing and acting like nothing ever changes, I can't be too shocked, can I?

"Jake's your friend, ask him." I shrug, trying to act unaffected.

Jake moves in between Trent and Ben. "Ben, now isn't a good time."

Ben's head moves from Jake to me and back to Jake.

"What am I missing?"

"Callie was in an accident." He swipes his hand in my direction. "Obviously, she's alright. But she scared us to death."

"What? You told me she didn't want to talk to me. You never said anything about an accident." Fire in his eyes is directed at my brother.

The breath vanishes from my body...*oh my God, he doesn't know.*

Ben brushes past Trent without looking at him and instantly kneels down beside me. "What happened?' Immediately encasing my hand in his.

"It was an accident. I wrecked my truck. Messed up my leg. A few bumps and bruises. I'm fine." Trying to act like it's no big deal, but all I want to do is fall into his arms.

He looks up at Jake, pleading to his best friend, "Why didn't you tell me?"

"She's been through enough, Ben. You've got your own shit going on and she doesn't need to be a yo-yo anymore." I think I gasp. *How about that, Jake Rae has been paying attention.*

"Jake, I'm a big girl. Besides, there is nothing going on between us."

"That's because he can't make up his mind. I know you two had a thing. It doesn't matter that you're my best friend, she's my sister and she doesn't need to be in the middle of your circus. She's got her own shit. Someone was targeting her and made sure her truck went over the hillside. She could have died. And all you ever care about is whatever you have going on in Las Vegas. Well, here's your chance to leave for good because you aren't needed here now."

His voice is hard, cold, menacing. I've never seen these two argue over anything, let alone me.

"Jake, it's fine." I don't like it. I don't like that I'm the one thing they are fighting over. This needs to stop.

"No. Callie, it's not fine. None of this is fine. These two assholes are both disrespecting you in different ways. I'm sick of watching the women I care about date fucking assholes. You both need to leave." He points at the door.

"Thank you both for stopping by and checking in on me. But Jake is right, you *both* need to leave. Now."

Without a word, Ben stands, his head to the ground as he walks toward the door.

Trent says, "I'll call you," and leaves first.

Ben looks over at me, hurt deep in his features. His eyes close as if he's steadying himself.

"I'm so sorry, I didn't know. If someone would have told me, I would have been back sooner."

But would he have? His past behavior says no.

"I hope whatever you left for, turned out in your favor."

He purses his lips. "It did."

He moves closer just as Jake moves toward me, playing a very overprotective brother.

"Let me talk to her. Please." His voice is strained.

Jake inhales a deep breath. "I'll leave you alone. But, Ben, I wasn't kidding when I said she's been through enough." The sincerity in his voice tugs at my heart. He then leaves the room and heads outside.

"Callie, I don't know what to say."

"Yeah, so what's new?" Unable to keep my snarky attitude to myself. I let the words slip out.

"That isn't fair. You wouldn't take my calls. You wouldn't let me explain."

"Explain? No...let me guess." I place my finger on my chin like a brat. "I'm sure it had something to do with Las Vegas, racing, and Becca. Am I right?"

His broad shoulders sag. "It wasn't like that. I had to go. I didn't want to but..."

I hold up my hand to stop him. I can't hear the same excuses over and over again, and I won't hear him say I'm not a priority.

"Please leave."

He steps closer to me. His familiar fresh scent surrounding me.

"Callie, please," he pleads.

"Leave..." I say, sternly this time.

He flinches. Nods his head, and does as I tell him. And as the sound of the door shutting makes it way to my ears, tears fall down my cheeks as I cry for the millionth time over Benjamin Carmichael.

***

A little later, after giving me some space, Jake comes back in the room, while I'm hiding under the blanket hoping to disappear, but he continues his tangent anyway. Starting with Trent.

"I can't believe you let that asshole into my house. What are you thinking?"

"Which one?" I joke, trying to lighten the mood.

He scowls at me.

"You know that he saved me, right? It's the least I could do."

"Saved you? The fuck he did. He saw your car from the road. It was by coincidence. He wasn't out looking for you like I was. Or even the rest of the town. He doesn't give two fucks about you. You're just a way to fuck with Ben and me. He is using you to get back at us. Our friends. Everyone we care about!"

"Look...I know you don't like him, that he's competition for you guys, but he is a friend."

He growls, actually growls at me.

"He isn't your friend. If you even think of dating him, I'll disown you!"

"You aren't my father."

"Then stop acting like a kid. Trent Harrison is trouble. You don't need him in your life. He can't be trusted."

I know my brother is right. He can't be trusted. The night at the salon, something wasn't right, but shouldn't people be given a second chance? I mean, I can understand the jealousy thing. I wanted to punch Becca in the face a few times. Things change and I'm going to give Trent the benefit of the doubt.

Ben, not so much. He's had his second chance and ruined it.

30

I've been home a little over a week now and thankfully, I'm able to walk around on crutches. I'm not winning any races, but it's nice to be more independent. I'm also running out of money, so the faster I heal, the faster I can get back to work.

Emerson picked me up this morning. We stopped for some bagels and now we're hanging out at the shop. Van and Jake are working on Ben's car. Even though Jake is pissed at Ben, he's still his friend and knows how important racing is to everyone.

"Are you comfortable?" Emerson asks me for the hundredth time.

"Yes, Mom," I say sweetly.

"I know, I'm annoying. I've just been in your shoes." Great, now I feel like crap. I wrap my arm around her shoulder. "I'm sorry. I know you love me."

We sit and talk about everything under the sun, but she hasn't mentioned Ben and I'm thankful for that.

"Callie, any news on who might have run you off the road?" Van asks as he's cleaning off his ratchet.

"The cops have no leads. I'm not much help. All I know is that one moment there were headlights, and the next I was waking up at the water's edge, confused and in pain."

Emerson grabs my hand. "They'll figure it out."

"It's going to be hard. I didn't see who was driving or even what model of car it was. Just that it was a car. It's the only information I have."

I'm interrupted when I hear a familiar voice.

"Hey, guys." His voice carries through the garage. He's behind me, and it's taking every ounce of strength not to turn and face him.

I notice Jake slides back under the car on his creeper.

"How is Annabella?" Van asks, I'm assuming to break the tension.

Before I can register it, Ben is in front of me.

"At a daycare program right now. That's why I can be here in the mornings." Damn him, as his striking blue eyes are now focused on me instead of Van. "She's asked about you, but I didn't want her crawling all over you until you were up to it. She has been wanting to see you." Ben smiles, making me want to give into every thought I've had over the last few days about how I want to be with him and only him.

"I don't want her to see me hurt and bruised. She's so young, I wouldn't want to scare her." It's the truth, even though it feels like an excuse because even though I've missed Ben, I've missed her just as much.

"I remember the time you broke your leg as a kid. Scared the shit out of me, Callie." His eyes soften at the memory.

I clear my throat, hoping to disrupt his stroll down memory lane because I remember that, too. He was sweet, kind, and took care of me.

"Van's working on your motor. The torque that it's giving out now is ridiculous." Jake slides back out from under the car, acting as if nothing happened the other day. As always, the car and the race overrule any kind of emotion.

"Yeah. He told me. Nothing really for me to do. You guys have a better grasp on that stuff than I do. I'll just do some computer stuff. See what kind of tune-up I can give it."

The guys continue to talk motors and tune-ups while Emerson and I chit chat about her latest makeup ideas. I glance at Ben off and on and can feel when his attention is on me. My heart rate picks up and warmth spreads over me. I'm just sitting in this chair, lighting up like a damn Christmas tree for this man.

Emerson interrupts my stupid teenage girl thoughts. "I'm headed out to grab some sandwiches. I'll be back in a few." I want to grab her by the arm and plead with her to take me with her, to not leave me alone. Not sure if I can be trusted to not gape at Ben with my mouth hanging open. I thankfully hold back the theatrics.

Only a few moments after she is gone, I grab my phone. Within a minute, Ben takes a seat beside me. I scroll through an app on my phone, trying to ignore the most delicious scent coming from beside me in the form of Benjamin Carmichael.

I swallow. Concentrating on the latest gossip news post.

"I know you are mad at me. You're doing that ignoring thing you did when we were younger. I hated it then and I don't like it now. We need to talk."

He places a finger under my chin, nudging my face in his direction.

"No, we don't. Especially not when Jake is around."

"I already talked to Jake. He said it was fine for me to talk to you. At least, he promised not to shove my head through a wall. Can we go sit outside?"

I nod. Finally giving in.

"Can I help you outside?" He looks hopeful.

I snap back. "No, Mr. Carmichael. I can handle walking by myself. If I waited for you to help me, I would fall over because you're never around."

He has the audacity to laugh. But I growl. How could he not find that mean? It was definitely meant to be just that.

Once outside, we sit on the bench that is far enough away from the other guys working on the car.

"Okay, then." I set down my phone and straighten my back. "So, let me guess, you left to deal with your baby mama when you said you weren't going to disappear on me again. We weren't together for long, and then, poof – you are gone." I make an exaggerated motion with my hands, gesturing into the air. "That seems to be your talent besides racing cars."

I can't look into his eyes, so I keep my eyes on his chest. His rock-hard chest that I want to touch. Keeping my hands firmly at my side.

"Please look at me. I'm sorry."

"No. You're not. And I've had a very hard few weeks, in case you haven't noticed." I want to shove my fist through his sexy face.

"I'm sorry that I left without telling you personally. I'm not sorry I went and raced one last time to make sure Becca wasn't coming back for Anna. I did it for my daughter."

His words surprise me. "You what?"

"I was able to convince Becca's dad that she didn't want to be responsible for a child. And that I wanted the sole responsibility. I kept trying to call you. To tell you what was going on, but you refused to talk to me."

"I couldn't do that to myself again. All you ever do is leave me." I sound so pathetic, but it's the truth. "I just want you to want to be with me. I know you have Anna, and I want to be there for her, too, but you can't keep pushing me away...and then come swooping back in like nothing has changed. You have your shit to deal with. It's always someone else. Anna is one thing because I think you *should* go to the ends of the Earth for her. Becca, her dad and your dad, they are all adults. They need to fix their own lives. You can't do it for them anymore."

"I left for Anna. Not for them."

"This time, but what about next time? It's what you do. It's what everyone does. And that's okay because that's who you are, but I can't be waiting for you all the time. I can't do that to myself."

"Callie..."

I hold back the tears threatening to fall. "I think you should go back inside."

"Callie..." he pleads again.

"I'm fine. Please, just go."

This time he listens.

When he's gone, I finally let the tears fall.

31

"You look amazing," Emerson tells me "When are you back to work?"

"Tomorrow is my first shift at the salon. I'll put in a few hours, sit when I feel the need." I've been resting but no I can't stand staying still. Hanging out at the house is losing its appeal, deciding to turn my attention to the lovebirds and get the attention away from me. "So what have you guys been up to?"

Emerson tells me how she's been helping Van with putting in a new accounting system to keep better track of spending.

"But I've been showing her how to renovate a car from scratch. We're working on the '68 Mustang." He kisses her on the cheek and she beams. Again, jealousy rears its ugly head. I can't help but want what they have. At one time I thought I did. Ben was everything I wanted, but we seem to never be able to get on the right track.

"Well, someone has to be the boss," I joke with them.

"I know, but let's hope she doesn't get the hang of it too fast, I really like the hands-on approach." Van winks.

"Okay, enough. I get it, you crazy lovebirds." We laugh.

Just then Jake walks over and he doesn't look happy.

"I've just heard that asshole Trent is racing. Is Ben's car ready to go?"

"Almost. We just have to test it tonight. Then he'll be all good. What's the big deal about Trent? It doesn't take a genius to figure out that he'd be the first in line to take on Ben."

"He's got a new car and a new motor. I just don't want that bastard to have a leg up on us. He's getting too close, and I don't like it. Do I, Callie?"

All heads turn to look at me.

"What?" I feign innocence.

"Don't act like he's a saint. You are letting him weasel his way back into your life. Sticking up for him because he happened to be on his way somewhere and saw your car down an embankment. We all searched for hours for you. It's not like you were easy to find."

"What are you trying to say?" God, I thought we were over this.

"I'm saying how did he just happen to see your car? It wasn't like it was visible through all the trees and the creek. It rolled and was submerged in the water. I drove on that same road looking for you. Van and the cops did, too, we didn't see you at all." His voice fades and I know that it bothers him that he wasn't the one who found me.

"It's okay, Jake," I say softly.

"No. No, it isn't. I'm your brother. I am supposed to take care of you. Not that asshole."

I touch his shoulder in an attempt to calm him.

He shrugs me off, heading over to his toolbox.

I'm guessing the conversation is over.

Van says quietly, "Don't worry about him. You just scared all of us. But it might not be a bad idea to stop hanging around Trent. I don't think he has your best interest in mind."

I'm taken aback by his blatant honesty and can't decide if I want to yell at him or give him a hug for worrying about me.

"I haven't hung out with him. I can't just ignore him. He found me. Without him, I wouldn't be standing here right now."

"I'm not trying to be a jerk. I just think he isn't good for you," Van tells me.

I can't help but want to tell him to mind his own business. I already have too many big brothers looking after me. But I don't because it's Van and he's family. So instead I ask Emerson if she'll take me home and tell her I'm tired as a way to stop this conversation immediately.

***

All that I want to do is run up to my room, but when Emerson drops me home, it seems there is a visitor on the front porch with Gran.

"Do you want me to stay?" A wide-eyed and concerned Emerson asks.

I let out a deep sigh. "I think I can handle it. At least I know Gran will."

Emerson still gets out to hand me my crutches. I hobble over to the step, taking them one at a time. Probably taking them slower than I should. I can't even fathom why she is here. The last time I talked with Ben, he made it seem like she was out of the picture. But he obviously lied to me.

I don't even want to look at Gran. Knowing that she's looking at me to do the right thing is exhausting so I say, "I'm sorry, Becca. I have a date with my bed, and I don't have the energy to argue with you."

She's dressed differently from what I've seen her wear before. She has on a tan suit, silk top, and white pumps. Interesting. Guess her wardrobe has at least changed, even if she hasn't.

"Callie, I know you hate me, but I was just telling your grandmother that this is the last time I will be visiting your little town. I'm giving full custody of Annabella to Ben."

I turned away from the door I was about to open. "Why would you do that to her?" I can't hide the pain from my voice. Reliving the feelings of my own mother's abandonment.

"He is a better parent. You have to know that. He can give her a good life and he knows how to do the family thing." She paces back and forth on our porch while Gran sits quietly on the swing.

"Then why are you telling me this? I don't have anything to do with Ben or Anna." The last part stings as the words escape my mouth.

"Callie, he loves you and I know you love him. All I ever heard were stories about you. Funny little memories that you shared. I could never measure up to *his* Sunshine. But the thing is, I never wanted to be his. My father wanted me to get married, take care of Anna. I don't want that life. We had one night that gave us a lifelong bond that neither of us wanted. I'm telling you this because I am officially out of the picture and so is my father. No more races, no big debts to be paid. That life for Ben is over."

Gran whispers, "Sit down, sweetie."

I do as she says.

"You want to tell me why I should believe you—or him—this time. His priority is whatever business he has in Las Vegas."

"I'm telling you, all his debts have been paid. I made sure of it. He needs you, Callie. Anna needs you too. Together you can give her a normal childhood." With sincerity in her eyes, I can see the unshed tears.

I freeze, I realize that I'm hearing my mother's voice. She always told my grandmother she couldn't give us a normal life. That's why she left us. Why she left me. My heart immediately splits into jagged pieces for Annabella.

I stand, and Gran grabs my arm. I cover her hand. Knowing she is supporting me like she always has.

"How can you leave her?" My voice raises in accusation.

"I'm doing what's best for her." She spits back, "I don't have to explain myself to you or anyone. But I want you to know that Anna needs someone to look out for her, and I know you would be the best suited for that. I'm going to kiss her goodnight and then I'll leave right after. I have a little gift for her, and I will visit when I am able—unless you both don't think I should—but it won't be anytime soon."

"Becca, you can't just leave her. She needs her mother." I've been Anna so many years ago, and I feel as if I am her right now, begging my own mother to stay with me.

"I just can't do it. I wasn't made to be responsible for someone's life. I want my own." She drops her head but turns back to face me. "He loves you. He only left because he feels responsible for everything that happened. I lied to him. I wanted to get pregnant. I thought it was my way out until the second I saw that damn positive test strip. He did the right thing. I know my opinion doesn't matter, but he deserves someone to finally do the right thing for him." She turns back around, making her way to Ben's house.

Once she disappears into the house, tears start to fall. Gran stands, holding me in her strong, loving arms.

"It's okay, puddles. Anna will be okay. She has Ben and us." As if she knows exactly what I'm thinking, she says, "Your Mama had to leave, too. You are fine, just fine," she whispers. Hushing me as if I'm a baby.

"She left me. She left Jake. How can a mother leave their child?"

"Some women aren't meant to be a mama." She lifts my chin, smiling, her eyes shining with unshed tears. "But baby, some women are born to be mamas, even if it's not their own."

I hug her. Needing to feel her arms around me.

It could be an hour or five minutes, but when I open my eyes, Ben's car pulls into his driveway. He opens the back door, pulling Anna out of the back car seat. I can hear her little voice from over here.

I tear myself away from Gran as I watch the sweetest little girl who is about to lose her mother, but I promise she will gain a new one.

I can't fight my feelings any longer. The people in front of me are the ones I want in my life, every minute of every day. They are my family, and I won't ever abandon either of them.

32

I've waited longer than I can stand. Becca has been gone for over an hour. I grab my crutches and cross the street to Ben's house.

"Callie! Callie!" Anna squeals, catapulting herself onto my good leg.

"Anna!" Ben scolds. "Be careful with Callie. She is still healing."

Heart melting and breaking again, I think to myself why must he torture me?

I pat her back. Savoring the toothless grin looking up at me.

"I'm okay. You can hug me all you want. I'll never turn you away."

I bend down to kiss the top of her head.

Ben's features soften. "How are you feeling? I haven't seen you in a few days. I'm glad you're here." He rubs the back of his neck as if he's nervous.

But he's the one who makes me nervous when he looks at me that way. As if he can see straight through me. It's hard to pull my eyes from him but I place my attention on Anna.

"How have you been, sweet girl?"

"Great! I got a new Barbie and a necklace from Mommy. Daddy has it. He said I'll lose it. He's silly. Me and Daddy went to the park today, and now I get to work on his car. My daddy is going to race his car."

All of her sentences run together, the pronunciation as expected by a three-year-old, and full of excitement.

"Wow. That sounds like so much fun." The fact that she doesn't mention her mom leaving comforts my worries. I know how I felt when I knew my mom was leaving for an unknown amount of time. I would stare out the window hoping her car would magically appear in the driveway, or that she would come home in the middle of the night and cuddle into bed with me so that in the morning I'd wake up to her smiling face. But none of those scenarios ever happened.

I can't help but wonder what they told Anna. Did they give her false hope? I pray they didn't.

"Are you going to watch? I can scream so loud, he'll be able to hear me from his car. He says I'm his best cheerleader," she says with pride.

"I bet you are. He is so lucky to have you in his cheering section."

"Are you going to cheer, too? It would make him so happy and probably help him win." Her guilt trips me into saying, "Of course, I will."

How can I refuse her?

"Did you want to come in?"

Pushing a strand of hair behind my ear, I nod. Not sure what I'm going to say.

"I'm glad you're moving around better."

"Me, too." There is an awkward tension between us. Almost as if we just met and haven't known each other for years.

He shifts to Anna, leaning down to her level. "Anna, why don't you go ahead into your room and let me speak with Callie for a few minutes. I have to tell her about your mommy." His voice breaks. "Okay?"

Ben watches her skip into her room. He stands up but doesn't face me. I reach for the back of his shoulder. I'm unable to see his expression. "I'm sorry Becca is gone."

"It's for the best. Even though she is Anna's mother; Anna doesn't really depend on her. It reminds me a lot of how your mom would come and visit you and Jake. I know he saw a lot more than you did growing up, but I'm sure it affected you, too."

"She'll always be Anna's mom. Just like my mom will be mine, but she has you...and she has me."

He continues, "We told her she was starting a new job and was going to be very busy. Anna will be able to FaceTime her and call whenever she wants." He sighs, "But I think the number of times she talks to her will lessen with each day."

My heart aches at his words. "I'm sorry." That's all I can think of to say at this moment.

"I can't bring myself to tell her the truth. I can't break her little heart." He takes my hand, warmth spreading through my body. "I remember what losing your mother did to you. I'm sorry you had to go through that."

I swallow back the tears. "It will break her eventually, but you will be there to pick up the pieces."

He takes a moment, turns to face me as his eyes roam over my features. He closes his eyes as if he's in pain. "I'm so sorry about everything. Leaving you. I didn't know you were in that accident. No one told me. Jake, Van, Ems, Gran—no one. I would have been here instantly if I'd known. You must hate me." He sounds defeated.

"I don't hate you. But I need the complete truth. Why did you need to leave?"

"I left to meet with Becca's father. To make arrangements for Anna to be with me." He lets out a breath. "There was a race set. I was in the race of my life – for my daughter." Ben pauses, gathering his thoughts. "My car was ready and at the last minute, Becca convinced her father that I should take Anna without any more interference from them. The other racer took my place and won him enough money to appease his greed. I have proven myself, my loyalty to his granddaughter. He was done with fighting for his daughter. My only promise was that they could see her once a year. They agreed that would be enough." He reaches for my hand. "For the life of me, I can't imagine that being enough time with your grandchild." He shakes his head as if trying to still understand.

He steps close to me. My body reacts, wanting to feel him closer.

"Ben."

"Listen. I didn't want to be a father. But now that I am, I will do everything in my power to protect that little girl. I've had to fight my whole life. My dad got us into more trouble than any father should. I made it my goal to never let that happen to my child. Then my child's mother turns out to be worse than my own father. So, I've been working toward getting Becca's father to see my side. To see that his granddaughter will be fine with me. Becca has so many problems, always has. I thought I could help her fix them, but she doesn't want to fix them. And I won't have her hurting Anna in the process." He exhales, almost in relief.

"She came to see me before she left earlier."

His eyes widened. "What did she say?" he asks, worry marring his expression.

"She told me she was leaving. That she thought you loved me." I take a step closer to him as he wraps his arm around my waist and leans his forehead against mine.

"Please forgive me for all of it. Especially for leaving you. I'll never leave you again. I have everything I want. Right here, right now." He takes a step closer. As if he could read my mind. He reaches a thumb and brushes it across my lower lip. "Callie Rae, I love you. I've always loved you. You are my Sunshine. I can't be the person I want to be without you."

"If I stay here with you..." I pause, not wanting to ask again; however, I do need some type of validation so I spit it out "If there is a chance you're going to be called back to that life—we can't be together."

"Sunshine, our relationship has been twisted and bent, but never broken. Don't for one moment think that I left you because I didn't want you. I've always wanted you. Since the moment those cute pigtails caught my eyes. It's always been you. I'm just so sorry it wasn't sooner. I'm sorry I left, but not for helping my dad or becoming Annabella's father. If I had to go through all of that to get to you—it was worth every moment apart to get right back to you...I want to build a beautiful family with you."

Even though his words are exactly what I want to hear, I have to confess to him the one thing I've been hiding.

"Ben, I can't move forward with you."

His face falls. "Callie, I..."

"No, it's not that I won't, but I can't hide the truth from you if we are to move forward."

"Truth? What is it?"

I inhale a breath. His jaw tics, waiting for me to find the words.

"I was pregnant with your baby. The first time at the lake. I got pregnant." I peek up at him for a reaction. There isn't one other than biting his top lip. I let the words rush out. "I lost it. I was only seven or eight weeks along, and by the time I realized I was pregnant, I lost it almost as quickly so I knew me telling you wouldn't change anything. I'm sorry I kept it from you."

He clears his throat; his beautiful blues meet mine. "You were pregnant?"

"Yes." I swallow.

"Sunshine, we made a baby?"

I nod.

He pulls me into his arms. I go willingly, wrapping myself around him.

"I'm so sorry you had to go through that alone." He pulls back and cradles my face in his hands. His thumb brushes under my eyes, swiping away the tears.

"You're not mad at me for not telling you."

He shakes his head. "No, baby. I wish you would have told me. I wish I could have been there for you. It must have been so hard for you."

"It was. I was scared but excited. I was ready to be a mother."

"I hope someday I can make that happen for you."

I don't hesitate and I finally let myself go to him, with nothing between us. He has been the only person I've loved. No matter how much time we spend apart.

And if there's one thing that I know…it's that no matter what happens, we always come back to each other.

33

Street racing is so different from regular track racing. Tonight we're on a new road. Thankfully it is deserted. Cops shouldn't be an issue even though they know we are here.

Every driver has brought their car hauler and trailer. Some cars can be driven, but others like Ben's and Trent's are not street legal so they are hauled here. Trailers are lined up, making up the pit area for each driver. I haven't seen Trent's crew yet, but I'm sure they are here. I know he wants me with him. I feel guilty because he saved me, but that isn't a reason to lead someone on. I won't walk away from my friends, my brother, and most of all Ben.

Ever since Ben and I made our feelings known, I haven't spoken to Trent. I know I have to do it today, finally put everything out in the open and tell him we are done.

Emerson is helping Van make the car shine by wiping a cloth over the paint. They laugh and he pinches her butt.

Jake is under the hood, checking over wires, plugs, and generally just a once over of the engine. It is what he loves to do. He's sometimes a driver and other times a mechanic. He loves to be in on the action, no matter the role. He doesn't have the money like Ben and Van to spend on the cars, engines, tires, and everything else it takes to make them run fast, but he enjoys being a support for his friends.

Ben was born to be a driver. Even though he only races on the streets, he's one of the best. Trent is good but has never quite reached Ben Carmichael status.

Anna catches my eye, as she skips over to me in a matching race suit to her dad's. Isn't that the cutest sight in the world? Black with red stripes, and Carmichael Racing written on her chest. Ben emerges wearing the exact same race suit. As he walks in my direction, that feeling of home washes over me. I've had it since I was eight. It's never gone away, only changed into something more intense as the years have passed.

Peeling my eyes away from him, I ask Anna, "Are you staying to watch your daddy today?"

Ben answers, "She's leaving in a few minutes. The babysitter, Lindsey, is going to take her. I won't be able to keep an eye on her. I don't trust her not to get into something or start crying of boredom." He winks at me.

Oh, that wink, those eyes, everything about him.

34

"Can I show you something?" Anna breaks into my thoughts and stops me from the inappropriate thoughts about her father.

"Absolutely, darling."

She pulls a strand of red beads out of her pocket. They seem to get caught on something, as she yanks a little harder until she reveals rosary beads.

"Very pretty." I tell her as she drops them into my palm.

Looking down, shivers run through me. A vision of rosary beads dangling from the mirror of a car intrudes my thoughts.

I stumble backward. A shadow of a face and a car are in the vision. It must be the car that swerved into me. A woman driving, a man in the passenger seat.

"Callie!" Ben calls. I can hear my name called over and over. But I can't seem to focus. There are people around me and I'm sitting on the ground. How'd I get here?

"Callie!"

I hear it again. Something touches my hand. Looking up, concern is etched all over Ben's face.

"The rosary..." I choke out.

"It's okay. Breathe, Callie. Baby, just breathe."

"They did it on purpose. Left me." My mouth burns as I say the words.

"Who?"

"I don't know. There was a woman driving. I saw them when the car sped up beside me. They almost passed me, but then they let up. That's when..." I inhale as much air as I can to get through this. "I saw the rosary dangling from the mirror."

Jake stands. "A rosary? So what?"

"I don't know, but if we find the rosary, maybe we'll find who hurt Callie." Ben is angry, almost like his mission has shifted into detective mode.

Van comes running over. "I need you at the car. Something isn't running right."

I nod to Ben. "Please, go, there is nothing we are going to do about it now."

Trying to reassure him, I realize that I'm so tired of feeling like a broken flower. This isn't me. Somehow, I've lost my fire. I won't let whoever did this take any more from me.

Emerson comes by my side. "Everything alright? You look so pale."

"I'm fine. I can handle this situation. It's time I realize it. I need to put my big girl panties on finish things with Trent tonight by speaking with him. I have to officially break things off. I know Ben doesn't want me around Trent without him there but I'm tired of waiting. I'll be back."

Emerson isn't happy. "This isn't a good idea. Whatever it is you're thinking of doing."

"Trust me, it'll be fine."

She stays put but I continue walking toward Trent.

Thank goodness my walking boot is all I need today. I don't think I could accomplish what I have planned if I was chained to a crutch.

Once I see Trent's race car, I know he won't be far away. As I approach, Trent ducks out from the passenger side. "Are you staying in my pit or his?" he huffs, nodding in Ben's direction. There he is. This is the real Trent. I knew his silence meant something or I knew him not contacting me meant something. I give a quick glance to make sure that no one from the Carmichael race team has seen me. Coast seems clear.

Trent is wearing a Harrison racing t-shirt, strutting toward me. His hat is on backward, which means he was under the hood a few minutes ago.

"I want to thank you for taking care of me and finding me. I'll never be able to repay you."

Smirking, he says, "I see you made your choice." Gone are all the sweet words from when he was trying to take care of me at Gran's.

"I m sorry, I wanted to talk to you about everything. To be fair, you haven't contacted me for a few days." I blink, raising a brow.

"I've been busy with the car. This race is important." He seems far too calm, and maybe a little uncaring, which is out of character for him. I expected a lot more theatrics from him.

"Well, good luck today. I know it's a big one."

He ignores my comment and grunts, "I don't think your friends want you over here wishing me luck, considering my luck and skill will be what wins this race against them," he says while lighting his cigarette.

"By the way, did you hear any more about who ran you off the road?" he asks, but avoids my eyes.

"No. Nothing. But I did remember something that could be important." His eyes widen and he steps closer to me.

"What?" He rubs his chin back and forth with his finger.

"Just something hanging from the mirror."

"Oh yeah, what was it?" He inches closer.

"Oh, it's probably nothing. It doesn't matter." I turn away from him, but he grabs me by the arm to stop me.

"What was it?" He grits through his teeth. I can feel the anxiety rolling off of him.

"It was... those silly stuffed dice. You know from the good ol' days. Everyone has those, ya know." I laugh. "I'm sure it's nothing. Who knows, I could have probably seen it in a movie or something." I know I'm rambling, but the way his eyes are flaring at me, I think it's best he doesn't know what I really saw.

He nods. Gazing off in the distance to Ben's pit area.

"Well, like I said, good luck today. I think you have a great shot today." As the words leave my mouth, I know that wasn't the best thing to say to him.

"A shot?" He repeats back, anger lacing his words. I've definitely chosen the wrong word.

"Yes. You'll finish in the top two, I'm sure of it. You know I've been watching races for as long as you've been behind the wheel."

"Better than Ben? You think he'll catch me?" He blows out another puff of smoke in my direction. He knows I hate smoke.

"I think you have an equal shot. That's all."

"So, you leave the pricks to wish me luck. I don't want any wishes from you. I see who you want to win. If you're not in my pit, at my back, then don't wish me anything."

Trent throws his cigarette butt to the ground and stomps away.

I stand for a moment, watching him. I hate that I've hurt his feelings. He was sweet when he wanted to be. We were just hooking up and he wanted more. As I'm heading back, I take a different route to try and buy a few minutes so that I don't hear it from the overprotective brother's crew. I can gather my wits and brace myself for Ben and my brother's reaction to talking to Trent without him.

I pass a few cars that are parked off to the side of the road and stop when I see Jackie coming out of a silver car. But she isn't what catches my attention. Rosary beads dangle from her rearview mirror. I'm in shock as she turns and locks her door. This isn't the same car unless they had it fixed. Surely it would have some dents from hitting my car. Then again Trent and his team can fix car bodies as good as we can.

She spots me right away. A fire starts to churn inside me. My feet start to move on their own. She's got a Trent Harrison t-shirt on, with a short pair of shorts, showing off her ass cheeks.

Damn this little wench. Even though it kills me to think she was behind the wheel of that car, I've not felt this alive in forever. I'm going to crush her pretty little makeup-caked face into the dash of her car and steal those rosary beads. Someone like her doesn't deserve that kind of religious protection, or maybe she needs it more than anyone.

She waves. "Hey there, Callie Rae." She frowns. "Aw... are you still unable to wear a cute pair of shoes?"

I chuckle. I mean, give her a good hearty chuckle. This little bitch has no idea that I just figured her out. What I can't figure out is how she was able to cover it up.

"Not. Yet." I responded to both her comment and to my question.

"Don't be surprised if Ben doesn't cross the finish line. Trent is a much better driver. Ben will never keep up." She comes to stand in front of me while digging for something in her tiny bag. With all the makeup on her face, I'd think she'd carry something bigger. "He'll never beat Trent."

"I guess we'll find out. But he at least beat Trent where it counts, with me."

"I'm going to my pit." She spins, her hair almost whipping my face.

When she gets to Trent, he looks angry. She's looking up at him. Asking him something, and he pulls her by the arm and they vanish behind a car that I don't recognize. Seeing them together, my thoughts clear. Was he in the car, too? Did he know the whole time? Was he covering for her, or did he put her up to it?

Ben is at my side before I can gather my thoughts.

"What the hell do you think you're doing?" Ben asks, smoke almost radiating from him.

"Nothing. He didn't fly off the handle, he didn't call me a name. He literally doesn't care. He only asked if I found out anything else about who could have run me off the road."

"Wow. That's unexpected, I thought for sure he was going to go crazy on you."

No, but I have a feeling I'm about to go a little crazy Callie Rae Sunshine on them.

35

Ben's face changes. His eyes fill with fury as I tell him and Jake what I found out. Van and Emerson also are listening intently, but not adding to the news. Thank goodness we are in the safety of the trailer so no one can hear us and witness the reactions of the guys.

"Now it makes sense. I've seen those hanging from her mirror. It was Jackie," Jake says, smacking his hand on the hood of the car. "I can't believe I didn't think of it sooner."

"Jake, we don't know if it was her for sure." I pause, unsure if I should say what they probably already thought of. "Do you think Trent knows?"

"Who else could it be? She has reason to hate you. Trent picked you over her. I knew it!" Jake says, pacing in front of me. "That bastard is going to die. He was just going to let Callie die?"

The words sink in, and the answer is yes. Yes, Trent knows it was her. Because he was in the car with her.

"What do I do?" I whisper.

Ben leans down. "We let the police know. Leave it up to them."

Jake jumps up, he's ready for a fight. His eyes are wild and his face is red. "Are you crazy? We need to beat his ass right now! He's in his pit. I'll beat him to death with my tire iron."

"No!" I yell, jumping up to stop Jake.

Ben puts his hand up, stepping in between me and Jake.

"We'll get him, but not that way," Ben tells him, pinning him with fiery eyes. "We all need to calm down. The last thing we need is for any of them to see us unhinged. We can't let them know we are on to them. They won't see us coming if we act normally tonight."

Jake nods, realizing what he's saying makes sense.

It's as if they have spoken in code. Of course, they have. I know what he means, too.

He'll get him on the street.

Jake is irritated beyond words. Ben is strangely calm. Working on the computer. Tuning his car to the computer program recommendations.

I'm relieved that the babysitter came and got Anna. She was a little startled about the way I reacted to her rosary. Thankfully, she has a loving father who directed her attention to her doll instead of my outburst.

"I can't believe you ever dated that asshole," Jake exclaims.

Guilt surfaces. He's right to feel this way. I started my relationship, or whatever you want to call it, to get away from my brother's shadow. To set myself apart from his friends. All I ended up doing was pissing everyone off.

"I'm sorry. I didn't think it would turn out this way."

Jake runs his hands through his hair. "What did you think would happen? You can't play both sides. Life doesn't work that way. You have to pick a side or a team."

"Jake...she's been through enough," Van speaks up. "She's your sister. I can understand her wanting to step out on her own."

Ben quietly works behind the computer screen of his laptop that is sitting on top of his race car. Definitely not jumping to my rescue. I'm annoyed because I was hoping those would be his words, not Van's.

"She could have picked a million other people to fool around with, but nooooo..." Jake drops his wrench to the ground and steps outside.

Van and Emerson stand. "We'll go talk him off the ledge. Don't worry," Van assured me.

Patting my shoulder as he passes. Ben and I are left alone.

"Are you mad at me, too?" I ask him.

"Truthfully, yes." His voice is nonchalant, his eyes never leave the screen.

I knew the moment the question was out; I wouldn't like his answer.

"Well, truthfully, it's not like you were around to stop me," I spit back.

Ben slams his laptop shut. His blue eyes meet mine. Anger etched on his handsome face. His intense stare cuts through me.

"You think I care that you messed around with him. That you wanted to see what another guy was like? No."

He steps closer to me. His big hands hold my hips in place.

"Yes, I do," I whisper.

"Baby... I'm pissed because I wasn't there for you. I'm upset that you ever felt the need to be with him, or anyone else, for that matter. He tried to hurt you. Left you to die. It's all I'll be able to do... to not smash my car into his—rolling him, then hoping to see him...unmoving. Hopefully...done or worse."

I place my fingers over his mouth. Quieting his words. He gently moves his hands from my hips to his face and lowers his lips to mine. Just having his lips on mine stops the chaos that Trent has brought to my life.

"We are going to do this the right way. They are going to jail," he says without a doubt in his voice.

A knock on the door makes us both jump.

"Sorry, you're up, man," Van tells us.

***

Both race teams are at the starting line. The cars are lined up behind us. They are idling as the coin rotates in the air. Trent calls heads and the coin drops to the ground.

"Heads, it is!" Dean, the race master, says. "And to make this race a little more fun..." He addresses the crowd. "We've decided to ask our very own Callie Rae to flag the race. She's been through a lot lately, and we'd like to honor her with the flag."

My throat goes dry. I haven't flagged a race in years. I don't want to do this, but it is an honor if you are asked by a race master. I've known Dean since I was little and can't insult him. I should do it because it would be poetic justice for Ben to win a race that I flagged.

But I nod in agreement. Dean swings his arm around my shoulders, giving me a quick peck on the side of my cheek. "You set these boys straight, girl!" He lowers his voice to say, "I'm glad you're here with us."

A knot of emotion forms in my throat. My father was his friend. I know he's glad I didn't suffer my father's fate. But he doesn't know that I almost did.

Dean takes both Ben and Trent by the shoulders. "Listen here, guys. I know you have a beef with each other. But it ends here. This is my fucking race, and you will not cheat in any motherfucking way." His head swivels between the both of them. "You got me?"

Dean is a big, burly guy. Bald, a long gray beard, and monster hands that easily can grab a racer in each.

They nod in agreement.

Trent is focused solely on me. He glares in my direction, causing an unease that I feel in my veins. I don't trust him to run a clean race. If he can watch me fall off a cliff after the slut of his crashed into me, he can surely find a way to cheat...or worse...wreck into Ben's car.

Ben pulls at my arm, breaking the trance Trent has put on me.

"You okay?" He yells over the sound of the engines and the crowd.

"Yes!" I plug my ears so I can hear my own thoughts.

"You don't have to do this." He steps closer to say into my ear.

"Yes, I do."

He grabs my hand, and we go to his car. He zips up his race suit and climbs inside and attaches the steering wheel to the steering rod.

I lean down, "Good luck." I tell him.

"I love you, Sunshine." He winks and puts on his helmet.

"You do?"

"You know I do. I've loved you from the first time I met you."

Glancing up at him, it's something I've known from the moment I met him, too. Ben is supposed to be in my life. Somehow I force myself to back away so that Van and Jake can make sure he's secure. Quickly checking gauges, switches, and whatever else they do. I've asked them a hundred times what all of that's for, but they always talk in race terms that I don't retain. Just because I don't understand it all, doesn't mean I don't love everything about it.

Dean hands the flag to me. The wooden pole is just as I remembered it. It's lighter than when my dad used to let me hold on to it. It felt like it would break my arm back then, but I was much younger, not much older than Anna. I smile at the small memory.

This is what I love. Watching the cars fly down this track. Nothing but a car and a road. People cheering on their favorite. Me at the center as the cars fly by.

The ground begins to shake, the cars roar to life. They are allowed a burn out to warm up the tires for better grip and traction. Trent goes first, he lets go of his throttle and the car lays a quick strip of tire. Smoke fills the air, causing my lungs to retaliate.

Jackie stands in front of Trent's red car, signaling for him to back up. She guides him back in place while he is in reverse. In a true back-up girl fashion, she's wearing the skimpiest of clothing. Her butt cheeks hanging out of her jean shorts and her cropped top barely covering her underboob.

Next Ben goes the same distance. They both back up to the starting line.

Getting my shit in order, I've got a job to do. I make sure they are both equal on the line. I give them each four waves of my hand. I run back a few paces, and raise the flag. The smoke, heat, roaring engines, and the crowd's excitement fill the air. I drop my hand as they push on their pedals and whoosh past me. Strands of hair fling into my mouth as I spin to watch them.

It takes only a few seconds. Trent's car looks to be veering to the left but he gets it under control. Ben stayed the course, straight as an arrow. Before I let out another breath, the red brake lights came on for both cars.

The race is done.

My hearing comes back as people ask who won, while others celebrate. Van and Jake run past me. "He won!" Their fists pump in the air.

Dean gets on the walkie-talkie. "Who won?"

"Left lane." The voice hollers back. Ben was in the left lane.

Ems comes running over and I grab her. We spin in victory.

Moments later, we move to the left lane to celebrate Ben as he returns. He drives slowly up to the line. Clapping as he drives up, then a fist pump. Pride swells in my heart. Even though I can't see Ben's face through his helmet, I know his eyes are shining bright. I glance up and spot Trent's car coming up the track. Only it's going faster than it should. The sound of an engine revving, tires burning through the asphalt. In an instant, Trent plows into the back of Ben's. Causing it to spin, and slam into the wall. My hands fly up to my ears to stop the ringing sound of metal. The air fills with pieces of both cars. The smell of smoke and rubber burn my nostrils. Everything seems to run in slow motion.

The pieces scatter around me as a large crowd gather. I can't seem to move. Oh no!

"What the fuck?" Jake screams, breaking through the fog.

"No." The words fall from my lips.

Ben's car door opens, and he falls on all fours to the ground.

Jake and Van run to him.

Trent untwists his car from Ben's by backing up and makes a sharp right into the field, thankfully avoiding any people or cars.

"Are you hurt?" Van yells.

Ben is on his knees. Panting to find his breath.

"Get his helmet off." Jake shouts. Van yanks it off, and Ben rolls over onto his back.

"Get a medic." Someone screams over the chaos.

My feet finally move as I slide beside him. My knees scrape the asphalt. But I barely notice. "Ben!"

"I'm okay." He pauses.

"Just."

"Give."

"Me."

"A minute."

Relief washes over me. He's fine. Everything is fine.

Once he's standing, Van helps support his weight as he walks him over to the trailer. I'm trailing behind, not wanting to interfere.

"Where the hell did he go?" Ben asks, his breath coming back sharper now.

"I have guys looking for him," Dean says. "I've never seen anyone do that before, man. I'm sorry. We have rules for a reason. He'll never race with any of you again."

Ben sits down on a stool. His head in between his knees. After a few moments, he lifts his head and looks straight at me.

My cheeks are soaked with tears. "Come here, Sunshine."

I step in between his knees and he wraps his arms below my waist and brings me close to him. His head up against my belly. I lean down to kiss the top of his head. "Are you okay?"

"Shh. It's okay. I'm alright." He tightens his hold on me. "I just got the wind knocked out of me."

I sniffle.

"I'm sorry you had to see that. You've been through so much."

"I'm just glad you're okay."

Relief and resolve wash over me. I've had enough. I can see my decision clearly and I know exactly what I need to do to stop this once and for all.

36

Dean explains that Trent was back in his pit.

"I'm sorry, Ben, but there is nothing we can do. Trent said it was a mechanical failure.

"I talked to his crew chief, too, right after it happened. They think his brakes locked up at the end there." He swipes his forearm over his forehead, removing the sweat that glistens from the streetlights.

"That's bullshit! You know it is, Dean," Jake spits out.

"I know that and everyone else does, too. But it's racing. There isn't anything we can do now. He lost the race. The best we can do is suspend him for races, but that's up to a vote with the other teams," Dean tells us.

"It doesn't matter to me. I'm more concerned with finding him...I want to talk to that asshole," Ben says while he paces in the trailer.

Dean huffs, "I think he's the last person you need to talk with."

"I agree." I say, rather demand. "We don't need any more interaction with him tonight. Everyone's emotions are running high. I think I'm going to grab a snack from that food truck I saw at the beginning of the road."

"Give me a few minutes, I'll come with you," Ben states, not wanting me out of his sight, I'm sure of it.

Not happening. I'm sick of everyone trying to watch over me, protect me, fight my battles. I'm a big girl. I can handle my own damn business.

Am I going to get a taco at the taco stand, yes. But on my way back, I'm going to see if I can find him. I'm headed over to pay a visit to Trent. The only problem is not letting the guys know where I'm going.

I wait until the guys are consumed with the computer data and packing up for the night.

This could go on for a while. They relive what happened, what could they have done differently.

"Hey, do you want me to come with you?" Ems comes jogging over. "I'm starving."

"No, that's okay. I can bring you something back, if you want?" Crap on a cracker, I don't want her to know what I'm doing.

Her eyes narrow, "Are you sure? I'd love to get away for a few minutes."

"Hey, Ems. Can you come here?" Van yells. "I need you." *Thank you, Baby Jesus!*

"Go on. I'll bring you back three tacos?"

She purses her lip. "Fine." Ems points her finger at me. "Callie Rae, do not go causing any more problems."

I huff. "What would give you that idea?" I feign complete innocence. She knows me better than I thought.

Her hands go to her hips. "Callie Rae, don't you dare try to find him."

"I'm not. I promise," I say as I hide my crossed fingers behind my back.

Once she turns away, I start to walk to the Taco Shack Food Truck.

I order the six tacos and pay for my meal. The unenthusiastic cashier hands me my change and places them in a bag.

Taking the long way back, I make my way to Trent's pit. Trent is there, but he's got Jackie with him.

He's putting away something in his toolbox and is very aggressive while he sorts through it.

Jackie is sitting in a nylon chair, picking at her long, sculpted pink nails. Slipping behind the black pickup that's at least six feet away so they don't notice me, I think I'm disguised enough by the shadow from the truck. I can't see them, but luckily, I can hear them. I set the bag of tacos on the ground to free up my hands.

"I don't know why this is such a big deal?" Her voice sounds as if she is bored. I'm sure she's still picking at her nails and rolling her eyes.

I hate that I'm cowered behind a vehicle. I'm wanting to hear some type of information that may slip from their iron lips. Maybe it wasn't him or her. Maybe I'm reading way into this.

"You don't get it, Jackie. He fucking wins everything."

"You mean her?" Pure venom spews from her lips.

"Callie. Say her fucking name," he snarls.

His tone sends chills through me. I hate the way he just said my name.

"I've kept your secret like I promised I would. Even though she almost died. Do you understand how serious this is?" His voice is low, but clear.

I gasp, covering my own mouth because I hope to God they didn't hear my gasp.

There is hushed whispering. My heart is racing. I know they're talking about me. They did it.

I back up a bit, my back hitting the cold metal of the truck.

Inhaling as much air as I can, my mind starts racing. I need to get out of here. I need to get to the police. I need to get to Ben and Jake before Trent decides to cause harm to them. I need to...

Before I can finish the thought, a hand covers my mouth and my back slides against the metal frame of the truck. Scraping and stinging my skin as I think to myself that I won't survive another incident with Trent and Jackie.

37

"I'm glad you are here?" Trent's voice penetrates every scared cell in my body.

Instinctively, I start to scream. In my head it's loud, deafening.

"Shh... Callie, it's just me. We need to talk."

I try to tell him to fuck off.

"I'll let you go if you don't scream for him."

I nod because what other choice do I have. Not going to keep quiet though.

"Okay. I'm not going to hurt you." He nods, but still doesn't let go of me completely, only my mouth.

"Why would you try to scare me like that?" I ask him with a hoarse voice when his hands slip from my face.

"I need to talk to you."

"Didn't your mama teach you some manners? Let go of me," I say, gritting through my teeth. What I really want to do is scream my head off for Ben or Jake or Van to come help me. I'm so tired of all of this bullshit.

"I want to explain. I had nothing to do with the accident. Jackie was drunk. She got behind the wheel." He's out of breath. "She was going on and on about how she hated you. How she hated me. I wanted to stop her."

I try to wiggle free by moving my shoulders from his grasp but it's no use. He's holding tight. "Yeah, what's new? I'm going to scream and a million people are going to come running to slap you upside the head for this."

He ignores me. "I tried to stop her. But she was so hell bent on getting to you. I promise I didn't know she was..." I freeze, is he going to confess to my face?

Another voice joins us. "Trent, you promised."

"Shut up, Jackie. I told you to stay hidden. You fucked this whole thing up."

Trent grips my arms tighter. I try shrugging again. "I knew it. She better pray to that rosary. She needs all the forgiveness she can get," I spit.

I try to move again, and again, it's not working. He yanks me back with him a few inches farther.

"I love you, Trent. You always picked her over me. She doesn't love you. I'll do anything for you." Tears stream down her face. I've never seen her made-up face look so terrible. Guilt finds a crack in my heart. I don't want to be the cause of her jealousy and this crazy revenge. She can literally have Trent.

"You don't love me, Jackie. You just wanted to win. Just like I want to win her." He spins and twists me so that I face him. He's got sweat dripping down his face. His eyebrows are knitted together. "I promise I tried to yank the wheel, but before I could she wrecked into you."

I gasp. He was in the car with her. That's how he knew to find me. The images of me falling, the crushing, banging sounds stabbing at my ears, the deafening silence that followed. The pain. Every second comes rushing back as if I'm living it again. Oh God. He knew all along. I didn't want to believe he could be such a heartless snake. I don't even realize it but I start banging on his chest. He grabs me by the wrists. "Stop. Baby. Stop. I know I let you down." He crushes me to his chest.

He's shushing me, rubbing my hair. I'm going to vomit. Knowing his hands are on me repulses every cell in my body. "How could you..." I mumble into his chest.

"I'm sorry. I looked for your truck, but I couldn't see where it landed. I had to get Jackie back home first, but I came back for you, babe."

Processing his words, shock, anger give way to a spark of strength, and I somehow manage to shove off of him. "You had to get her home? What about me? I could have been dead?"

"I know. It wasn't the right thing to do. But I was drinking, too." His normal at-ease features are now tense. He reminds me of a wild animal that's about to be caught. Looking erratically around us.

I rush at him, this time shoving him with all my strength with both hands. "You were fucking drinking? That's your excuse for almost letting me die. You were worried about you. You would rather let me die than lose your license?" I don't give him a chance to answer. "You stupid piece of shit. I hope you two spend the rest of your lives rotting in hell!"

I go to turn, but he grabs my wrist. "You're not going anywhere!"

"You stupid selfish prick, let go of me!" I scream.

His hand comes over my mouth again, and I'm right back where we first started. He's trying to get me to move. I dig my heels in the gravel, hoping to stop him from getting far. They slip through the rocks as he moves me along.

Hells bells, it's not slowing us down one bit. Causing more pain because this damn boot is digging into my skin. "Jackie, get that strap and that crowbar," Trent orders.

She picks them up. Obviously forgetting her earlier mental breakdown of how mad she was at him. Apparently, it's a little more directed at me now.

I try to move my mouth to bite at his hands. I need to be free. Dear God, what are they planning on doing with a crowbar? Panic starts to run wild inside me. How is this going to end? They've already indicated that they had no problem letting me die, and here I am again.

A loud banging sound comes off the trailer, causing Trent to tighten his hold on me. Spinning me against his back. I'm dizzy from being dragged around like a rag doll. Ben moves slowly toward us with a baseball bat in his hand.

"Trent...take your fucking hands off of her before I kill you. This is between you and me."

He chuckles. "No motherfucker. This has nothing to do with you."

I'm fighting against his hold, but nothing is working. Every time I move, he moves, and the vise of his hold gets stronger.

Jackie comes into view, tossing the strap to him. He wraps it around my upper body.

"You really want to die today, don't you?" Ben asks in a voice that I've never heard from him. It's menacing, sending fear into the air.

"You have no idea what you walked into. Just leave us to finish our talk. I'll let her go. We just need to come to an understanding." Trent is nothing like I thought he was. He doesn't care about anyone but himself.

Ben's fist turns white as he holds the bat.

Jackie still has the crowbar. She's holding it with both hands, ready to swing at the air if so much as a light breeze touches her skin.

Ben slams the bat into Trent's race car. Pieces of it come flying at me. Something scratches my leg. "Come on, let's fucking go! Prove how fucking fast you are by dodging my punches to your face."

Jackie takes a swing at Ben. He grabs the crowbar midair, picks her up by it, and wraps her in his grasp. Now we're in matching positions. Except she's pinned by a bat and a crowbar.

Trent lets out a spiteful laugh. "You think I care what happens to her? I want Callie."

"Trent!" Jackie screeches. "Do something!"

Her voice becomes far away. My eyes snap up and notice that there is another person here dragging her away. Jake. His dark eyes nod over to Ben. "You take care of that motherfucker and I'll make sure this gets what she deserves." He drags her away from us.

"I got him."

Ben nods at their unspoken words. Sure of himself. It's undeniable the vigor in his voice.

Jackie tries to fight him, but they quickly vanish from our sight. Taking her into the shadows. I can hear her muffled screeching.

Ben takes this distraction to dive into us. All three of us fall to the ground. Gravel digs into my arms and my head bangs off of something. My vision blurs. Ben's fist pounding into Trent's face comes into view, then fades. Something wet slides down my cheek. I go to swipe at it just as something bumps into me.

I try to focus. Trent is standing over me, Ben on the other side of me. I try to sit up.

Trent stares above me. His chest heaving as he tries to catch his breath. Fear paralyzes me. Ben's struggling to get up beside me. "Look at you, Carmichael. You think you're so damn tough. A crowbar to the head will fuck you up a bit. Won't it." He laughs in the vilest way I've ever heard.

Ben groans from beside me. I try to move to his side because I know I need to check on him.

Trent grabs my injured foot, tugging my leg almost out of its socket, and I slide again. Pain shoots up my back. I feel as if it's on fire. Oh God, is there any skin left?

I take my other foot, trying to strike at what I hope is Trent, but nothing is helping.

"I'm taking you with me. Stop trying to fight me. You're just making it worse." He lets go and spins, opening another drawer of the toolbox.

Rolling to my stomach, I feel around me. I don't know what I'm doing. I just know I don't want to go with him. I never want to be near him again.

My hand reaches something familiar and I grab a hold of it and roll it to my side, out of his vision.

Trent then leans down, shoving a rag in my mouth. "Beautiful."

He swipes his disgusting hand down my face, and I take that moment of putrid disgust and use the butt of the bat in my hand to shove it into his forehead, knocking him down and out cold.

He falls back and so do I.

I knew that baseball bat would come in handy someday.

38

My eyesight clears. Ben is to my right. He's moaning. I somehow manage to crawl over to him and run my hand down his face.

"Ben, I'm here. Open your eyes," I beg, desperation pouring out of every bone in my body.

He moans again, but moves. His arm comes up to his face. "Shit."

"Come on, Ben. Open your eyes. We need to get help."

His head turns toward, me and by the grace of God, his eyes open. "Sunshine. Ugh."

"Come on, we need to get up, Trent is still out cold." I double check, glancing in his direction. He's sprawled out and looks worse than Ben. He's also motionless.

With all my might, I place my arms underneath his shoulders, pushing him up into a sitting position.

He shakes his head. "Okay. I'm okay. Getting up."

"Come on."

We stand up together. My legs are weak. Hurting. But we manage to get to our feet.

"That baseball bat came in handy." He chuckles in a sarcastic way.

I mirror his chuckle. "I was thinking that, too."

Ben seems to be more stable than I am and is able to walk over to him. He calls his name, then kneels down on one knee. Placing two fingers on his neck, he looks back at me and says, "He's got a pulse."

Ben then slaps Trent's face with the back of his hand.

No reaction.

He reaches for the phone in his pocket and tells the person on the phone our location and that we were attacked.

Jake then calls my name and dashes toward me. He engulfs me in the best hug that I ever received from my brother.

"You're okay, Callie. You're okay," he repeats, I think more for him than for me.

"I am. Where is Jackie?"

"I have her locked in my car. She's flipping the fuck out. But she knows she's in deep shit."

I almost forgot about her with Trent being the main issue right now. Seeing Jake made the memory come rushing back.

"Thank God. I just want this to end." The tears start to fall. He sweeps me into a hug again.

"I know you do. Officer Alex is on his way."

Ben stands over Trent as the red and blue lights of the police cars shine over them. They quickly come into view.

Relief washes over me. It's unlike anything I've ever felt.

"It's over, it's really over." I can finally breathe.

Once the police show up, Trent wakes up. He's groggy and hasn't said a word. The police keep asking him questions, but he's just staring at the ground. Alex places handcuffs on him and pulls him up to his feet. Trent looks at me, standing next to Ben. Then he stops.

"I'm really sorry, Callie. I didn't mean for all of this to happen. It got out of control. I never would have hurt you."

I'd rather spit in his face or punch him in the nuts, but instead, I say, "You did more damage than you can ever imagine. But you know what, in the end Ben's the winner...of not only the race, but of me."

"Come on," Alex orders, shuffling Trent along by the elbow. Not allowing him to speak another word.

Ben takes my hand. "Let's let the paramedics take a look at you. You knocked your head pretty good."

The paramedics look me over. They say I don't have any signs of concussion, but they still want me to look out for any signs and to not go to sleep for at least an hour or two. All I want to do is go to sleep. But as soon as I close my eyes, I know all I will see is Trent.

We tell the police officers our version of what happened. They question us for what feels like an hour, then finally let us go. Trent is on his way to the hospital with a concussion, before dealing with the cops. And Jackie has been taken to the station for questioning.

"I'm so glad to be going home," I tell Ben.

"Will you stay with me tonight? I need to watch over you."

"I wouldn't be anywhere else but with you and Anna." Because, it's true, there is no other place I'd rather be.

***

Gran is relieved to see us. How she knew what happened to us, I don't know. And I'm too tired to ask.

"How was Anna for you?" Ben asks Gran.

"She was an absolute angel. The babysitter was apologetic that she couldn't stay the whole night with Anna, she said she wasn't feeling well, but I couldn't have asked for a better little girl to spend the evening with. Now, you two need to tell me everything."

"Gran, I'm exhausted. Besides, I'm sure you already know everything." I yawn, proving my point.

"Okay. I'll let you get some rest."

She kisses my cheek and gives Ben a hug. "Anna is all tucked in tight."

He kisses her on the cheek. "Thank you for taking care of her tonight."

"Thank you for bringing my girl home safe. I could just spit nails at those two heathens who hurt my little girl," Gran tells us, and by the redness creeping up her face, I believe it.

Once Gran is gone. Ben and I sit on the couch.

He grabs a blanket and wraps it around my shoulders. "You look exhausted. I'm sorry I didn't stop that bastard from coming after you. But damn it, Callie Rae, why did you go to him in the first place? You know it wasn't safe." His forehead crinkles with concern. The little V on his forehead is in overdrive at the moment.

"I just wanted to tell him off. I had no idea it would get out of control like it did. I'm just glad it's over." Another big yawn finds its way from my lips.

"Come here." Ben pulls me closer to his side. "You have no idea how perfect it is having you here."

This is everything I've ever wanted to hear from him. I'm tired of playing this game and I want it to be more than just a night. I want us to be a family. So I ask, "What time do I need to leave in the morning before Anna wakes up? Is there a time limit for how long I have you tonight?"

"That's the thing, babe, the only time limit you have with me and Anna is forever."

Epilogue

BEN CARMICHAEL

Today's the day and I'm nervous as fuck. We've only been technically together for five months, but we've spent our whole lives loving each other.

Callie moved in with me and Anna a month after the night from hell. She amazes me every day with her strength and determination. But damn, do I love her fiery spirit.

Jackie went to a mental facility for a few weeks after the incident. She was dealing with mental illness on top of a drug and alcohol addiction. Trent, on the other hand, got out of it with minimal jail time.

He did own up to everything, but his lawyer got him off pretty easily. I've tried everything to keep him there, but with overcrowding in the jail, he was let go for good behavior.

The only saving grace is he's moved out of state to compete on another race circuit since he can't race here any longer.

With those obstacles behind us, we are finally able to focus on the future.

"Daddy, I found it!" Anna rushes toward me, holding a big red bow.

"Nice job, kiddo," I say as I wrap her in my arms. "You've got a big job to do. Are you ready?"

Her dark curls tickle my nose, and I wouldn't have it any other way.

Callie comes trudging out of the bathroom, pale, holding her stomach. She takes a straight line to the fridge. Plucking out a can of ginger ale.

"Are you okay?"

"My stomach isn't so good," she says quietly.

She plops down on the couch. Thankfully she's distracted by her upset stomach, and she doesn't notice that I slipped the bow behind my back.

Anna jumps off my lap. She climbs up on the couch until she's nuzzled against Callie's side.

They have formed a special bond since the moment they met. Now that Callie is an everyday part of her life, it's undeniable.

Callie has been more of a mother figure to her in a few short months than Becca ever was. Becca is back in Las Vegas and has decided that she wants very limited contact with Annabella. What kind of person says that about her child?

But I don't want to wait another second. I pluck the ring from my back pocket and I slip it on her middle toe.

She looks down and gasps. But then laughs. "What did you do to my toe, Mr. Carmichael?"

Anna's eyes widen with excitement. "Daddy, are you going to give her the present?"

I nod.

"Callie Rae, I love you with everything that I am. I know I'm doing this backward, but I've got everything I could ever want." I take the ring off her toe and place it on her ring finger. "Will you do me the honor of marrying me?"

Tears glide down her cheeks, morning sickness forgotten, as she says, "Yes, Benjamin Carmichael, I will marry you."

Anna claps and I wrap my arms around Callie, picking her off the seat as she says, "Whoa, I'm going to puke!" And I laugh because nothing is more perfect than this very moment.

My family is now complete, and I know I can do this thing called our crazy life with her by my side.

I stand up, bending down to touch Callie's face. I tip her chin up to look at her. Her sparkling blue eyes are puffy, and her cheeks are red. Her usually perfectly styled blonde hair is pulled up into a messy bun. She's never been more beautiful as my hand lands on her swollen belly.

We found out a few weeks ago we're expecting a baby. We haven't told anyone but Gran. Callie doesn't want anyone to know until we hit the second trimester in case something happens to the pregnancy.

"What can I do to make you feel better?" I ask as she rubs Anna's back.

She lets out a moan. "Rub my feet, please," she asks with a whine.

I lower down to one knee and start to rub her feet. I glance up at her tired face, but watch as she picks up Anna's favorite book beside her and starts to read.

Even though she's sick, she is putting Anna first. Nothing is as important as these beauties in front of me.

***

Did you get a chance to read Van and Emerson's story. Read it now https://www.amazon.com/Beautifully-Restored-Trisha-Madley/dp/0996680969

Forced into a loveless marriage due to a business deal, Emerson has always done what was expected of her. Even if that means submitting to her controlling husband and his vindictive family.

Yet when she is ordered to oversee a car restoration at a shop on the other side of the country—she meets mechanic, Donovan Bradley. The chemistry between them is instant and undeniable. Beneath his rough exterior and bad boy ways, Emerson finds a kind-hearted man, full of compassion and a protective nature she's never experienced before. It doesn't take long for him to become everything she never knew she wanted.

But can their love survive the wrath of her husband? Or will his family's malicious agenda destroy their chance at happily ever after?

Read Beautifully Restored

Follow Me!

I'd love to hear from you! Follow Me!

To sign up for updates and my newsletter, go to https://www.trishamadley.com

Website: https://www.trishamadley.com

Facebook: https://www.facebook.com/trishamadley

Facebook Group - Madley's Mob

Tiktok: https://www.tiktok.com/trishamadleybooks

Instagram: https://www.instagram.com/trishamadley

Pinterst: https://www.pinterest.com/trishamadley

ABOUT THE AUTHOR

Acknowledgements

I want to thank my girls, Madison and Hayley. They are always so proud to tell someone that their mom is an author. Although they are not old enough to read my books, I write so that they know whatever they want to do in life, no matter how challenging, they can accomplish it.

To my mom, no words will ever be enough to express the strength she has shown throughout her life, but I've learned so much from her. Love you, Mom, and I'm so proud of you.

To Nana, thank you for being the first person to read my books, and helping me become the person I am. May you be dancing in Heaven with Grandpa Joe.

Kathy Blinkiewicz, my second mom, who is the best Trisha Madley book promoter and one of my biggest fans! Thanks for all you do for me.

To Jason, the love of my life, my partner and best friend. Thank you for supporting my passion.

Most of all, to you, my readers:

Thank you to all of you who have read and purchased *Safer With You* and *Fearless With You and Beautifully Restored*. I can't tell you how much it means to hear people ask me, "When is your next book available?" Thankfully, I can finally answer, "Today!"

So, thank you.

Amy Dobbs is a wonderful author, and the proofreader of *Fearless With You, Beautifully Restored, and Beautifully Built*. Thank you for the countless things you did to help make these books possible. I can't wait to see your books in print.

My beta readers: Mary Balmer, and Amy Dobbs.

Thank You, Everyone!!!

Enjoy!!!

Visit trishamadley.com for more information.

Trisha Madley Books

Trisha Madley Books

BEAUTIFULLY RESTORED

Beautifully Restored –

Forced into a loveless marriage due to a business deal, Emerson has always done what was expected of her. Even if that means submitting to her controlling husband and his vindictive family.

Yet when she is ordered to oversee a car restoration at a shop on the other side of the country - she meets mechanic, Donovan Bradley. The chemistry between them is instant and undeniable. Beneath his rough exterior and bad boy ways; Emerson finds a kind-hearted man, full of compassion and a protective nature she's never experienced before. It doesn't take long for him to become everything she never knew she wanted.

But can their love survive the wrath of her husband? Or will his family's malicious agenda destroy their chance at happily ever after?

Fans of forbidden romances sprinkled with the spiciness of opposites attracting are sure to love Beautifully Restored by Trisha Madley!

THE WITH YOU SERIES

Safer With You- Book One –

Nora Skye must start her life over again. She notices that her boyfriend Luke has become distant and secretive, leaving her with no other choice than to spy on him.

When Luke learns of what she has done, he discards her. Forcing her back home. Upon her arrival, she attends her sister's wedding where she meets the sexy, charismatic, and outrageously out of her league Jase Madsyn.

She knows his reputation, the mystery that surrounds him, but that doesn't stop her from experiencing the best night of her life. But she soon discovers that he may be the person responsible for her pain.

FEARLESS WITH YOU - Book Two –

Nora Skye has survived the unimaginable. Now that the chaos has settled, she is free to enjoy her new life, with the man who saved her in more ways than one—Jase Madsyn.

Jase killed the man who hurt Nora, but now new obstacles arise. His career starts to wear on their relationship, but the problems don't end there when Samantha, his ex-fiancée, shows up with a surprise of her own, and his mother disappears without a trace.

Nora tries to be supportive, but too many secrets cause their fragile relationship to crumble. Can their love survive his secrets...but most of all, his past?